CHRISTMAS IN COCKLEBERRY BAY

NICOLA MAY

Lightning Books

Published in 2020
by Lightning Books
Imprint of Eye Books Ltd
29A Barrow Street
Much Wenlock
Shropshire
TF13 6EN

www.eye-books.com

British Library Cataloguing in Publication Data
A catalogue record for this book is available from the British Library

ISBN 9781785632204

For my dad

PROLOGUE

'I think she might have carked it, mate.' Danny Green's face was as puce as that of the smartly dressed, curvaceous woman who was currently lying spread-eagled and lifeless on top of the sumptuous blue velvet throw.

Lucas Hannafore put a hand to his forehead. 'Shit. If this wasn't so serious, it would be hilarious. I can just see the headline in the *Gazette* now: *Hotel Inspector Found Dead in the Titanic.*'

Danny gulped. 'What the hell are we going to do?'

CHAPTER ONE

'Christmas crackers? It's only October.' Titch carried on topping up the Corner Shop till with change.

'Now that I'm a grandmother – even though it makes me feel old, just saying that – I want to get organised early this year.'

'Well, you're lucky, Mary, because I have actually just ordered in quite a few boxes. They should be here in the next couple of weeks. I'm also going to set up a Christmas Corner, just like Rosa used to. I've lots of little trinkets coming and special flashing Santa lights for the window. I do love it when it starts to get festive down in the Bay.'

'Ooh, me too. Well, save me a box of crackers, love. I want good ones, mind. Decent presents that don't just get thrown in the bin.'

'"This is the lovely gift I got from my cracker present last year" – said nobody, ever,' Titch laughed.

'Hmm, you've got a point there.' Mary took a puff on her inhaler, waited a few seconds then put it back in her coat pocket. She blew out a long whistling breath before saying, 'I can't believe you've been in here a year now, duck.'

'I know – mad, isn't it?'

'And you're nearly cooked with another little one too. Just

goes to show – life turns on a sixpence. You never know what's around the corner.'

Titch rubbed her heavily pregnant belly. 'In this case the Corner Shop. Did you want anything else while you're here?'

'Ah. Yes, I do. Some of those special savoury dog biscuits for Hot Dog please, for when my girl visits. And that reminds me, here's some cookies for the biscuit tin.' Mary reached into her bag and handed Titch a plastic container full of scrumptious home-made treats. 'You don't want to be getting a sugar lull in your condition, now, do you?'

'Aw, that's kind. I'm actually seeing Rosa later; I'll take some with me.'

'Perfect. Send her my love.'

'I will, and have a good day, Mary.'

The older woman went to leave, then turned around to caution Titch. 'Christmas may be a-coming and I know you'll be busy, but don't you be overdoing it with a baby on board, Titch love.'

CHAPTER TWO

Rosa Smith peeked her head around the nursery door and listened; on hearing her son's soft little sleeping breaths she tiptoed back down the winding wooden staircase of Gull's Rest.

Thank heavens for a best friend like Titch, who had guided her every step of the way through mothering her four-month-old. She had been completely unaware that a baby needed so many naps. Rosa got herself a cup of tea and sat down at the kitchen table. With luck, she would be able to concentrate on her charity paperwork before the little munchkin woke up and consumed every second of her time.

On seeing her coming down the stairs, Hot, the Smiths' lively dachshund, bounded off his bed and started to bark, hoping for a walk. For a small dog, he could make an ear-splitting amount of noise. Closing the gate which stopped the mini-dachshund from attempting to climb the steep stairs, Rosa rushed over to the noisy hound, picked him up and gently closed his soft brown whiskery snout with her hands, rubbing her nose against his. 'Shush now, Hotty boy,' she told him, 'or you'll wake Little Ned and then there will no W.A.L.K.' She spelt the trigger word out, so as not to cause any more doggie delirium.

'Here, come on.' The little wiener dutifully pitter-pattered behind her to the kitchen door, where she set him free to run around the secure garden in search of seagulls, which of course he never caught; just barked incessantly at the mere sight of one flying overhead.

Yawning loudly and running her hands through her curly brown mop, Rosa came back through to the open-plan modern living area and popped a couple of logs into the basket next to the log-burner. Lifted by the autumn sunlight streaming in through the wide, sea-fronted bay window with its curved window-seat, she allowed herself a massive, noisy stretch.

The window-seat was probably what had most excited her when they viewed the house. It was here, in rare moments of peace, that she would sit watching the comings and goings of Cockleberry Bay beach life against the rhythmical ebb and flow of the tides. Resting her small body along the comfy blue-and-white seagull-printed bench cushion, she yawned again. Pain from her son's sore gums had caused him to wake twice in the night and she was knackered. Maybe a little snooze was what she needed before she embarked on the day's chores.

Taking in the glorious expanse of water in front of her, she then turned her gaze to her beloved Rosa's Café and reminded herself that she must talk to Nate, her brother and now manager of the establishment, about putting the Christmas lights up. With her newfound excitement around everything Christmas, in Rosa's eyes it was never too early to start decorating. Plus, it was the legendary Cockleberry Bay fireworks display the following weekend, so even the beach wall would be illuminated.

This reminded her to ask Mary, her mum, if she could babysit and dog-sit then, too. It would be nice to have some free time without the responsibility of Little Ned or Hot. Plus, she had planned with Nate that this year they would serve hot dogs as well as hot chocolates with marshmallows out at the front of the café, so it would need all of their hands on deck.

It was a relief to her that now Little Ned was taking his bottle without a tantrum she could leave him for a few hours. She felt no guilt in doing this, any more than she had about giving up breastfeeding. She had struggled with it. The baby wasn't taking enough milk and they were both getting uptight and stressed every time a feed was due. Did changing to a bottle make her a bad mother? Surely not. Rosa tried to tell herself that it made her a sensible one. To her, motherhood was about practicalities: getting through each day in the easiest way she could, with the best interests of her baby at heart, of course. She had always vowed that she wouldn't be one of those mothers whose baby literally took away their identities as soon as they were born. However, she was beginning to understand exactly how that happened. A baby certainly was for life and not just for Christmas!

On seeing that the newly refurbished Ship Hotel had beaten her to it with their white twinkly lights, she made a little disgruntled sound. They had also already lit their open fire, as she could see the sweet-smelling woodsmoke billowing from its chimney into the bright but chilly late-October afternoon. The path that led up to South Cliffs and the magnificent views over the English Channel was empty, aside from one lone dog-walker. The beach was quiet too; a high tide had thrown varieties of slimy green and black seaweed up onto the wet, dark sand. A small blue fishing boat could be seen way in the distance. And then she spotted a single cormorant, its wings spread wide, flying towards West Cliffs with a fish hanging from its curved yellow and grey beak.

Now that winter was almost upon them, Rosa was thankful for the sea wall in front of the cottage. It acted as an adequate defence, apart from the one terrible storm they had had the summer before last, which had not only flooded the café, but had caused carnage on the beach and to sea life, including many of the gulls.

She'd noticed recently that the tides were definitely getting higher and had thrown up more than just seaweed, especially around the time of a full moon. The sea would sometimes completely engulf the Bay, thrusting boats right up close to the wall in front of their house, disappearing as quickly as they had come with the ebbing tide. She couldn't recall this ever happening when she had first moved here.

With its fantastic array of shops and eateries, and its stunning beach and cliff location, Cockleberry Bay was a sought-after area in which to live. There were generations of families who had been born here and would never leave, so the sea-fronted properties rarely came onto the market. When they did, it was usually city-dwellers on the look-out for a second property who, on promising hungry estate agents back-handers for immediate information, snapped them up quickly. So it had been fortuitous timing that the detached and desirable Gull's Rest should come up for sale just when she and Josh were looking for a new home before the baby came, and that they should get wind of its availability before anyone else.

Gull's Rest had been owned by a rich city gent, Sandy Hamilton-Jones, and was previously being lived in by his estranged wife, Bergamot. The agent had unprofessionally told Rosa that Mr Hamilton-Jones, despite making his wife sign a pre-nup, had come a cropper. A massive divorce settlement had gone in her favour and, with regret, he had had to let the house go. Rosa was disgusted that the very same woman who had stolen money from her Corner Shop last Christmas had lucked out in this way, but was also incredibly grateful that Bergamot had moved out and left the Bay long ago so there would be no onward chain.

It had originally been Josh and Rosa's plan to move to nearby Polhampton Sands. However, Josh had quickly realised that it made no sense to move out of the Bay as Rosa didn't drive, and if he wasn't around it would mean her travelling backwards and forwards by bus or taxi to help run the café or the Corner Shop, and see her friends. Rosa was delighted at their final decision to stay in Cockleberry Bay. She loved it here. Far removed from the deprived area in the East End of London in which she had grown up, this vibrant seaside town was somewhere she was now more than happy to call her home.

Gull's Rest had a cornflower-blue front door with a silver starfish knocker that Rosa had insisted on adding, and, with its beachfront location, offered magnificent sea views from every angle, upstairs and down. After living in the compact flat above the Corner Shop in the main town, being in this place, with its large living space and underfloor-heated wooden floors felt like living in a mansion. The back garden was perfect for a young family and dog, too, with its lawn leading down a small hill to an orchard of apple and pear trees.

On viewing the property, Josh had randomly got excited about the greenhouse that the old owners had left, and had been insistent that he would grow tomatoes, chillies, peppers and cucumbers – in his whispered words to his wife, 'as long as my cock'. None of which had yet materialised. Although her husband of two years had said that moving to the new place would allow him to slow down and help her with their Cockleberry businesses, he had just taken on a contract in New York for the old firm he had worked for previously, with Carlton, his mate and work colleague.

With Little Ned being so young, the married couple had discussed the pros and cons long and hard, but in the end the ever-resilient Rosa had been fine about Josh going. A few weeks in New York would earn him a particularly good income, which in turn would buy him time at home. A lucrative contract like this would see him through for the next year at least, and with their café share and his many investments, the Smiths would be in a more secure financial position than ever.

If Rosa was completely honest, the thought of spending quality time alone with Little Ned, their son, quite appealed to her. It would surely be easier only to have to think about feeding the pair of them, and if she wanted to go to bed as soon as the baby was sleeping, she could do so, guilt-free. The other bonus was that she and Josh had a lot more to talk about on their Skype calls, and as long as he was back in the middle of December as planned, she could count down the last days until his return with the Advent calendar she was intending to purchase.

Considering how busy life was with a young baby, Rosa knew the few weeks would fly by. Josh was a good man. A hard worker and great provider, and that was one of the reasons she loved him. He made life easy. Not that she wasn't a hard worker herself; far from it. Yes, Titch now had the Corner Shop, and Rosa's newly discovered brother Nate was managing the café, but Rosa still very much had a hand in the running of both businesses. And now, as well as trying to concentrate on spending as much time with her son as she could, she was dedicated to making a success of Ned's Gift, the charity she had set up in her great-grandfather's name; the same Great-grandfather Ned Myers who had originally bequeathed her the Corner Shop in Cockleberry Bay. The very man towards whom, despite never meeting him, she felt so much admiration and gratitude. It was in his memory, and with Josh's complete approval, that she had named their first-born Benedict Christopher Smith ('Little Ned').

Rosa awoke from the deep slumber she had fallen into on the window-seat to a tapping on the front bay window. A voice was saying urgently, 'Rose, Rose! Wake up and let me in.'

The sleepy mum didn't even need to open her eyes to see who it was. There was only one person she knew who called her Rose.

Hot was barking and scratching at the back door. Little Ned had just started to cry upstairs. Rosa opened the front door, then with eyes half-closed sloped her way up the stairs to return a few minutes later after changing and comforting the baby, to find Titch holding out her arms to her pink-faced baby and pointing to a steaming mug of tea on the kitchen table. Hot had been let in and was now calmly chewing at a toy in his dog bed in front of the log-burner in the other room.

'I was sparko. I never usually miss him crying,' Rosa moaned.

'Hardly. You woke up just as he started. Teething, I guess. Poor little lad.' Titch cuddled the baby against her neat pregnancy bump, allowing him to push his sweaty head right into her breast, leaving a line of dribble as he did so. 'He's going to be a big, tall boy like his daddy, this one, I reckon.' Titch rocked him gently.

'And the Worst Mother Award goes to Rosa Smith.' Rosa splashed a bear-shaped teething toy with boiled water, waited until it was cool, then handed it to her friend to see if Little Ned wanted to gnaw on it. 'I wish I had a manual that told me exactly what to do and when to do it. And the state of his nappies too, at the moment! Fluorescent green we had this morning. Why does nobody tell you about these things?'

'I did try,' Titch said, 'but until you experience it, you don't realise how bloody hard being a mum is. Have you got any biscuits?'

Rosa dug out a clean muslin cloth from a kitchen drawer, handed it to Titch for the dribble then fetched a dachshund-shaped biscuit tin from the side.

'Ah, that reminds me,' Titch said. 'Look in my bag, Rose.'

'Mary's ginger and raisin cookies? Yum!' Rosa emptied the Tupperware into the biscuit tin. 'Good old Mum.'

'She sends her love.' Titch immediately reached in and grabbed two. 'And if there's a competition running, I will always beat you in the Worst Mother category. Do you remember that night we got drunk in the Ship when Theo was only a couple of months old? My poor mother; she had to have him nearly the whole of the next day, I was in such a bad way. He could have thrown himself out of the cot and I wouldn't have noticed.'

'Where are Theo and the dogs today, then?'

'This is why I've dropped by to see you. I come bearing great news.' Titch grinned. 'A Cockleberry Crèche, also known as Little Angels, is now officially up and running in a room off the church hall five days a week. It's so much closer than the one I used to put Theo in and the woman who runs it is so laid-back and flexible. Gladys Moore, her name is, and she's one of our tribe, Rose. She's so lovely, very experienced, has all the qualifications, and also has a great sense of humour. I trust her implicitly with my Theo. He's been twice now. He bloody cries when he has to leave her. The little sod.'

'That's surely a good sign, isn't it?' Rosa sat down at the kitchen table. 'Don't tell me she takes dogs too.' She lowered her voice. 'That would be just the best.'

'Not quite, I've left my two with Mum today. Sometimes it just gets a bit too much for all of us, doesn't it? So don't keep beating yourself up, Rose.'

'I hear you, sister! I can't believe we missed that amazing item on the old Cockleberry grapevine about a new crèche in town.'

Rosa took a drink of tea then admitted, 'Saying that, I'm in a daze half the time at the moment.'

'I think it all happened very quickly, but it's a blessing, I tell you. Having a toddler and running the shop just wasn't working. At least when they are this age, they sleep for hours.' Titch was enjoying her cuddle with Little Ned, who had fallen asleep. 'Ritchie is great but juggling his chip-shop shifts has been challenging as his mum has got some kind of flu bug and he's had to cover for her. He's just doing an hour for me now as I wanted to spend some time with you.'

'Aw. That's nice. I can't even imagine what it will be like for you with two of them to look after.'

Titch groaned. 'Tell me. I could never deny my Ritchie having a child of his own though, how could I? He's such an angel. This one has definitely got his gangly limbs; he or she is forever kicking me.'

'A Christmas Day baby will be so sweet.'

'For whom, Rose? This one isn't going to be too happy when they realise it's one set of presents every year. But at least me and Ritchie will be off for a few days when the birth happens – if our baby is on time, that is. And hurrah, I'll be able to have a drink on New Year's Eve.'

'Er – and if you are breast-feeding? Maybe just the one.'

'Look at you being the sensible one.' Titch smiled.

'I think it's so great you are waiting to find out the sex.' Rosa carried on.

'You know what? There's not so many surprises in life these days, so we thought it would be fun.'

'I agree. I reckon it's another boy though. Do you?'

'I think it's a bloody giraffe.'

They both laughed.

'Was Theo early then?'

'No, but he flew out without warning, didn't he? Right on the Corner Shop floor, where I now stand every day serving customers.'

'That seems like years ago now.'

'Two years, five weeks to be exact. Talking of twos – and I know this is the question every mother hates – but when are you planning to have another one? Josh wants a football team, doesn't he? And how lovely if our little broods could all be friends together.'

'Give me a break, mate. Josh may have to call on a substitute if he wants one this early. I'm only just about coping with this little bundle of fun.'

'It will get easier,' Titch soothed. 'I keep being told that anyway.' She had a think, then added, 'Saying that, if he's not back until December, even if you get up the duff straightaway, you've got at least another year with just Little Ned.'

'Thank God!' Rosa replied. 'I wanted to get the accounts sorted for Ned's Gift today, but that ain't going to happen now, isn't it?' She finished off the last of her mug of tea. 'Nice to get a sneaky nap in though.'

'How's it all going with the charity anyway? You haven't mentioned it lately.'

'Well, I still have the thirty collection tins around here and Polhampton in various shops and cafés, et cetera, but as Christmas is coming – the season of goodwill to men and all that – I need to think of something that will bring some cash in to support them. They are all such great causes and I feel I've been letting them down slightly.'

'Rose, just remember that looking after a baby is a full-time job.'

'True, true – but you know what I'm like. I have to be busy and I'm forever thinking of new ideas rather than just relying on the charity-box donations. So, if you have any ideas, answers on a postcard, please.'

'Lucas is going to turn the rear car park of the Ship into a grotto, apparently,' Titch came out with. 'Father Christmas, a hut for kids to write letters to Santa and even talk of reindeers.'

'Real reindeers?'

'I guess so, unless he and Danny are dressing up like a pantomime cow.'

Rosa laughed. 'The kids will all love that, for sure.'

'Maybe you can tie something in with that; a Christmas raffle or another event?'

'I was thinking more along the lines of involving the community, like setting up a festive fête or concert maybe. I just need to get my head around it.' Rosa stretched her arms out in front of her and yawned again.

'Talking of pantomimes, how about you organise one of them?' Titch said eagerly. 'Do Peter Pan! I'd make a great Tinkerbell, flying through the air on a wire.'

'What, with that belly? You'd never take off. Anyway, we can't do a pantomime, not in the church hall anyway. It's banned.' Titch looked perplexed as Rosa went on: 'You must know about this – Mary told me. It went down in Cockleberry history over twenty years ago, she said. What happened was that the guy playing Joseph outed his wife onstage for having an affair with the Angel Gabriel; in his hurry to escape the humiliation, Gabriel got his wings caught in a wise man's walking stick and fell off the stage, breaking his ankle.'

Titch cried with laughter. 'That is bloody hilarious!' She wiped her eyes. 'Can you imagine being in the audience. Classic. So why the ban?'

'Because Joseph, aka Mr Gunter, is still the verger. He never got over the shame of it. Saying that, he lives with the woman who does the church flowers now and is very happy. So maybe it was meant to be.'

'I can't believe that juicy bit of gossip has escaped me for all these years.' Titch reached for her tea.

'To be fair, you weren't born when it happened.'

'And my mum keeps herself to herself, living right up the top of the hill.'

'I will hold that thought though,' Rosa promised. 'Maybe I can go and see Mr Gunter and assure him that if we do have one, it will be a staid affair.'

'Don't mention the word affair!' They were both laughing now, causing a little whining noise to come from the sleeping beauty on Titch's lap.

'Just a little bit longer, precious one, please,' Rosa whispered with slight desperation in her voice. Then she added, 'Titch, is it terrible to say I get a bit bored of being a mum sometimes?'

'Of course it's not. You have to fill your mind with other stuff, or it will just become eat, poop, nap, drink, playtime, another nap, another poop, playtime, bath, sleep, repeat.'

'You missed out scream,' Rosa said. 'I do love him unconditionally though.' She leaned across to stroke Little Ned's soft hair, as, awake again, he now calmly chewed and dribbled on his teething ring.

Titch took another one of Mary's wonderful biscuits, then said, 'I got away without putting any weight on with Theo, but I really must stop snacking.' Letting out a little burp, she put the lid back on the tin with her free hand. 'Remind me what charities make up Ned's Gift again. Sea & Save, of course. They were so amazing after that storm, weren't they? Looking after the wildlife and clearing the beach.'

'Yep, and South Devon Lifeboats, who were my saviours when I fell down the cliff.' Rosa grimaced as she recalled that fateful day. 'How times have changed. I was in a bad way mentally then.'

'Yes, you were,' Titch said sensibly. 'But you were lucky, and look at you now, girl. A happily married sober mother of one, businesswoman and charity CEO extraordinaire.'

Rosa blushed a little. 'Ha. That makes me sound very grand. Going back to your question, I have also included the Carrot Footprint, as they are creating awareness around climate change in schools and workplaces, followed by the Cockleberry Bay Residents' Association, as they do such good work for the community, and I also, after much thought, decided to include Polhampton Paws. This is because although Vegan Vera used them in her underhand way in her mission to try and get the Corner Shop, they are a respected dog and cat shelter, and I was grateful that she brought them to my attention.'

As if Hot knew his kindred paw-folk were being talked about, he plonked himself down in front of them on the heated kitchen floor, making a contented snuffling noise as he did so.

On seeing his favourite creature in front of him, Little Ned, now wide-awake, started to make all sorts of delighted noises.

'Aw, cute,' Titch cooed.

'I know. He is funny. I still can't believe he's mine sometimes. I used to brush off new parents when they said that you don't know what real love is until you hold that little bundle of flesh and blood in your arms.' Rosa paused. 'Titch, do you think he's a handsome baby? – And please be honest.'

'Er, yes, he's a stunner. He's got so much hair and the cutest features. Looking a bit like his dad already, I think.'

'Oh, I don't see that yet. I only ask as I've seen some downright ugly babies before, and parents just think they are the most amazing things on the planet. So maybe he is ugly, and I don't see it.'

'He's not ugly, Rose. How could he be, with you and Josh as his parents. He is beautiful both inside and out.'

'Aw. Don't you be going soft on me. Ugly or not, after my long dark road of growing up in foster homes, I intend to give him the share of love I missed and then some.'

Titch stuck out her bottom lip. 'That's lovely, Rose, but don't spoil him too much, will you.'

'I won't. I love him too much for that. And I love this one too.' Rosa went down on her haunches and lifted Hot so that Little Ned could see him properly. Without warning the little lad reached forward and grabbed sharply at one of the hound's soft brown ears, causing the usually placid pet to bark sharply in the baby's face.

'On the other hand, Little Devils, did you say?' Rosa shouted above Little Ned's screams. 'Have you got their number?'

CHAPTER THREE

'Good moaning, the Ship Hotel, how can I help yew?' Tina Green announced, trying to disguise her Hackney accent with an over-pronounced posh one. 'One room, one person for two nights on November the fourth, is that right, madam?'

Danny, Tina's thirty-four-year-old son, was hovering close to the small reception area at the right of the entrance of the old pub building. He earwigged as his mother continued politely, 'Perfect. Yes, yes, we take cash, cheque, card' – and here she risked a joke – 'or you can do the washing up instead if you like. Ha, ha.' Danny made a face at her. 'Yes, Ms Swift, thank you very much. See you on the fourth. Check-in is at two precisely.'

'Ma. You don't have to put on that voice every time you answer the phone,' her son grumbled. 'This ain't the chuffing Ritz.'

'It is to me. We are just into month two of opening and we need to make a good impression. And not everyone likes the London accent, you know.' Tina took a sip of the cold coffee in front of her. 'Ugh! Do you know what, son? I'm the happiest I've been for years. Look at us! Me and you have got jobs down here, a roof over our heads and a lovely new school for our little Alfie. I mean, who'd have thought it, eh?'

'I guess so. We've worked bloody hard to get this lucky though, right?'

Tina laughed at her son's astute observation. 'Yes, you've done yourself proud with the renovation work. Lucas still goes on about you getting him such a great discount on all the building supplies, what with you having worked at C&V back home.'

'Life's a funny old game, ain't it?' Danny mused, running his hand down the deep scar on his right cheek.

'It won't be if the rooms aren't ready for tonight's guests,' Lucas Hannafore answered as he came down from upstairs. 'Two rooms need turning around up there and the public areas need a good hoover. Maybe I should look at getting Edie Rogers back to clean, if it gets too much for you both.'

'We can manage without that boot-faced old misery, ta very much. Me and my boy are used to a bit of hard graft,' Tina Green replied. Her face was still pretty despite being lined from too many years smoking and too many years struggling, and right now a smart grey cropped haircut and bright red lipstick complemented her usual happy demeanour. She made soft fists to hide chipped red nail polish from her boss.

'Also, while I have both of you here,' Lucas went on, 'I wanted to let you know that, so that we can compete on a consistent level with the Lobster Pot, I have applied for one of those Three-Star Seaside ratings.'

'OK,' Danny nodded, not really having a clue what that meant. Lucas, who in his time had been a plumber and part-time publican, but not a hotel owner as such, was however very streetwise, and picking up on Danny and Tina's ignorance on the matter, he explained: 'This is a big deal for us. Seaside Stars are really sought after in the hotel trade and will definitely secure us more guests. And with three stars comes higher room rates, so more profit, which equates to bigger staff bonuses.'

Danny nodded in appreciation, as Lucas went on, 'But to get this extra star rating, everything – and I mean *everything* – from the outside step to the gents' toilets, to the back corner of the restaurant and to the smallest shot glass in the bar: all have to be spotless. In the rooms, the bedding has to smell fresh, there are to be no cobwebs and absolutely no hairs of any kind *anywhere*. In the restaurant, the food must be consistently excellent. The staff have to be courteous, polite and smart, so no chipped polish – all right Tina?' She unfurled her hands guiltily as Lucas finished with: 'We have to think *Four in a Bed* combined with *The Hotel Inspector*.'

'Oh, I love them two TV programmes,' Tina piped up. 'But shit, we don't want the likes of that Alex Polizzi coming here with her "darlings" and her effing and jeffing to get us at each other's throats.'

She laughed, but Lucas was deadly serious.

'And there'll be no swearing here either, not while we're on duty, or someone will report that on Tripadvisor and it will damage our standing. But you've hit the nail on the head there, Tina. Because that's part of it. To get this rating, the company who set up the awards send a mystery hotel inspector.'

'Oh fu– I mean, oh dear.' Danny raised his lip, likening him to a young Elvis.

'Yeah,' Lucas nodded.

'Mind you, I hope it is Alex Polizzi. She is one sexy Italian.'

'You and your thing for older women, my boy,' Tina said with a sigh.

'Yeah, experienced, can't get pregnant, and they love us young bucks.'

'That's enough of that.' She went to swipe her son, then remembering where she was, stopped herself. 'When will they come then, Luke?' she asked.

'That's the whole point, Ma,' Danny interjected. 'We dunno. The clue is in the word "mystery", right?' He put his hand up to high-five his boss. 'OK. We've got this, Lucas, mate. We're a winning team.'

'Yes, from now on, we need to be vigilant,' Lucas told them both. 'Davina said she'd help out when she could. Make sure the female touch is on show.'

Tina raised her eyes and quickly lowered them again; luckily only Danny saw. Neither of them was enamoured by Lucas's girlfriend of ten months. There was something about her they didn't trust. The fact that she was a policewoman didn't help either, as the Greens had been brought up trying to keep out of the way of the boys and girls in blue. Danny had even done a stint in prison, through no fault of his own. He had been protecting his ex, Leah, and mother of his child, who was now working on her addiction demons while living with her family in Wales.

Lucas was now saying, 'And my brother Tom will give us some input, I'm sure. They – the inspector, that is – will come alone and pretty soon, I think, so from now on we just have to up our game and be vigilant.' He paused. 'I also need to talk to you about how we are going to manage the Christmas Grotto set-up, but let's get this place shipshape first.'

While Danny and Tina headed upstairs to start on the bedrooms, Lucas went behind the bar to grab a coffee from the new whizzy machine he'd just installed. He then sat himself at a table in the window and looked out onto the beach. What a difference a year had made. Since their mother, Sheila Hannafore, had tragically died and left her two sons the old pub in her will, Lucas's older brother Tom, despite living in Bristol with his family, still had a big say in the goings-on of the business and, as an accountant, made sure that the books were in apple-pie order.

It hadn't taken a huge amount of money to do the old place up, and in the capable hands of Danny as project manager, and with Lucas's plumbing skills, the two men had basically renovated the bedrooms and added a couple of en-suites by themselves. Sheila had left them a tidy sum of cash too, so as well as it covering the renovation work, Tom's suggestion of hiring an interior designer had worked out well. The rooms and en-suites had been transformed into different seaside themes, with spanking new furnishings and bedding to bring the Ship bang up to date. The four en-suite bedrooms had been named after famous historic ships: the *Mary Rose*, RMS *Titanic*, the *Golden Hind* and HMS *Victory*, allowing the charm of the old building to shine through, but with modern comforts.

Freelance marketer Carly Jessop was also now on board to maintain the website she had recently created and to continually promote and update the hotel's services online.

The place was unrecognisable from when it had been the Ship Inn. Even Lucas's bedroom was like a posh hotel room. He had named his room HMS *Belfast*, purely because he had remembered sneaking a girl down to the engine room and snogging her there, while on a school trip. The imposing Air Force-grey warship, permanently moored on the River Thames, had also been a landmark to his life when he had lived in London.

Despite it being a great space, with the large lounge and newly modernised kitchen area also for his sole use, he quite often thought of moving out and getting a place not linked to his work. He always immediately changed his mind, however, for this place felt like home, and the memories of his mum and dad were still very much alive between its old walls. That made him feel safe – not quite so alone, somehow.

Taking a sip of coffee, he wondered what his forthright and quite often misunderstood mum would think of the place now. She would have hated it, probably. She had loved her old boozer, with its long-standing traditions, local clientele and family appeal. Despite grumbling about the changes and the price hike of spirits and wines, the locals did still frequent the hotel bar, with its roaring log fire and beach views. Lucas on the whole ignored their moans, but out of respect for them and knowing that the locals' custom was key during the long, cold winter months in the Bay, he had kept all the draft ales, aware that if he dared to change any of them, there would be a revolt. They might even shift their loyalties to the Lobster Pot up the hill. No way would he allow that to happen.

The original plan had been for Danny and his family to live above the pub in one room but, working on the business plan, Lucas's brother had said it made no sense to lose a room that could be used for guests. Instead, Tom would keep the rambling old place in Cockleberry Bay that he had bought a few years ago and was now only used for Hannafore family holidays. Danny, Tina, and Danny's nearly six-year-old son Alfie could move in there, he suggested, and pay a peppercorn rent that was taken directly out of their wages. Nate, Rosa's brother, who was also looking for accommodation, could live in the converted summerhouse at the bottom of the garden, so it was a mutually beneficial arrangement. Lucas liked the fact that his staff were close to hand at all times if he needed them. And Tom was happy that the rent paid for the expenses and a bit more on his property.

The Greens with their working-class London roots had been saviours to Lucas Hannafore. Rough and ready they might be, but they were cut from the same cloth as him and Lucas knew he could trust them not only to work hard but also to always have his back. This was no doubt helped by Lucas's close bond with East-Ender Rosa, who had bravely saved Alfie's life during the terrible storm of two summers ago.

Lucas's thoughts were interrupted by a familiar high-pitched barking and on looking out of the front window and down to the sea's edge, he could see Rosa, in bright yellow wellies and with Little Ned in a papoose on her front, running alongside Hot, dodging the waves as they came in. She was, quite clearly, without a care in the world. He had known all along that she would make a great mother; free and loving and fun. Fierce and protective. It was just a shame it wasn't to his children.

Sighing, he drained his coffee and stood up. Rosa had played such a massive part in his life already. Had once said to him in his deepest moments of grief for his mother and unrequited love for Rosa herself, that you had to keep breaking your heart until it opened fully. That was pretty hard to take from the only woman who had ever broken his. But he was lucky to have her as a friend. A friend for life, whom he knew he could rely on.

Reaching for his ringing mobile phone, he grinned and said playfully, 'Ah, if it isn't the elusive and gorgeous Miss Filth. What can I do you for today?'

Davina Hunt laughed down the end of the phone. 'I'm off shift at four and wondered if you fancied taking me from behind in the *Golden Hind*.'

CHAPTER FOUR

'Remind me when Little Ned's birthday was again.' Jacob opened up an embossed red leather diary, labelled *Lobster Pot Restaurant Bookings*. 'And what would he like for Christmas?'

'It was only in July,' Rosa looked quizzically at her friend, then down to Little Ned who was sleeping soundly in his pram, 'and now it's Christmas already?'

'You know me, I like to be organised. If my presents are not all bought, wrapped perfectly and under the tree by December the first, I come out in hives. It's all right for you, being semi-retired; some of us have to work, you know.'

Rosa could hear Hot upstairs causing chaos with the Duchess, Ugly and Pongo, the camp publican's dogs, as Jacob went on, 'And the trouble with being rich, gay and childless is that I have at last count seven god-children, including your little fellow here, three dogs and one husband. I don't even believe in God and He certainly doesn't believe in me, so it's all a bit of a farce really. To top it all, I can't stand half of the little bastards. That's why I have to write everything down.'

Rosa's shoulders started to shake with laughter. 'I do hope that my boy fits into the "stand" category.'

Ignoring her, Jacob carried on with his rant. 'I'm even

thinking of making this pub a child-free zone, but as half the holidaymakers are families, Raff told me rather firmly that it would be career suicide.' On hearing his name, Jacob's handsome Italian husband peered through the kitchen hatch and blew a kiss at Rosa.

'*Ciao bella*, I'm busy making pasties to freeze for the Residents' Association tent at the Fireworks Night party, so I won't come out. And you tell him, Rosa. Say it's for *la famiglia* – it's all about the family.'

Rosa blew him a reciprocal kiss and turned back to Jacob.

'You may be rich, but I'm certainly not after your money so you don't have to worry about that, at least.'

Jacob leaned over the bar and squeezed her shoulders. 'Darling girl, I didn't think that for one minute. Considering you own the café and are now in situ in that lovely pile of bricks on the front, you are becoming rather the Devon landowner. In fact, I might have to start calling you the Queen of Cockleberry Bay.'

Rosa said, 'Oh, I think you're quite safe with that title, don't you?'

Jacob smiled wryly. 'You'll never guess what else has happened. I'm so bloody stressed.' He let out a massive sigh. Raff was smirking to himself in the kitchen at his husband's dramatics.

'Now as you know there was never any love lost between me and Sheila Hannafore. I always suspected her of burning down my storeroom. Anyway…'

'That was years ago,' Rosa interjected. 'And you shouldn't speak ill of the dead. But go on.'

'Well, that gorgeous bear of a man, Danny Green, told one of my punters that the Ship has also applied for a Three-Star Seaside rating. I mean, how can they even consider that they will be on a par with us?'

'Oh Jacob, there's plenty of room for you both to have guests down here.'

'Maybe so in the summer, but in the winter not so much.'

'You have lots of repeat business, you'll be fine.'

Jacob ran a hand through his hair. 'It's more the principle than the money, darling. They've also got somebody working on their marketing.' He shuddered. 'I can't imagine anything there will be up to our standard. You know how I insist on every one of my one-thousand-thread Egyptian cotton pillowcases, sheets and duvets to be preened and positioned to perfection and not once, let me repeat, *not once* has a pubic hair EVER been found in a shower cubicle. That reminds me, we've just had a letter to say that our annual inspection is due before the year is out too.'

'It's good you get a warning though.' Rosa tidied Little Ned's blankets.

'Yes, but they still send a bloody *mystery* inspector, so we have to be constantly on the ball. On that note, I must get the dogs groomed.' He sucked in his breath. 'Can't have that good-looking scallywag Lucas Hannafore getting one over on us now, can we?'

Jacob's excitable voice caused Little Ned to stir and Rosa to get tetchy.

'Shush. We mustn't wake him,' she hissed. 'I've got at least half an hour of peace left and then I'm taking him to meet the owner of the new Cockleberry Crèche.'

'Oh yes.' Jacob cheered up. 'The woman who runs it is a hoot. She popped in yesterday to check out our menu.' He busied himself wiping down the bar. 'What does your husband think of you dumping your child with someone else?'

'Did you really say that out loud? And anyway, my husband has flown across the Pond and left us to fend for ourselves, so

I'm sure he will be perfectly fine about it. If it worries you so much, maybe I can leave Little Ned with you two?'

With a tight, 'I think not,' Jacob minced purposefully to the other end of the bar to get himself a bottle of water. Then he came back grinning to say, 'Fancy some lunch before you go and sell my *favourite* godson to someone else?'

CHAPTER FIVE

'Goodbye Stephanie, what a good girl you've been today. See you tomorrow, Bertie. Catch some more spiders in that tin, please. Mrs Hatt, can you please make sure you pack more nappies tomorrow and can you tell your sister that no, I don't supply vegan snacks for under-fives, for under anyone actually, but we'd love to have her little Bobby if she wants to provide some herself.'

With the door shut firmly and all her infant charges gone for today, Gladys Moore plumped her large backside on the sofa at the rear of the nursery and stretched her legs out, needing a few minutes' peace and quiet before she roused herself to tidy and clean the place ready for tomorrow's intake. Her ebony skin was so flawless that Rosa couldn't exactly guess her age but thought she might be in her late fifties. Her natural afro was soft and wild. Her breasts large and full. The long-sleeved red and white polka-dot dress she was wearing suited her affable personality to a tee.

Rosa, who had been keeping out of the way, waiting with Ned asleep in his pram while the others left, coughed to get the woman's attention. Gladys sat up with a start, her open smile brightening the whole room.

'Sorry, didn't see you there. Can I help you, dear?'

'I hope so. I'm Rosa Smith and this is Little Ned, my son, and I just wanted to see if you provide vegan meals before we discuss anything further.' The young mum's face remained deadpan for a second, then on seeing the woman's dismay Rosa quickly explained, 'Sorry, but I couldn't resist. You see, I overheard your conversation. The nearest we get to veganism in my household is eating an apple.'

Gladys Moore let out a loud throaty laugh. 'Rosa, I like you already. I needed that. It's been a bloody tough morning.'

'I can imagine, I have trouble coping with just the one.'

'I do have a young assistant, Claire, but Pablo Escobar bit her, so she's gone to the hospital to get a tetanus jab.' Gladys pointed to a cage across the room where a grey chinchilla was munching on some hay. 'Our resident pet. Thankfully, he took to car travel, as he was originally just here for the day, but he's been such a hit that he's one of our resident Little Angels now.' Gladys could sense what Rosa was thinking. 'And don't worry, he doesn't usually bite, but Bertie stuck a pencil in his eye and Claire was trying to pacify him – Pablo, that is, not Bertie.'

Rosa couldn't help but smile. Titch was right, Gladys Moore was definitely one of their tribe. Also, she grinned to herself on recalling how Josh sometimes called her 'my little chinchilla'.

'Little Ned? So is his dad Big Ned, then?' the nursery owner asked.

Rosa explained, 'No, that was my great-grandfather. The name on his lordship's birth certificate is Benedict, but that's quite a mouthful and I thought there would be fewer Neds around than Bens, so Little Ned just stuck. When he goes to school, I dare say I will have to drop the Little, but that's OK.'

'They stay little boys all their lives, girl, but let's not say that out loud or the PC police will be knocking on our doors.'

Rosa was amused: she loved this woman already. Then looking at the cage in the corner, she frowned and queried, 'Pablo Escobar? That's an interesting name too.'

'That's my husband for you. I said, "Frank, we can't be explaining to children who Pablo Escobar is – him being the world's richest and most successful crime lord." "Yes, my dear, I realise that. But you can teach them about South America where both he and the chinchilla come from." Anyway, I just call the little fluff Pablo in front of the children, who are all under four and care more for crayons, cars and cookies than countries – or chinchillas for that matter.' Gladys then looked closely at Rosa. 'I recognise you.'

'You do?'

'Ah, yes. Rosa, isn't it?' The woman was animated: she spoke incredibly fast. 'The Corner Shop owner, you're *that* Rosa, aren't you? And yes, Ned was the great-grandfather who left you the shop. I saw an article about you a while back in the *South Cliffs Gazette*. What a lovely story that was. In fact, we were living in Harberford at the time. Do you know it?'

Rosa shook her head, and Little Ned started to stir.

'It's inland a bit from Polhampton. Hearing about Cockleberry Bay, well, me and my Frank have always wanted to live by the sea and one of those mobile homes came up in the park at the top of the hill – you know, by the garage. I never thought you could live in them as a resident, but you can. Ours even has two bedrooms. He's on the bins, my Frank that is, and a job came up in Polhampton for him, so here we are. I used to childmind at home in Harberford and I also worked for several years running a nursery there, but this big church room is lovely and so much easier to clean up, plus we have a kitchen adjacent, as well as two child-sized toilets and one for the adults, cots for the babies a great enclosed bit of outdoor space here too, where the children can run around, drive our little plastic vehicles and stretch their legs in the sun. It's perfect. And how lucky was I to find it was vacant. You changed our life too, little lady. See?'

'Wow. That's amazing.' Rosa felt a warm glow inside. 'So, have you always lived in Devon?'

'Born and bred. I met my Frank at Polhampton High. Fell in love over a Bunsen Burner experiment in the fourth form. Quite a day that was. I leaned forward, my hair nearly went up and he had to douse me with a can of orange Fanta.'

'Some would call that love at first light, no doubt,' Rosa said, surprising herself at her own joke.

'Yes, yes.' The woman's contagious laugh rang around the hall. 'And how about you? I can detect a London accent.'

'Yes. I've been here three years this Christmas now and married to Josh for just over two.'

'And let me guess...' Gladys looked into the pram. 'Four months to the day, I reckon.' Rosa reached under the end of the covers for Little Ned's bottle. 'You're so close. On the ninth of November he will be four months old. Could I just warm this somewhere, please?'

'Of course. Give it to me.'

They went through into the small but spotless kitchen. Gladys took the bottle, shook it, and put it into the microwave. 'So, I guess you want me to take this little man under my bingo wings?' She lifted her right arm and wobbled it under her sleeve. 'Luckily, I have plenty of room. Fancy a cuppa?'

Rosa grinned. 'No thanks to tea, I just want to find out a bit more first, if that's OK. Do you have children of your own, Gladys?'

Gladys blew out a huge noisy breath. 'I'm saying this fast; it's easier that way. I lost a few babies; couldn't hold on to them. There were complications. A hysterectomy – you know.'

Rosa bit her lip. 'I'm so sorry. I had an early miscarriage and that was bad enough. I can't even imagine what you went through.'

'I had two choices, I could flail around on the floor punching it, saying woe is me, or I could get up, brush myself down and live a full life. All of these children are my own real-life little angels now. And there are many advantages. I get to enjoy them all and then give them back, so me and my Frank can have a nice quiet evening together. Oh, and holidays, and to get jiggy when we want it. We love our me time, you know.'

Rosa tried to get the vision of Gladys and Frank's *me time* out of her mind.

'He's always called me his exotic flower. I just say, "Frank Moore, enough of the exotic and more of the erotic. Just give me more of the Moore". Gladys let out another one of her marvellous throaty laughs, causing Rosa first to smile, then to reflect that her usually rampant sex-life with Josh had almost vanished without her even noticing.

The vivacious and likeable nursery owner looked down and started cooing over the now wide-awake and hungry baby loudly announcing himself to this new face. She lifted him out of the pram and stroked his cheek gently. 'So, what's all this fuss about, baby Smith, you handsome little fella?' The large lady made a shushing noise and, as if being lulled into some kind of trance, the baby immediately stopped crying. Then, testing the temperature of the milk on the inside of her wrist, she went and sat down on the sofa again, got Little Ned comfortable and gently pushed the teat into his mouth and held it there. 'You enjoy that,' she instructed him, 'while I tell Mummy exactly what else she needs to know.'

Rosa took a deep breath of relief and said, 'Can he come tomorrow?'

CHAPTER SIX

'Oh Merlin, don't you be starting that old nonsense again,' Mary Cobb scolded as her big black cat swiped a quarter-full glass of water on to the kitchen table with his paw to get her attention. 'I know it's breakfast-time. Give me a minute, will you! You know I like my tea and toast before I do anything.'

Tutting, she reached for a cloth to soak up the spill, then with Merlin now loudly meowing his hungry discontent, she opened a sachet of food and squeezed it into the moody moggy's metal bowl. She then turned up her radio to hear the *South Cliffs Today* weather presenter announcing, 'A bright and sunny day, with temperatures of seven degrees and a chilly easterly wind. Torrential rain after dark. And don't forget, all you boaters out there, a full moon will bring with it a high tide tonight. So, to summarise, it's a sunglasses and wellies kind of day.'

'For goodness sake, can I get no peace!' Mary exclaimed as her landline phone started to ring. She pushed her long wiry black hair away from her ear to answer it.

'Mum, it's me. I'm on my way up the hill and going to pop in for a cuppa. Is that all right?'

'Course it is, duck,' Mary replied resolutely, quickly shoving the last mouthful of toast and chunky marmalade into her mouth. Then, draining her favourite yellow teacup, she quickly checked the tea leaves that lay all around the thin bone-china base.

On noticing the massive pumpkin and other Halloween decorations that adorned the front window of Seaspray Cottage, Rosa smiled to herself. Then, scrabbling to find her keys in her messy handbag, she let herself into her mother's cosy home.

'Oh, just you, is it? Where's my boy and that hound of yours?'

'That's what I've come to tell you. Little Ned's in the new nursery in the church for a couple of mornings this week. And I gave Hot a run on the beach before we came up, so he's flat out at home. I just needed a break from the pair of them.'

'If you'd have just asked, I could have…'

Rosa interrupted. 'No, Mum, you couldn't. You love working your few shifts at the Co-op and I think it's good for Little Ned to have company. He's being a little terror at the moment.'

'Probably because his father is away again. Tea, dear?'

'That's not fair. Josh is a great dad. And if a couple of short contracts a year keeps his toe in the finance world and himself sane and happy, then that's fine by me.' Rosa sat at the kitchen table. 'And yes, tea would be lovely, thank you.'

'She's got no children of her own, you know, that Gladys Moore.'

'Oh, so you knew she was there then?' Rosa said as her mother continued without listening: 'So, are you sure you trust her with yours?'

Rosa bit her tongue. Mary's alcoholism had seen to it that Rosa had had the most terrible childhood, so who was she to put this warning to her own daughter now? But Rosa had no wish to hurt her feelings by reminding her of this.

'Yes, Mum, I do. Titch trusts her with Theo so that's good enough for me. And I'm usually a decent judge of character, you know that. Gladys Moore seems a lovely person. Straightforward and kind.'

'Two words. Joe Fox.' Mary put two fresh cups of tea down in front of them. 'You so trusted him, didn't you?'

'Mum! What's the matter with you today? That was ages ago and my heart made that decision, not my head. And he got his comeuppance, didn't he? His family left him and went to Spain to live.'

'He's back from Manchester, so I've heard.'

'Well, bully for him. I certainly won't be having anything to do with him, that's for sure.'

Mary yawned. 'I'm sorry, Rosa. I don't know what's wrong with me at the moment. One minute I'm happy as Larry, the next I'm snappy as a biscuit. I'm worried that's maybe why Titch hasn't asked me to do any more shifts for her at the Corner Shop.'

Again, Rosa didn't want to hurt her mother, this time by telling her it was because she kept forgetting to give Titch messages or update the order sheets.

'No,' Rosa replied kindly. 'I think Titch is being mindful about finances and the shop's never as busy in the winter; we both know that.'

'I'm always tired too at the moment, but I don't help myself, as I was up until the small hours, getting the window ready for tonight's trick-and-treating. So maybe you're right, I probably shouldn't take on too much babysitting at the moment.'

'Well, you do like to sell yourself as the witch of Cockleberry Bay,' Rosa teased, but also now slightly concerned about her mother's ailments. 'And what did you tell me about All Hallows Eve? That the dead return to the living world and reconnect with their families, wasn't it? You probably won't sleep tonight either.'

'Maybe you should come up later and see if we can talk to Queenie. Your great-gran would have loved our Little Ned.'

'As much as I'd love to,' Rosa lied, 'I can't, as the boy will be fast asleep. Oh no – that reminds me.'

'What is it, duck?'

'Sheila Hannafore died a year ago today. Bless Luke. I was going to pop in and see him later. He took it so hard.'

'That was a rum old business, wasn't it? Those poor boys of hers.'

'Let's not dwell on it now,' Rosa sighed. 'Have you got all your goodies ready for the kids?'

'I made hundreds of Critter Cookies with currants as flies last night. I just need to get some bags of sweets now.'

'If there are any cakes left over from the café, I'll get Nate to drop them up to you, if you like.' Then Rosa added, 'That reminds me – I must pop in and see how he's getting on later. A woman's work is never done and all that.' She threw her coat on the back of her chair, sat down, and started to drink her tea. 'So much to do. But for now, can I have some toast, please? I'm starving.'

'You know where the toaster is, missy,' Mary tutted, then on seeing the bags under her daughter's eyes she got up and went to the bread bin. 'I can read your leaves for you too if you like?'

'No, you're all right.' Rosa took a big drink of her tea. 'Why does nobody tell you how time-consuming having a baby is? I literally have so much to do every day and I only ever get half of it done.'

Mary sat down. 'I wish I'd have experienced it properly and I could advise you a bit more,' she said in a low voice, and put her hand on Rosa's arm. 'You do realise that I will make time to look after your little one whenever you ask me to? I can juggle the supermarket shifts if I have to. I may have failed you, but I want to be the best grandmother ever.'

'Actually, yes, you've reminded me, can you have him on Fireworks Night, please, and Hot as well? You know how much I love it and the café will be extra-busy as we are doing food and drinks this year.'

'Of course.' Mary grinned. 'I hate it in equal measure to you liking it. All that thick sulphur-filled air plays havoc with my breathing.'

'How is your COPD at the moment?'

'Since my attack last year, that lovely doctor at the hospital makes sure I have all the right inhalers and drugs on hand in case I start to go downhill. At last I feel it's under control.'

'Good.' Rosa started to butter her toast. 'Remember to keep them with you at all times though, won't you? They're no use in the medicine cupboard if an attack comes on quickly, like last time.'

'Yes, daughter.'

'So, I have a few hours now to pop by to see Titch, go up to the café and sort out the charity finances. Luke may have to wait.'

'Well, make the most of the time, won't you.' Mary shuffled in the kitchen chair. 'And Rosa?'

'Yes. What is it?'

'I've been meaning to tell you something.'

'Go on.'

'Christopher Webb, you know, your…your dad.'

'You mean the man you had a one-night stand with and mistakenly created li'l ole me?'

'Rosa.' Mary looked upset. 'Don't you be saying things like that. You are so loved and he is a good man. You just need to give him a chance. Anyway, he's decided to take on the old funeral director's business at the very top of Main Street.'

'He's moving to live in the Bay!'

'Yes. You never think of what happens to a funeral director when he dies, do you? Old Eddie Bailey only had one daughter and she emigrated to New Zealand years ago. It's all set up for someone else to just move in.' Mary put the kettle on again. 'Christopher doesn't want you to think he's forcing anything on you, but with your brother here too now, he feels he wants to be nearer to his family – and that of course includes you and Little Ned.'

'So how often do you see him then?' Rosa asked flippantly.

'I…er, we keep in touch, as he wanted to be kept in the picture about you and, of course, his new grandson. I've only met him once, for a drink last year, when you'd just found out about him. We talk on the phone and I send him photos of you and the little one.' Mary sounded a little nervous. 'I hope you don't mind.'

'Wow. You kept that quiet.'

'It's not that I was being deceitful. It was made clear to you that the door has always been open for you to meet him properly. When you are ready. He is a sensitive and kind man, Rosa. He hopes when the time is right, you will go to him. He'd love to meet his grandson in the flesh too, of course.'

'I'm surprised I didn't pick up that he was coming to town on the Cockleberry Gossip train.'

'Nobody knows. The estate agents who dealt with it are in Polhampton and I wasn't going to say anything that might jeopardise the peace of my family; you know that.'

'When does he move? Where will he live?'

'He actually arrived yesterday and there's a flat above the Chapel of Rest that he's going to stay in for now.'

'That's a bit spooky.'

'I think it's marvellous in many ways.' Mary looked down

to hide her blushes. 'I can't wait to see if it's haunted.' At that moment, Merlin screeched in through the back-door cat-flap and jumped right onto his mistress's lap.

'Something just spooked him for sure,' Rosa noted, getting up and putting her coat back on. 'OK, I'm off. Thanks for breakfast, Mum, and I will pop in with the little man soon. And are you sure you're happy to babysit and dog-sit on Fireworks Night?'

'Yes, duck, I'm sure. I'll keep them safe from the loud noises. It's a full moon tonight, by the way.'

'Halloween and a full moon. It's a witch's paradise, isn't it?'

Rosa faked a cackle, as her mother went on sombrely, 'This time of year, that tide will be right up against the sea wall, you mark my words.' She got up without another word, went to the kitchen counter and handed Rosa a plastic bag with some biscuits in.

Then, watching as her only daughter sped down the hill and over to the Corner Shop, she smiled a watery smile. A mother's love – so nourishing, so magical but also, at times, so bloody complicated. She then looked inside her daughter's teacup, saw the way the few leaves in the bottom were sitting and a prickly feeling of spirit went right through her. Closing her eyes, she took a massive breath and made a low moaning noise. Merlin jumped off her lap and ran upstairs, hissing. This time of year had always brought with it some sort of consequence for her daughter, and it looked like this one was going to be no exception. She must write herself a note, so as not to forget to warn her.

CHAPTER SEVEN

Rosa bumped into a stressed-looking Ritchie Rogers coming out of the Corner Shop as she made her way in.

'All right, Rosa?' he greeted her. 'Glad you're here. Titch is insistent she can cope, but I'm worried about her. She seems to forget she's having a baby.'

'Ritch, I know you love her dearly, but she's young and tough and still got seven weeks to go. I worked up until a week before I dropped, and I was fine.'

'OK, but tell her to wait and I'll unload the delivery that's just come in. My mum's still not right so I said I'd do her shift at the chippie.'

There was no sign of Titch when Rosa entered the shop. Guessing her pregnant friend must be in the loo, she went through to the familiar back kitchen, put on the kettle, and deposited Mary's Critter Cookies into the battered old biscuit tin – the same one that had seen the friends through many a drama over recent years. Titch had been insistent that when Rosa moved out, she must leave the biscuit tin behind so they could carry on their tea and biscuit counter-talks tradition. Saveloy and Mr Chips, Hot's offspring by Jacob and Raffy's dachshund bitch the Duchess (with her full name being Lady

Dolce Vita Petunia Duchess Barclay), were sleeping soundly in their dog bed at the back of the shop. They were very much part of the family Titch and Ritchie had created for themselves.

The shop bell rang. On seeing it was Davina Hunt, Lucas's girlfriend, Rosa put on her best fake smile. She'd taken an instinctive dislike to the woman the minute Lucas had introduced them, and this was the first time she had been in close proximity to the WPC without Lucas in tow.

'Hi Davina, can I help you?'

'Oh hi, Rosa. I didn't know you still lowered yourself to do shopwork.'

Rosa's smile remained fixed as the spiteful one went on, 'Lucas has sent me up to see if you have any Halloween masks of all things. I thought this place just did pet supplies?'

'Titch caters for all sorts of occasions. I think she's put the masks in the children's section over there.' Rosa pointed. 'There are some sparklers for Fireworks Night too, if you're interested,' she added, wishing she could light one and stick it up the rude cow's arse. An hour had already passed since she had dropped Little Ned off at the nursery. She hoped he was all right. He had gone straight into Gladys's arms without a whimper, so Rosa had felt no angst on leaving him. In fact, she was feeling rather guilty at how free it felt not to be at his every beck and call. There were only three children there this morning, and Claire, the young assistant, was helping two toddlers to do some finger-painting.

Rosa looked on as Davina started picking up and scrutinising the masks one by one. Seeing them reminded Rosa of the legendary Halloween parties at the Ship Inn. It had been a pub then, not a hotel. On one of those nights, she remembered Lucas apprehending her on the beach and trying to kiss her, one of the many push-pull scrapes that she had experienced during her complicated 'relationship' with the young plumber. A relationship that had initially been based purely on lust and sex, and if it hadn't been for her getting together with Josh could have grown to be so much more.

Rosa couldn't deny she still found him attractive, with his brooding hazel eyes, long lashes, full lips and taut, stocky body. But she loved the equally handsome Josh with all her heart, and now that a baby had cemented their love, straying couldn't be further from her mind. Lucas was a friend and would stay a friend. However, if she was honest with herself, when the sexy plumber had told her about Davina, she had felt a bit strange. It could only be a good thing for Lucas to direct his feelings to someone else and she wanted him to be happy, of course. But despite her feelings of love for Josh, there was still a minute amount of jealousy around anyone getting close to Lucas – and if anyone hurt him, she wasn't sure what she would do.

With Davina concentrating on choosing masks, Rosa had a chance to look her up and down. Her well-coiffured hair was everything that Rosa's wasn't. Long, straight, blonde and in perfect condition. Her long slim legs fitted nicely in her tight blue Levi's. Rosa was sure that she had had lip-fillers, and her breasts looked too round and perfect to be real. The rest of her rather pointy features made her attractive rather than pretty. And despite her being a police officer, there was something about her that Rosa could not trust.

'I'll take these, please.' Davina Hunt plonked five different masks onto the counter. 'Oh, and one of those Halloween goodie bags too. Lucas said he wanted something to give to the demon child.'

'Alfie, you mean?' Rosa questioned. 'He may not have had the best start in life but I think he's a good kid really.'

Davina harrumphed. 'You don't have to spend time with him

like I do.'

'You haven't discussed having children with Lucas then?' Rosa cringed at her involuntary question.

Davina turned her nose up. 'God, no. Why would anyone want to sacrifice their freedom in that way?'

Knowing how much Lucas would love a family of his own, Rosa didn't dare respond, instead commented, 'I didn't know you were having a party at the Ship tonight?'

'We're not, but we are having a themed dinner for guests who want it, which will no doubt lead to drinks at the bar, and Lucas thought we should make some kind of effort. Actually, while I'm here...as you know him quite well, Lucas, that is, I just wondered if you'd know what he'd fancy for Christmas. It was early days into our relationship last year and his present was...' She paused. 'I'll just say we were too busy to feel the need to give each other anything of a material kind. He just got a blow job for his birthday too. His favourite.' She ran her tongue around her teeth. 'But I guess you know that already?'

Davina then laughed out loud, causing Rosa's initial dislike of the coarse woman to accelerate up to a firm hatred. Taking a deep breath, she went in for the kill. 'You mean to say that you've known him for eleven months and you've not an inkling of what he'd like?' Power regained! 'And er, no – I've never bought him a present.'

'That surprises me.' The blonde woman sighed. 'I'm not stupid, Rosa. I see how he looks at you still. I also know what happened that night in the house next to yours on the front. You're lucky your husband forgave you.'

Rosa replied calmly, 'You, stupid? Of course not.' She lowered her voice. 'But I would think twice about believing everything you hear in this small town. I don't feel I should have to explain, but for the record, WPC *Hunt*, I love my husband very much and my relationship with *Luke...*' as if by saying the nickname she had always used for him, tightened their bond '...is purely platonic.' Rosa scanned the woman's purchases hastily through the till. 'That will be twelve pounds fifty, please – unless you were wanting anything else?'

'Bitch,' Rosa said aloud once the shop bell had confirmed Davina's departure. Her face was flushed with anger; her throat tight from holding back what she really wanted to say. To this day, she didn't remember exactly what had happened with Luke that night, apart from kissing him, but that was ancient history and it felt strange to be even thinking about it.

Rosa checked her watch. She called out for Titch, but there was no reply. A little concerned, she put the *Back in 10 minutes* sign on the back of the shop door, locked it and made her way up the steep stairs to the flat above. Since Titch and Ritchie had taken over the shop that she had gifted to them a year ago, they had done a sterling job to keep it running the way she and her great-grandparents before them had done so competently. Rosa had found out from experience that it was no mean feat to take on a new business and make it a success, and for this she was extremely proud of the couple and grateful to them.

'Titch?' Rosa called softly, walking through the beloved upstairs flat where she had spent her first years in Cockleberry Bay. She checked the lounge, then the kitchen, and when she got to the bedroom and there was still no sign of life, she began to panic slightly. Then, on pushing open the bathroom door, there was her mate, pants down on the toilet with her head resting awkwardly on her baby bump, away with the fairies.

Rosa gently touched her shoulder and whispered, 'Titch, wake up, mate.'

'What the fuck!' Titch's head shot up. 'Oh my God, I must have fallen asleep. What's the time? Was the shop door open?

Where's Theo?'

'It's all right, you've only been up here a very short while. Theo's safely at nursery and the shop has had either Ritchie or me in it. Are you feeling OK?'

'Yes, yes. I'm fine. I've been up since five with *Thomas the Tank Engine* and his lordship, that's all.'

'Bless you, and don't worry, I crossed Ritchie on the steps, so, like I said, you've not missed anyone. I just served Lucas's dear darling girlfriend and that was it. Look, you're obviously knackered, so why don't you get into bed for an hour? The kids are at Little Devils, so I can put the order away and pick up Theo for you when it's time, if you like?'

'Oh Rose. Only if you're sure.' Titch yawned hugely.

'I'm more than sure.'

'But what about your charity stuff?'

'I'm my own boss, it's fine. That can wait.' Rosa put her hand on her friend's arm. 'Maybe you are overdoing it a bit? Do you want me to have a word with Luke and see if Danny's got some time to spare to help you out when you need it?'

'Hmm, I may not be able to bear that.' Titch gave a wry smile.

'Why not?'

'I won't get anything done, will I? I'll just be perving at him; he's so hot.'

'Titch Whittaker – I mean Rogers – what are you like? And anyway, he'll be working when you're not. That's the whole point – to give you a break.'

Rosa went out of the bathroom, so Titch could sort herself out. The cropped-haired blonde soon reappeared, saying, 'I kind of prefer Whittaker and all it stood for. Do you remember when I very first met you and said I'd introduce you to the few single cocks of *Cock*leberry Bay?'

'Yes, I do.' Rosa laughed. 'You were reckless, and the *cocks* were all feckless, back then.'

'I don't recall you being a complete angel to be fair,' Titch said, straight-faced.

'What a difference a couple of years makes, eh?' Rosa sighed. 'It will be my last year of being in my twenties next birthday too – how did that happen?'

'Yeah, you old bint,' Titch teased her. 'I guess the joy for me about getting pregnant as a teenager is that at least Theo will hopefully be off my hands before I'm forty. Anyway, only regret the things you don't do, I say. We lived it, girl, and we still are. Anyway, back to Danny Green.' Titch smirked. 'There's nothing wrong with fancying him, is there? Even with Lucas, you surely still have your own little fantasies?'

'I don't feel that way about him any more,' Rosa said swiftly.

'Oh? Truly, Rose? I think if you have that fire in your loins and that soul connection with somebody, it never really goes, does it?'

Rosa bit her lip and suddenly burst out with: 'How often do you have sex with Ritchie at the moment?'

'Hmm…around once a month if he's lucky, but I may be ramping it up soon to help get the baby giraffe out.' Titch put her hand on her friend's arm. 'Sex and babies aren't good bedfellows, Rose. You're either too tired, too busy, or too scared of having anything near you that may create another little monster. And ignore me harping on about Lucas, it's clear that you and Josh are made for each other.'

'Saying that, we did manage it the night before he went to New York. I thought the least I should do was put out before he went away for nearly two months.' Rosa forced a smile. 'But yeah, sex aside, we are an exceptionally good team, and thanks for saying that. I love you, Titch.'

'I love you more, and I feel fine again now. Amazing what a

little power-nap on the bog can do. There's no need for you to stay, honestly. You go and have an hour or two to yourself.'

'What about the order that's come in?'

'I've promised Ritchie I won't lift, so I won't. I shall just unpack the boxes out the back and bring stuff through individually.' Titch went to the kitchen and downed a glass of water. 'Go on, Mrs Smith, get down those stairs,' she instructed Rosa. 'I'd have a kip if I were you, while you have the chance. I know, let's reconvene at Little Devils at one and hope that Pablo Escobar hasn't torn off either of our offspring's limbs.'

CHAPTER EIGHT

Bailey's Funeral Care was located at the very top of Cockleberry Bay's Main Street. Inside the pristine front office was an antique red-leather-topped desk and a comfortable seating area with a glass coffee-table. Brochures outlining all shapes and sizes of coffins and headstones were neatly stacked in the middle of it. A sign above the desk pointed to a door marked *Chapel of Rest*. A small kitchen and toilet were situated to the rear of the office, where another door opened out to a car park housing a battered hearse, which looked old enough to be pulled by horses.

A tall, white-haired man in his mid-fifties, wearing a long black coat and sucking on an empty Meerschaum pipe, was standing in the window, chatting on his mobile. With his debonair good looks and somewhat spooky appearance, he could quite easily have passed as a younger version of the famous Dracula actor, Christopher Lee.

'So yes, I've sent you an email but I just wanted to confirm that it should read Webb *& Son*, please.' The man's voice was deep and precise. 'Yes, black writing on a white board. And "Son" is to be singular, not plural. I have one son and last time the signwriter misheard and put an s on the end, and by the time I got back from a funeral, it was up and there was no time to take it down and…my son, just the one son, hasn't joined me yet but… Oh, you're in a hurry, sorry to go on. Nobody's ever in much of a hurry here.' Both men then laughed.

'Thank you very much,' Christopher Webb finished, 'and yes, tomorrow is perfect – and you'll fit it by midday? Good stuff, good stuff. Goodbye now.'

He went over to his desk and sat down, then, taking off his rimless glasses, he rubbed his eyes, all the while continuing to suck on his pipe. It had been the hardest thing in his life to give up tobacco, but if just sucking in air was now his only vice, then so be it. He certainly didn't want to use one of those vape things which caused a trail of smoke so massive, it looked like your head was actually on fire.

The front window of the upstairs flat offered a great view over the narrow street which made its steep and winding way down to Cockleberry Bay's beach. In fact, if he stood on a chair, he could not only see the Corner Shop, but if he craned his neck to the left, he could also just about see the sea. 'Sea views,' the estate agent had said. Bloody liars, the lot of them, but he was happy: happy that he was now living so close to his only son and daughter, both of whom he felt he had failed in some way, although part of that had come about through tragic circumstance.

What with Rosa's mother being an alcoholic and not alerting him to their daughter Rosa's existence, and him selfishly sending his son away to boarding school when he couldn't handle the trauma of his now ex-wife abandoning them when Nate was just five, neither Mary nor Christopher had been the parents their children deserved. However, thanks to Rosa, he and Mary had found a way to try to repair the damage. It was Rosa who had taken the decision to find her birth father, but being the man he was, Christopher Webb bore Mary no ill will for not telling him that Rosa was his. They had been given an opportunity to put things to rights – and by moving here now, he hoped that would soon be the case.

What was it about Mary – or Polly Cobb as he had known her back in the day – with her long black hair flowing down her back and her beautiful, far-seeing mermaid-green eyes? They had met just the once, over a year ago, when it had all come out that he was Rosa's father. Physically, Mary was unlike any woman he had been attracted to since their encounter nearly thirty years ago. And even their subsequent telephone conversations about their new grandson Little Ned had been stilted and a bit weird. But there was something, something about her that he felt drawn to. And if he was put on the spot, he would have to admit that the reason he had sold up his place in North Devon to move across to the South was for more than just to be closer to his children.

'Right!' he said aloud, smacking his hand down on the desk and sending his spectacles bouncing onto the tiled floor as he did so. 'I'd better get on.' With his assistant of the past ten years understandably not willing to commute from North Devon, he had a great deal to sort out, especially as he was meeting his very first client here in a matter of minutes.

Without all his systems in place, he knew the first funeral would be a logistical nightmare to arrange, but he could use it as a good marketing ploy too. He would drive the hearse with coffin and flowers down and up Main Street, before heading to the crematorium or church. The locals would then be very much alerted that despite Eddie Bailey's sad demise, Webb & Son were very much back in the business of death.

He was just scrabbling around on the floor to retrieve his glasses when the front door opened.

'Oh, good morning, Mr Carlisle,' Christopher said, on his

hands and knees. 'Please forgive me – I'm just searching for my spectacles. Blind as a bat without them, I am.'

He peered up as the blurry figure in front of him reached down to the floor.

Hearing a female voice shocked him. 'Here they are.'

He hurriedly stood up, nearly banging his head on the desk, reached out for the glasses and put them on. 'Rosa – it's you! Hello, hello.' His eyes were now fully focused on the pretty curly-haired young woman in front of him. 'What a wonderful surprise.'

'I was just at Mary's and well, she told me you were here and well, as you are nearer to hers than mine…' Rosa stopped and took a breath. More calmly, she said: 'I just wanted to say welcome to Cockleberry Bay.'

'I can't tell you how happy this has made me,' Christopher said emotionally. 'I feel so terrible though, because I have a client coming in literally five minutes. It's going to be a hard one too – although none of them are easy to be fair – since it's a case of sudden death. But oh, my goodness, I would love to see you again, soon. And obviously meet Josh and my little grandson.'

At that moment, the door opened to a man in his late forties, with the build of a rugby player, the beard and hair of a Neanderthal man and blue eyes that were so swollen from crying they resembled pink golf balls.

'Mr Carlisle?'

'Yes. Felix Carlisle – from Polhampton and Chelsea, London. Celia Carlisle's only son and heir,' he stated dramatically, holding out his hand, his posh and effeminate tone alien to his strong masculine appearance. His smart Barbour jacket was, Rosa noticed, straining at the seams.

The funeral director shook his hand. 'Christopher Webb, pleased to meet you. Do take a seat.'

The big man groaned as he took the weight off his feet. 'Could I trouble you for a coffee? I was up with the tits, drove down from Chelsea and I'm so tired and so...' The big man burst into tears.

'Of course, Mr Carlisle. I was just about to offer you some refreshment,' Christopher said soothingly, aware that he had a crier on his hands. He could categorise his clients quite clearly into genuine but controlled grievers, over-emotional clients who needed a lot of hand-holding like Felix here, silently stoic ones, and then the ones he despised – the hard-hearted money-grabbers. 'My assistant is not here just yet. One moment, please.'

'I'll get it,' Rosa suddenly piped up, thinking that this poor man should not be left alone for a second and she was too tired herself to deal with grief of such enormity. As she was rooting through the packing box marked OFFICE KITCHEN, she listened in to the skills of her father as he talked to the man calmly, but with the utmost compassion.

'Sixty-nine! She was *only* sixty bloody nine!' the man boomed. 'I can't believe it.

Mummy was far too young to be popping off anywhere.' He fished out a large white handkerchief from his coat pocket and blew his nose loudly before carrying on. 'Mummy was in the middle of arranging this charity Christmas do for a church in Polhampton, you see. She loved the community life.' Felix Carlisle exploded into wracking sobs. 'I told her it was too much for her but she wouldn't listen. She said she had started getting it together and already people were showing lots of interest. There was even talk of a celebrity opening it. "I'm fit as a flea," she would say and like a fool I believed her. I blame myself! I went off back to London and left her in Devon alone, when I should have been watching her every move!'

He blew his nose again, mopped his eyes and said, 'I just can't believe it. She *only* ate fish, never touched red meat or a greasy chip, and the other week had even boasted about her prowess at the Downward Dog.' Discarding the sopping wet hanky, he grabbed a handful of the man-size tissues that Christopher had thoughtfully put on the desk for bereaved customers.

Felix gulped and confided in a shuddering voice, 'And then for her to die *in flagrante* like that, on *top* of her gardener of all people! A tradesman! Young enough to be her grandson! The shame!' He hugged himself in torment while Christopher and Rosa remained frozen, not knowing how to react, barely able to take it all in.

'I mean, I can't even *imagine* what our local vicar would think. But we can't bury her at the church close to our home here – no, no, no. All her friends will know how Mummy died. It's too embarrassing. We have to bury her here, in Cockleberry Bay. I insisted on that scoundrel Jamie the gardener telling me her very last words,' he drew himself up, 'and wished I hadn't now.'

Rosa almost felt that a round of applause was due at the dramatic delivery. She bit her tongue so hard it hurt, but at least it stopped her from laughing out loud. Goodness knows how her father was keeping it together.

Felix was far from finished. He went on, 'Mummy was adamant she could organise these things all on her own. She absolutely *doted* on her charity work for the church. They need a new roof, you see, and I'm too busy to take the project on for her. I'm an opera singer, you know. *Rammed* with work until Christmas, so I can't be away for too long. So, Mr Webb – it is Webb, isn't it? – how quickly can we get this thing sorted out?'

Rosa walked through to the glass-fronted area and placed two mugs of fresh black coffee on the table. She had located some random milk and sugar sachets in the bottom of the box and just one plastic spoon.

'That's all I could find,' she mouthed to Christopher who gave her a big wink and nodded.

'Thank you.' Felix Carlisle sniffed and looked at Rosa, who was still itching to know his mother's last words. 'This must be your father, I take it. You have the same lovely smile. Look after each other, won't you.'

Rosa felt an involuntary tingling sensation run from head to toe and then to the back of her eyes; she had to blink hard to stop her tears from falling.

'I'm so sorry for your loss,' she managed, then making a half-waving gesture to both men, scurried out of the door and back down the hill towards the beach and home.

CHAPTER NINE

'Where's my favourite nephew then?' Nate asked, as Rosa poked her head around the door of Rosa's, the café that she jointly owned with friend and colleague Sara Jenkins.

'He's at Little Angels, his new nursery, but me and Titch have renamed it Little Devils.'

'You and Titch would.' Nate grinned. 'Time for a cup of something?'

'Yes. Do you know what I really fancy?'

'Tell me dear sister, what do you really fancy?'

'A hot chocolate with some of those mini-marshmallows in, please.'

'Coming up. Anything to eat?'

'No, I'm OK for now, ta. You've had your hair cut,' Rosa noticed. 'You look more like me than ever with those short brown curls.'

'They work far better on you.' Nate whisked up the hot milk on the coffee machine.

'What do you think of the new funeral director in town then?' Rosa said, taking off her coat and sitting herself down at the table nearest the counter.

'Quite shocked actually. He literally only told me as he was leaving the old place. But it's good, I guess. We've started to get on so much better now that I have a focus and I'm earning my own money.'

'I just went in to see him.'

'Wow. I bet he was surprised.' Nate laughed.

'Yes. We didn't talk long. He had to see to a customer whose mother had had the life shagged out of her, by the sound of it.' Rosa giggled as she carried on, 'It's so wrong to laugh but this bloke's mother died while having it off with her toy-boy gardener. I felt so sorry for her son, but he was so stuck-up, and just the way he was telling the story cracked me up.'

'A fine way to go, I say.' Nate nodded approvingly, then walked around the front of the counter and placed the creamy hot chocolate in front of his sister. He sat opposite and clumsily reached for her hand. 'Sis, I've been meaning to say this and never ever found the right time – but thank you for saving me.' He bit his lip the same way Rosa did when she was feeling awkward.

'What's brought this on?' she asked. 'And I hardly saved you.'

'You did. Tough love and all that. I don't gamble any more. I respect what I have and most importantly, I now respect myself. I will never forget you giving me the chance to run this place.'

'That's family, isn't it,' Rosa shrugged. 'We are a good team, me and you.'

'Yeah. I've always got your back, sis.' Nate stood up and went back behind the counter. 'I guess chatting to Alec recently has caused me to mention it. He's made me see the light through the trees.'

'He's a bloody good counsellor and there is no shame in talking to one. He pulled me out of the depths too, you know that.'

'I haven't seen him for a while, or Sara,' Nate offered.

'My baby brain! I meant to tell you – they decided at the last minute to go to Australia. Sara hasn't seen her brother for years, and while they are over there, they are hiring a camper van and plan to travel around.'

'Nice one. It's summer over there too, lucky bastards. They've been kind of talking about it for a while, so it's good they've taken the plunge.'

'I think they were waiting for Brown to die before they went. SO sad, but he was an old fella, and it will take their mind off of losing him.'

'Yeah, it will. Talking of dogs, where's Hot?'

'I needed some peace. He thinks he's lord of the manor now he has a big house to tear around in, but I will walk him again when I get back.' Rosa looked around. 'It's quiet in here today considering it's half-term, isn't it?'

'That's because I've just sent everyone off on one of our legendary Spooky Café Cave Tours. You know, the same ones we did for the kids last year?'

'Sorry, you did tell me you were doing it. How's the uni student getting on being the tour master?'

'He's a good lad actually. Said he's happy to help during the Christmas holidays too.'

'Sara seemed to think you could manage without her few shifts.'

'Yes, well, I said that to her so she didn't feel guilty if she did decide to go off travelling. Let's see how I get on. I can always advertise for someone part-time if need be, if that's OK?'

'You do what's best. So, what did you feed the Spooky Tour gang with this year then? We did pumpkin soup last time.' Rosa made a gagging sound.

'Not this year, too bloody messy with kids, so we kept it simple with just some bat-shaped ham or cheese sandwiches, a bag of Monster Munch and a Halloween goody bag with a mask, a sweet treat and a giant toy spider in.'

'You've spoilt them. They'll have so much fun with that,' Rosa beamed. 'Keep an eye on that tide today, won't you though?' She still felt nervous about the power of the sea at this time of the year.

'Yeah, I said to Brad – he's the uni student – that he needs to keep a check on it. He's doing the ghost walk along the caves as we speak. He's not alone, sis – there's enough parents between them to make sure the kids are safe.'

'That's a relief. Right – now, about Christmas. I need to talk to Josh about it, but I've decided I'm doing Christmas this year at mine,' Rosa came out with. 'There's so much space at ours and I don't want to be going to Josh's parents with Little Ned. It's too far and if we stay here I can just put him in his own bed and he'll be far more settled. You are obviously invited.'

'I'd love that, of course.' Nate brightened up. 'Thanks, sis.'

'Talking of Christmas, I know it's only November the first tomorrow, but can we get the fairy lights up outside before the Fireworks Night, do you think?'

'I had that on my To Do list. I think we may need some new ones; I remember a lot of the bulbs going last year. I'm also planning to decorate in here as soon as the fireworks are over. We will have a Christmas Grotto to compete with that lot over there for the whole of December.' He pointed over to the Ship.

'I must check with Luke what they are doing foodwise,' Rosa mused. 'Maybe we can do a joint offering of some sort of voucher for a coffee and mince pie or something here with their entry price.'

'Always thinking, aren't you?'

Rosa put a finger to her head. 'Thinking.' And then to her feet and added, 'Dancing.'

They both laughed. 'And as for lights and any new decorations,' she went on, 'just order some online and put them on the business credit card, that's fine. We need some more tea lights too; they always look lovely and festive in the red holders. They should be in the Christmas box in the storeroom if we packed it all away properly last year.'

'OK, I'm on it. Actually, will you invite Dad?' Nate said bashfully. 'For Christmas Day, that is. I'm usually with him and don't like to think of him being on his own.'

'It sounds so weird, even using the very word "Dad", let alone him being a part of my life. I don't even know him yet. That's why Mum is Mary to me, half the time. It's crazy. I've gone from being just me and Hot to having a mum, dad, you, a husband and baby in less than three years.'

'When you put it like that, it is a bit mental.' Nate raised his eyes. 'But time will make things easier – about Dad, I mean. He's one of the good ones.'

'I hear you – and as for inviting him, I only just learned that he's living up the road from us. So, give me a chance, eh, brother?'

At that moment, a delivery van pulled up outside the café. 'Right, best get this order in before they all come back wanting their hot chocolates.' Nate headed towards the door, with Rosa following.

'Do you need a hand?' she asked.

Nate lovingly ruffled up his sister's curls, saying, 'I think you've got enough going on at the moment, don't you? Now, get yourself home and try to relax while you have the chance.'

CHAPTER TEN

Rosa stopped midway down the hill and pulled up the hood of Little Ned's tiny green anorak, and to shield him further from the biting wind she tucked in tight the soft blanket that Mary had knitted for him. He looked directly at her from inside his pram and let out a little scream of delight, causing Rosa to put her face right down close to his and give him a big wet kiss. He hadn't even acknowledged her when she had first gone in to collect him from Little Devils. Gladys told her that he had been a joy to behold, which was hard to believe, but whatever he had been, her little lad was sleepy now. He'd been fed too, so it was a perfect scenario. In theory, she could from now on drop him at eight a.m. and have peace until at least two-thirty.

Arriving back at Gull's Rest, Rosa shivered and turned the heating up. Winter was most definitely on its way.

She felt a weird sense of achievement – something she hadn't felt for quite some time – as she had not only spent time with her mum, Titch, Christopher and Nate, but she had also managed to give Hot a quick walk, plus sit down afterwards with him warmly coiled on her lap so she could stroke his silky coat for comfort while she went through the charity accounts and got the year-to-date total that she had been meaning to sort out for at least a fortnight. The figures hadn't been as high as she had hoped, but with ideas now buzzing around in her head about organising a Christmas event, she knew she would be able to top up the pot substantially over the festive period. She must speak to Christopher to see if she could maybe tap into the event that Felix's mother had been working on before she met her sudden end.

Getting up and placing Hot down on the floor, she knelt at the log-burner, putting a couple of logs in for later.

'*Yesss!*' she said aloud, having a sudden eureka moment. She could arrange an event and advertise it by putting a label around each of the charity boxes. Maybe place a tray next to each box containing small festive gifts – a bit like those boxes with buttonholes for breast cancer or the Marie Curie Foundation – and ask for a donation in return. After all, the charity was called Ned's Gift. She could make it charity-specific, with brooches maybe? A dog with tinsel around its neck for Polhampton Paws, a seagull with a cracker in its mouth for Sea & Save, a lifeboat with Father Christmas in for the local crew.

While she was deep in thought, Hot trotted up to her and whined, brushing against her ankles.

'Here.' Thinking he was looking for it, Rosa passed him his favourite toy, the chewed-up, grubby-looking remains of a yellow duck with huge eyes that drove him mad. Ugh, it was wet where he'd licked and torn away at it. But he took no notice. So it must be walkies he was after. 'I know, boy, but it's freezing, and we've been out already this morning.'

The mini-dachshund started to make I-need-a-poo-and-wee agitated noises. He was practically crossing his tiny legs and obviously bursting to go. Rosa looked down at Little Ned, who was now sleeping so soundly in his pram that she didn't want to take him out in the cold again. She picked up Hot's lead and checked that she had poo bags and door keys in the pockets of her coat. She pulled on her red bobble hat, and checking that Little Ned was still sparko, she crept towards the door.

'Two minutes, you spoilt hound, and that's it. Next time you just go in the garden,' Rosa warned him as she lifted him down from the beach wall and on to the damp, dark grey sand. Conscious that she had never left Little Ned before but confident that he rarely woke from his afternoon sleep, she cleared up after Hot, threw the little black poo bag into the doggie bin, then let the dachshund off the leash to chase gulls at the water's edge while she lurked near the house so she could go and check on the little lad if Hot disobeyed her return whistle.

The tide was now coming in fast with the easterly wind, which swept around her cheeks and snapped at her earlobes. She looked across to the Ship Hotel and noticed the familiar shape of Luke, who was up a ladder fixing more lights to the wall, by the look of it. 'Bugger,' she said aloud; she had forgotten to go and see him earlier. With Hot still running around she popped back into home again, sneaked a peek at Little Ned, picked up a carrier bag then went out again and made her way over to the hotel. She shouted Luke's name loudly to get his attention.

'Hey, you!' he called back, balancing the lights on the guttering, and climbing down the ladder backwards at speed.

'Mind you don't get blown away up there,' she said. 'I've got something for you.' She reached into the carrier bag and handed him a plain brown gift bag, completely unaware of a spying Davina, who was viewing the pair of them intently out of an upstairs bedroom window. He looked inside quizzically to see his brand of cigarettes, a miniature bottle of brandy and a Toblerone.

'A survival kit. Thought you might need it today.' Rosa

shivered.

Luke felt his eyes sting and looked away for a second. 'Thanks, bird. That means a lot. I went up to her grave this morning. I can't believe how much I still miss her.'

'Of course you do, it's only been a year.' Rosa put her arm on his. 'I'd better go, I've left Little Ned sleeping at home. I'm always around if you need a chat; you know that.'

Leaving the bag at his feet, Luke nodded and headed back up the ladder, as quickly as he had come down it, glad that the wind was noisy enough for his sobs to be drowned out to anyone but the darkening afternoon sky.

Feeling her friend's pain, with a heavy heart and a happy Hot, Rosa pushed open the door of Gull's Rest to be confronted by Little Ned screaming louder than she had ever heard him scream before in his short life.

'Oh my God, darling boy, what is it?' She ran over and immediately unclipped the baby from his pram. Little Ned was bright red and hitching his breaths in complete distress. His blankets and clothes were covered in sick. Rosa held him tightly to her chest, not caring about the mess she was getting on her coat. 'My little boy, I am so sorry. Mummy will never leave you like that again.'

She walked him upstairs, ran a tepid bath, and undressed him on her bed. Throwing her coat to the floor, she then held his little trembling naked body tightly to her, until he calmed right down, making contented whimpers while pushing his face into her neck.

She can't have been gone for more than fifteen minutes, she thought. It was a lesson. The biggest lesson she had ever learned in her life. Her baby could have choked; he could have died! She gently lowered the now-smiling infant into his bath support, the soothing warm bubbles causing him to kick his legs frantically in delight. With the little parenting she had had herself as a child, she had always been concerned that she wasn't going to be a good mother. And this had proved it. What was she thinking, leaving him alone? Poor little mite. She could have waited to see Lucas, but no, instead of putting her child before anything else, she had to get another job done and ticked off her list.

Titch had warned her how demanding motherhood would be. But until she was actually faced with having this little person to be her total responsibility for twenty-four hours a day for at least the next eighteen years, she didn't realise the enormity of it. It was terrifying. How would she know if she was doing everything right? Josh was great with their baby. He was the one who had read all the pregnancy books and some of the early parenting books. Maybe she should get him to come home? She immediately batted away that thought. Titch said she had felt like this. In fact, Rosa now remembered the conversation she had had with her about Titch never wanting another baby, and now she was pregnant with Ritchie's giraffe, so it must have got easier for her. She could do this. Rosa Smith, *née* Larkin, was a survivor.

Thoughts rushed through her head. Maybe she should talk to other mums about their experiences. But she wasn't sure she could be bothered with all the polite chit-chat. It had been bad enough going to the antenatal classes at the local hospital and having to converse with strangers then. Directing her anger towards her own mother, she felt tears of frustration stinging her eyes. If Mary hadn't been so drunk, then she could have advised her more now. Of course she was going to be a bad mother! This was all her fault!

She took a deep breath and allowed Alec's words of counsel

to fill her mind. 'You cannot blame anyone for making you feel or act the way you do; you are your own person, you do that all by yourself.'

Little Ned was still kicking with delight in the warm bubbles. As she leaned down to kiss him, he looked right at her, then pulled at her curls. 'No nursery for you tomorrow, my little one,' she directed at her son. 'No. Me, you and Hot Dog are going to see someone who will know all the right things to say.

'Ah, boo.' She blew a raspberry into the baby's chest to a bout of giggles. 'Ah boo.' She did the same again to a similar reaction.

Then without warning, a feeling of both love and fear engulfed her with such an intensity, she picked Little Ned up in a huge warm towel and hugged him to her as if she would never let go.

Rosa could hardly hear Josh for the torrential rain hitting the two big skylights that took up the ceiling of their Gull's Rest kitchen. Once she had fed and settled Little Ned, she had put a jacket potato in the oven, topped up his bath with very hot water and got in it herself. Now, with a full tummy and sitting in her dressing gown in the window-seat, she felt a whole lot better.

Rosa scrolled down to find her husband's number on WhatsApp.

'I did try and Skype you before I called but I think the weather may have affected it. You know me and technology.'

Josh laughed. 'You're not as bad as you think you are, you know.'

'It really is crazy weather here,' Rosa went on. 'I can't wait for the rain to stop as I won't see the full moon otherwise.' A big swathe of rain smashed against the front window.

'Wow! I heard that. It's dry here in the U S of A. Just cold.

How are you doing? How's the little man?'

'Um. We're fine.'

'You don't sound too sure.' Josh knew his wife so well.

'You know, it's tough. His little gums are sore with his first teeth coming through, so I'm going to have a really early night myself tonight.'

'Aw, bless him. He's in bed now though, is he?'

Rosa raised her eyes and snapped, 'Of course he is. I do know how to look after my son.'

'Whoa! I wasn't for one moment saying you didn't. I miss you both so much.' And when Rosa sighed, 'Hey, Rosalar. Are you sure you're all right?'

She batted the visions of coming home to Little Ned screaming and covered in sick to the back of her mind.

'Yes, yes, honestly. I'm fine. There's a new nursery opened up at the church, and he went for the morning today. That gave me a bit of a break, which was nice.'

'Oh,' Josh said flatly. 'You didn't think to discuss it with me first?'

'Josh. Not now. I just need a little bit of time to myself. I needed to regain some sanity and I wanted to get the charity accounts up to scratch. Theo goes there, it's a great little place and the woman who runs it is lovely. Little Ned loves her already.'

'OK, good. Make sure you put the costs on the monthly spreadsheet though, won't you?'

Rosa felt annoyed. As if she didn't have enough to do already. 'Fine. Actually, I have news other than baby news today.'

'Go on.'

'I went and saw Christopher. He's taken over Bailey's – you know, the old funeral directors at the top of Main Street.'

'That's a surprise. And a nice one for you, I hope.'

'Yes, Mum just told me this morning. It's time I spoke to him.

He seems really nice.'

'How do you feel?'

'More emotional than I expected, to be honest. We didn't have long; a client came in whose mother had died.'

'Ah, right.'

'She carked it while on the job with a young gardener apparently. I know I shouldn't laugh but it was so hard not to.'

'Love it. And I think it's great that your dad is nearer. Maybe you can spend some quality time with him – if you want to, that is – and I bet he would love to meet his grandson.'

'Yes. I owe them both that. Actually, I've just remembered, I also want to ask what you think about something.'

'Fire away, wifey.'

'So, the woman who died.'

'On the job?' They both laughed.

'Yes. On the job.' Rosa giggled. 'So bloody funny. Anyway. Her name was Celia Carlisle. They're Londoners but have a second home in Polhampton where she lived most of the time. Well, she was arranging a Christmas concert locally of some kind, even trying to get a celebrity to open it by the sound of it. So, I was thinking maybe I could offer to finish what the poor woman had started. Her son was so stressed about not having time to run with it and of course I'm looking at it as maybe being of advantage to my own endeavours with Ned's Gift.'

The ever-wise Josh was quiet for a minute. He had seen how his wife was struggling with motherhood at times and knew this kind of challenge would make her happier again. He was also beginning to realise that leaving her and their son for seven weeks was a selfishly long time for her to cope alone with a young baby. Also, how much was he missing by not being with her and their beautiful boy? Babies changed day by day – and he wasn't there to see any of it.

'I think it's a bloody great idea,' he said, a little sadly, since he wouldn't be there to help.

'Really?'

'Yes. Especially now you have found a good nursery. Just split your time wisely. Don't take on too much. And keep it local.'

'Ah yes, good idea.'

'Maybe you can be Rosa Smith, Charity boss extraordinaire in the mornings and Rosa Smith, best mum in the world in the afternoons.'

Rosa felt herself welling up. 'Am I a good mum, Josh?'

In a massive surge of love towards his insecure partner, Josh said chokily, 'The best. And to be honest, as wives go, I kind of hit the jackpot there too.'

Rosa hung up and put her mobile down on the seat, peered through the curtains and looked out into the dark night. The rain was easing slightly but she could see that the tide had brought the sea right up to the sea wall. Suddenly, a bright glistening light was in her eyeline. It moved up and down with the swelling tide. Straining her eyes to see where it was coming from, she thought she could make out the shape of a boat. There it was again – a light, as if it were flashing a warning…and then a static orange glow remained bright in the gloomy mist that had now formed above the black water.

She looked again and saw nothing; the mysterious light had disappeared as quickly as it came. She was so tired; maybe she had imagined it. Or maybe the full moon was playing tricks behind the clouds. If Mary were here, she would be telling her it was the ghosts and ghouls of All Hallows Eve. The lost souls who had been taken by the sea and were coming home to find their loved ones. It was, after all, as her mother had taught her, the night on which the wall that separates the living from the dead was at its thinnest.

Rosa hadn't had time to get a pumpkin carved to delight any trick-and-treaters, and tonight she was in no mood for frivolity, so she had instead left the outside light on and a note on the door with a big basket of treats and some of the plastic spiders that Nate had had left over from his spooky goody bags.

Scary monsters, witches brew
A spider or treat, it's up to you.
A new baby lives here, so I'm going to hide
While the ghosts and sea demons come alive.

She hoped that at least parents accompanying their kids would understand. It was such a vile night that she doubted many would venture right down to the houses on the seafront anyway. But, in the spirit of her mother, she thought she'd better do her bit.

Exhausted, she turned off the indoor lights and after checking that all the doors were locked, she picked up a sleepy Hot, who stretched his long wrinkly neck and nuzzled her under the chin, slapping his tongue around her nose and making the special creaking sound that she loved to hear. And so the two best friends made their way up to bed, with Rosa determined that tomorrow she would be a better mother.

CHAPTER ELEVEN

'Hold, talk and sing to your baby cheerfully,' the nagging voice instructed, causing Rosa to think that this self-righteous-sounding woman had never been anywhere near a baby in her life. 'Put toys close by so your baby can reach for them or kick out his or her feet. Place a rattle in your baby's hand to hold. Act excited and smile when your baby "talks" and copy their sounds so they learn to copy you.'

On hearing this, Rosa felt guilty; she was already concerned that Little Ned's first word would be 'bugger'.

So engrossed was she in listening to her newly downloaded *Things to do with a four-month-old baby* podcast, that she didn't hear Danny Green jogging along the beach path behind her. It was rare that Hot couldn't run on the beach, but the high tide from the night before was still nearly right up to the sea wall, so she had attached his lead to Little Ned's pram and he was trotting along beside her, his tail waving jauntily.

Rosa nearly jumped out of her skin when the fellow Londoner put his hand on her shoulder. 'Jesus!' She turned her wireless earbuds off. 'You scared the life out of me.'

'Oh sorry, sweetheart, I didn't realise you had your ears in.' Danny was puffing. 'I decided I ought to get some beef *off* before

I start shoving the turkey and mince pies *in*.' He grinned. His accent was pure London and edgy. 'It's bloody beautiful up the top of that cliff today.'

The tracksuit and trainers look suited him, Rosa thought, and she could understand why Titch was attracted to the rough diamond in front of her. Yes, Danny Green certainly crossed the T with testosterone. With his twinkling light eyes, large but firm body, hair short as stubble and the kind of scar you were too scared to ask about, he certainly had something about him.

'How are you doing?' Rosa enquired.

'Yeah, totally fine. Love it down here. Who'd have thought you saving my Alfie from drowning that day would change our lives so much.' He looked down at Little Ned who was now awake and bashing a teething rattle on his blanket. 'He's got your boat and attitude, that little one, I reckon.'

Knowing he was using 'boat' as in 'boat race' for 'face', Rosa was pleased. 'Talking of boats, did you see a boat out here last night?' she asked.

'Nah, we don't get the luxury of a sea view from Tom's place. I've seen 'em before out here though, on a high tide.'

'Yes. I thought I saw one with a flashing light but maybe I imagined it. Just hope they weren't in trouble. Actually, while you're here, do you reckon you might be able to spare a few hours a week to help Titch out in the shop? She's about to drop and she's bloody knackered with a toddler on board. She'll obviously pay you the going rate.'

'Hmm. Not sure. I'll have to check with the gaffer. We're on the alert for a hotel inspector so it's all go at the moment. But it's possible. I've been there 24/7 for him lately, so I reckon he'll be all right about it. Actually, Rosa, why don't *you* ask Lucas? He won't be able to say no then, will he?' Danny winked at her.

True, that had been her original plan. 'OK. Is he around now, do you know?'

'Nah, he's at the cash and carry. I'm keeping out the way just like he is while Davina, our friendly neighbourhood filth, is interviewing Father Christmases for the grotto we are setting up out in the back car park through December.'

'I think it's such a great idea. The kids will love it. I'll let Gladys at the nursery know too so she can get permission for her and Claire to take the little ones there. That will while a few hours away for them and their charges.'

'Yes, we've got reindeers coming down at weekends and all sorts. I'd best try and get in the Christmas spirit.'

'You've got the Fireworks Night extravaganza to deal with first.'

'I could do with some fireworks myself, I tell ya,' he said meaningfully. 'Not many single birds around here, are there?'

'That's the problem with living in the sticks. There's not quite the same opportunities here to meet your match.' Rosa had also felt like this when she had first arrived.

'Yeah, I was just telling my mates back home that Cockleberry Bay is so bloody quiet you can hear yourself dream.'

'Mind you, these days everyone is meeting online, aren't they?' Rosa said, adding, 'I was so lucky to meet my old man through being his lodger for a while in Whitechapel, which meant I got to know him properly.'

'Sounds good, yeah.'

'Maybe you should interview for a female Santa's little helper?' Rosa winked at him, then, on checking her watch, 'Shit! Is that the time? We can't miss the one and only bus to Polhampton.'

'Do you wanna lift to the bus stop?'

Rosa started to powerwalk. 'Nah, you're fine, but thanks. By the time we've loaded me, baby, the pram, and the dog in the car, we will have got there already. See ya.'

Vicki Cliss was one of those people whose calming voice sent you into a little bubble of peace the minute she opened her mouth. In her mid-thirties, she was plain but pretty with no make-up, and despite now having four boys under seven, she always dressed well, still sported a neat dark bob and there wasn't a drop of mud or sick on her.

She quickly locked the door to the veterinary practice that she owned in Polhampton, then held her arms out to Rosa as she saw her approaching with pram and dachshund. Little Ned was sitting propped up with pram pillows behind him and Hot, whose short legs were tired, was sitting in front of him, to the baby's delight.

'Oh my God, it is so lovely to see you!' Vicki cried, kissing both of Rosa's cheeks. 'I can't believe I've only met this little fella once, too. That's what having babies does for you, especially twins! I come to work for a rest. And hello you, you little sausage. I hope you're being good for your mummy.' She tickled Hot behind his ears and slipped him a dog treat, causing him to snap it up and look for more, and his whipcord tail to wag even more furiously and the baby to chuckle.

'You OK?' Rosa asked.

'I will be when we get settled.' Vicki sighed. 'I've booked a table at the café on the front, is that all right? They are dog-friendly and there is a quiet corner if you need to feed Little Ned.'

Together they made their way to the light-filled café and chose to sit in the quiet corner.

Rosa took a sip of coffee and smiled at Vicki across the café table. Hot was sitting on Vicki's lap and thankfully Little Ned was sleeping peacefully after all the excitement. The expansive Polhampton Sands stretched out in front of them, seeming huge in comparison to Cockleberry's little bay.

'It's full on, isn't it? Motherhood, I mean,' Vicki offered. 'But no regrets, eh?'

Rosa shuffled in her seat awkwardly. 'I'm struggling a bit, to be honest. I always used to think that women were making a fuss about it being so hard. But it is hard, isn't it?'

Vicki took Rosa's hand. 'Let me guess, it probably seems that every time you pick up something to wear, or reach for your phone, he needs his nappy changing again. If you run a bath, he starts crying, so by the time you get back, the water's cold. Then you're so busy feeding him that you forget to feed yourself and after having had say, four hours good sleep a night, you wonder why you are so tired and hungry?'

'Have you got a camera rigged up in my place?' Rosa laughed.

'No, I think you are forgetting I've done it twice before and now I have six-month-old twins. Imagine what you are doing times two!' Vicki took a big drink of her coffee. 'It is slightly easier as I know what to expect, but I remember when I had Arthur, I felt the same as you, so don't worry. It will get easier.'

'I haven't told anyone this, not even Josh, but I did something terrible yesterday.' Rosa felt she couldn't carry on without confessing to someone, and she trusted Vicki with all her heart.

'Go on,' Vicki urged.

'I left Little Ned safely sleeping and went on to the beach with Hot, who needed a poop. I then went quickly over to the Ship to see Luke.' Rosa gave a moan. 'I only intended to be gone for literally two minutes. I came back and the baby had been sick all over himself, and he was screaming. He could have choked, anything...' Tears fell down her cheeks.

'OK. That isn't good, but you were lucky this time. He was fine, and I bet you'll never do it again. In fact, you can't – they are too young to leave for a single second at this age.' Vicki was kind, but stern.

'I know that now. I am such a bad mother.' Rosa cringed.

'No, you're not. It's all a massive learning curve. We are both lucky to have such good partners – or just imagine how hard it would be. Hats off to all the single mums out there, I say.'

'Josh is in New York working at the moment. I didn't realise how much he helped until he went, but I want him to feel he can get on with his own life and for me not to have to rely on him.'

'That's all very well, but Little Ned is his too and you will have to rely on each other. Parenting is hard work, and ideally, it takes two.'

Rosa pulled herself together. 'So, where's your brood today?' she asked. 'I so wanted to see the twins again, I bet they've grown so much.'

'Arthur is at school, Stan is at nursery and my darling Stuart is a full-time house-husband now, so he's got the babies. I promised him I'd be back by two.' She reached for her phone, checked the time, then showed Rosa a photo. 'Here are all the little darlings.'

'You can tell they are brothers! You are so lucky having Stuart at home, but Josh will be home soon, and I've just got one, not four to deal with, so I need to shut up and get on with it.'

'Yes, you do.' Vicki laughed. 'I'll happily do a house swap.'

'Does Stuart still do his volunteering on the Lifeboats?'

'Yes, of course. That's his outlet for sanity even though it is so dangerous sometimes.'

'You've nearly got a five-a-side already. Josh would be so jealous. Are you going to be one of those women who keeps trying until you have a girl?'

Vicki put a hand to her forehead in mock horror. 'From now on, I am sticking with animals. If I even suggest having another baby, I beg of you to turn me from the error of my ways immediately. Motherhood is not for the faint-hearted and that's a fact.'

Rosa laughed out loud. 'That's another thing: I don't think I want another one.'

'You mark my words, you will. Once he's through the baby stage, you'll forget all the difficult bits and just remember the smell of his lovely baby skin and the snuggling into you while he feeds and those little looks between mother and son that are just so priceless. I even missed winding mine and hearing that satisfying first burp.'

'Let's see, shall we?' Rosa looked down at her sleeping bundle, and for the first time saw Josh in him. 'Aw, he is such a good boy really.'

Vicki put a menu down in front of them, her voice now serious. 'But Rosa, if he is enough for you, then so be it. There are no rules.'

'And I've been so good at breaking those in the past.'

They both laughed. Rosa carried on. 'I really want to start working on my charity stuff and there is a potential new opportunity with it, so I am going to put Little Ned into the new church Little Angels nursery every now and then.'

'It does them good, I think. And you good. A happy mum means a happy baby. I love being a vet. It's what I do, it's what I'm good at and I know I'm super-lucky to have Stuart at home – but he even puts Stan in nursery a couple of mornings a week or he'd go mad.'

'As always you make me feel better,' Rosa told her. 'I knew you would.'

'Good – and remember back to when you were so worried you wouldn't be able to conceive. You really wanted this baby, Rosa.'

'Be careful what you wish for and all that,' Rosa added, then:

'That was a joke! Are you coming down to the fireworks? Mum is having Little Ned and Hot so I'm free. Well, I say "free" but I might have to help Nate in the café for a bit.'

'The plan is to, yeah. Stuart's mum is going to have the babies and we will come with Arthur and Stan.'

'Excellent. I don't see you for months then twice in a week. That's nice.'

'I'm always at the end of a phone, Rosa, so please do call me if you need to.'

'I will. Thank you.' And Rosa felt so supported. 'Now, are we going to order some cake before mister here wakes up, or not?'

CHAPTER TWELVE

Even Gladys Moore's beaming face couldn't raise a smile from Rosa as she dropped Little Ned off at the nursery.

'What's up, young lady?' Gladys took the baby bag from her and placed it on the labelled rack with all the others. Her helper, Claire, lifted Little Ned from Rosa's arms and took him over to the baby corner, where there were soft coverings on the floor and lots of differently textured things to touch and explore. There were two other babies, one of six months and one of a year, both crawling, and, looking over, Rosa could see that Little Ned was transfixed by them. He'd completely forgotten about his mother already.

'You've got a face like a smacked arse,' Gladys commented.

Rosa's lips twitched. 'Josh messaged me last night saying he's decided it makes more sense financially to not come home for any weekends and just get the work done with the hope of finishing the project sooner. I've heard that story before.'

'Oh. Well, on a positive that means he will be home earlier,' Gladys said briskly, 'and you said your mum was having the baby Saturday night, didn't you? So at least you can have some fun then.' But she could see the misery on Rosa's face. 'Bloody men,' she said to her. 'I love my Frank to pieces but when I do get a night off, I relish it. Your Josh will be back in no time and you'll be wishing him away again. Just enjoy it, eh?'

Feeling slightly better as she walked up the hill, Rosa bumped into Mary who was tidying the trolleys outside the Co-op.

'Hello, my duck. What you up to?'

'I've just dropped your grandson at nursery and I'm actually on my way to see Christopher.'

'That's nice.'

'Yes. I like him.'

'Well, that's a good start.' Mary smiled. 'Has he met Little Ned yet?'

'No, not yet. I need to discuss something with him about my charities, first.'

'Oh. OK. And when will I get to see my grandson again? It's been far too long.'

'Mum, you are having him and Hot on Saturday night. You surely haven't forgotten, already?' At the mention of his name, Hot let out a little bark and promptly sat on Rosa's foot.

'Oh, OK. Of course I haven't.' Mary was flustered. 'It will be on the calendar. That's the thing – if I don't write anything down these days, it just goes.'

'Is this happening a lot, then? You forgetting things?'

'Hmm. It's little things, like I will walk into the bedroom to get something and then forget what I was going in there for. It doesn't happen often. I daresay it's because I'm not sleeping well. I shall try turning the heating off earlier, I get so bloody hot, which in turn wakes me up when I do eventually get off to sleep.'

'I think you should go and see the doctor.'

'Don't be daft. You know I sort these things out myself.' Mary added philosophically, 'I'm just getting old, that's all.'

'You're forty-eight, Mum! That's hardly old and if you're

losing your marbles, we need to know about it so we can get you sorted.'

'Brrr, it's cold today,' Mary shivered. 'Go on, get on with your business and I'll get on with mine, daughter, OK?'

'Water my melons with that big hose of yours,' Christopher announced in a dead-pan voice on Rosa's arrival at the newly written sign, *Webb & Son*.

'Sorry?' Rosa screwed her face up. 'I've just left my mother thinking she's going barking mad. And now you are too?'

'Celia Carlisle's last words.'

Rosa collapsed into hysterical laughter. 'Oh, my goodness, how did you find that out?' Hearing his mistress totally losing it was making Hot nervous. He kept looking up at her anxiously, his tail between his legs.

Christopher suddenly started sneezing uncontrollably. 'I'm allergic to dogs, sorry,' he managed between explosions, launching the front door open to allow cold, fresh air to flood in. 'Pop him in the back of the hearse, go on, he'll be fine for a second. It's open and one of the windows doesn't shut properly anyway.'

'You should have told me. I would have left him at home,' Rosa said, hurrying through the back door, glad she had taken time to put on the little sausage dog's warm tartan coat. Giving him a chunk of carrot to chew on and promising the little hound she wouldn't be long, she left him in the archaic funeral car and, trying not to hear his whines as he demolished the carrot in seconds, went back through to her father, who, to her relief had now shut the front door.

'So go on, tell me all about those famous last words.' Rosa sat down at the desk opposite him.

'Well, the young gardener rang me actually. Nice young

feller-me-lad. Of course, none of her family would talk to him so he made some enquiries, found out through the crem that I was doing the funeral, and rang to say he wanted me to put something in the lovely Celia's coffin.'

'Surely you can't do that without her son's permission?'

'Of course I can't.' Christopher's face remained straight.

'But please tell me you did?' Rosa urged.

'By the sounds of it he had a good relationship with the woman. Being the softy that I am and the signs of grief he was showing, I have to concur that I think his feelings were genuine.'

'Aw. Bless him. So, what did he want put in with her?'

'A sprig of fragrant jasmine.'

'Oh. Is that it? How dull.'

'Lessons learned about my daughter today, number 1: she's not a romantic,' Christopher said. 'He told me that the jasmine flower is associated with love.'

'Now that is sweet and not just the action of a man who was getting his big hose out to water her melons,' Rosa decided. For some reason she wasn't remotely embarrassed about sharing something a bit risqué with her father. 'How on earth did you get that out of him, by the way?'

'Once I had taken him under my fatherly wing, I just asked him outright.'

'So, are you going to put it in with her?'

'If he gets it to me in time, of course. But *dad's the word* on this one, eh?' He winked.

'Dad is quite a big word for me to say at the moment,' Rosa blurted out; it came from the heart.

The wise man smiled. 'And truthful lips endure forever.' Rosa gave him a quizzical expression. 'Proverbs 12:19. I could quote the whole Bible I've been in this game so long.' He squeezed her hand briefly. 'And I do understand that "Kit" might be easier for the time being. Whatever feels right to you is fine by me.'

Rosa bit her lip. 'Well, thank you for telling me the gardener's tale…Kit. It's cheered me up, in a macabre kind of way.'

'And why do you need cheering up, pray tell?' The funeral director walked through to the kitchen to put the kettle on.

Rosa called after him, 'Oh, just my mother getting forgetful and my husband not coming home for any weekends.'

'There's a solution to everything apart from death, my dear. This job has made me realise that. Don't sweat the small stuff.'

Rosa could see where she had got her own usually forthright attitude from. 'You're right. I can manage without Josh and I've told Mum to book in to see the doctor.'

'You've made me feel better as well.' Christopher reached for two mugs from the cupboard. 'Mary promised to ring me back the other day and didn't. I thought she'd got the hump with me. She's a good sort, your mother.'

'Yes, she is, but that's a worry. Imagine if it's dementia. I can't lose her; I've only just found her.'

'I doubt very much if it is at her age, but I'm one to face up to things. If it is, then we get all the facts and deal with it.' The man's use of the word 'we' gave Rosa the same warm tingling feeling that she had experienced the other day. 'But you can't force anyone to do anything they don't want to do,' Christopher added. 'Your mother is not stupid. She will confront it in her own time, I'm sure.'

They both now sat at the red-leather-topped desk, a lovely hot cup of coffee in front of them. Christopher pulled a blue folder from one of the drawers. 'I have good news, by the way,' he said.

'Great.' Rosa took a tentative sip of her hot drink.

'After our conversation, Felix handed this over to me and said he's more than happy for you to pick up on it. His one wish was that you could update him if you think it's a viable proposition, and also if it does go ahead, he'd like to perform at it.' Christopher then took on the man's effeminate and pompous attitude. 'I am a renowned opera singer, don't you know.'

They both then fell about laughing again, during which Rosa caught her dad's eye and held his gaze for a split second.

'I'm glad you moved to the Bay,' she said spontaneously. The man looked down, then shuffled some other papers on his desk.

'Like I said, Rosa,' he replied, with a slight croak to his voice. 'There's always a solution.'

CHAPTER THIRTEEN

'Team meeting time!' Lucas shouted up the stairs of the Ship Hotel to Danny and Tina, who were preparing the rooms for the new arrivals. The pair scurried down the steep stairs, then sat on the opposite side of the bar to their boss. Big mugs of coffee and a plate of chocolate digestives were already in front of them.

'You spoil us with your biscuits, sir,' Tina mocked, then laughed.

'You're both working your nuts off, that's why.' Lucas looked at his handwritten piece of paper. 'Basically, there are three main things on the agenda. The hotel inspector, Fireworks Night and the Christmas Grotto, OK?'

Tina and Danny nodded as their boss continued. 'There is a Ms Swift booked in for two nights. She's our first solo guest for a while, so just in case she is the inspector, I want you to put her in the *Titanic* room, which is not only the best room, but has the slightly better bathroom. I've got a half-bottle of champagne and some of those posh chocolates that supplier left us the other day, so put those on the bedside table when you're done getting it ready, thanks.'

'Better not put any ice in the champagne bucket,' Tina

quipped. 'We don't want her going down hard on this ship.'

'Not even funny, Ma,' Danny replied.

'Oh come on, it was quite,' Lucas grinned. 'The room has to be spotless, so wipe the paint down on the skirting boards and even check the top of doors for dust too, please. New bedding has just arrived from the laundry, so it will be smelling fresh. That's it really, and if she orders anything in the restaurant, then Danny, you pull out all the stops, OK? And her breakfast has to be perfect.'

'Yes, boss. Do you think an inspector would stay two nights?'

'I don't bloody know; this whole game is new to me, too,' Lucas said. 'I just hope we haven't missed somebody coming in already?'

'Nah,' Tina replied. 'It was all half-term holiday families last week. Thank goodness no kids are booked in for a while now. I found crayon on the walls of HMS *Victory* this morning and the *Mary Rose* headboard was covered in bogeys. Ugh.' She shuddered. 'Little perishers, or maybe it was their chuffing parents. Henry VIII would have beheaded the lot of 'em.'

'Good history knowledge, Ma.' Danny chinked his mug with his mother's.

'Have you ordered in all we need for the fireworks barbecue, Dan?' Lucas asked.

'Yep, all in the freezer, mate. And to confirm, we ain't doing any menu food that night, are we?'

'Correct, we always make a killing on the burgers. The café is doing hot-dog rolls this year and the Residents' Society are selling pasties, so it should be a good 'un. I just need to find a good Spotify playlist and we're sorted. I've interviewed a couple of lads to run the bar, so that leaves me and you to do the cooking, Dan. And that reminds me, I've ordered 200 fresh burger baps from the bakers. They will deliver the morning of the fireworks.'

'Noted, boss.'

'OK, we are getting there.' Lucas drained his mug. 'Grotto-wise, it is to run from December the first to December the twenty-third. We need to make sure we then focus on the bookings that we have in from Christmas Eve onwards.'

'Good idea. We are fully booked for the Christmas and New Year packages now,' Tina piped up.

'Thank you, Tina, that's great news.'

'Lucas, I do need to talk to you about me and Ma working our shifts to make sure Alfie is our prime focus at Christmastime,' Danny said.

'That goes without saying,' Lucas replied kindly, 'and I think we will need to take on a couple more people to help if the grotto is as busy as I envisage it will be. Danny, have you ordered supplies to build the makeshift huts out there?'

'Yep, it's all coming next week. There'll be a hut for kids to write letters and a hut for Santa – that's right, innit? I've worked out we can run electricity out there, so they will both be heated.'

'Yep – and good work with the electrics. We still need to leave some room for a few cars and also a pen with hay for the reindeer if we can get them. Davina wants to be involved too.' Hearing this, Tina let her hackles rise and fall discreetly. 'I think she has just one more prospective Father Christmas to interview,' Lucas went on, 'and she is seeing if we can source reindeers from somewhere.'

'Our Alfie will love it.'

'Great.' Lucas put his page of notes down. 'I just need to contact Carly, our marketing lady, so she can start promoting it.'

'We will need some signs for the huts,' Danny said. 'Maybe she can do those too. And we'll need a couple of decent chairs in each.'

'Yeah, we can't have Father Christmas getting a numb bum,' Tina guffawed.

'Good call. OK, leave the chairs to me. I think that's it for now then. We've an hour before we open for you to get cleaning. All happy?'

'Yeah,' the mother and son said in unison, as the front door opened, letting in with it not only a big whoosh of cold, seaweed-laden air but also a very pretty woman. Lucas and Danny caught each other's eyes in appreciation of the female standing in front of them. She was in her mid-twenties, with long dark hair, a shade of bright green eyes not dissimilar to Rosa's, and a naturally pretty heart-shaped face. She was wearing a long beige trench-coat that cinched in her tiny waist and accentuated her neat little breasts. Heeled ankle boots and a swipe of thick clear lip gloss on her rosebud lips finished off her look. Her smile was friendly but shy as she took in the two men standing looking at her.

Tutting to herself, Tina waved, smiled, then made her way upstairs with the bag of clean bedding that the laundry had just dropped off. There were things to be getting on with, and if the blokes wanted to stand there like tits in a trance, that was their business.

Danny automatically held out his hand to the new arrival. 'Danny Green, pleased to meet ya.'

'You've got work to do, mate.' Lucas's voice was firm.

'Carly Jessop. Good to meet you too,' she called after Danny as he reluctantly made his way upstairs.

'You can't get the staff these days,' Lucas joked, then, 'I didn't realise you were coming in today. Your ears must have been burning.'

'Really? I was just having a cup of tea with a friend in Rosa's Café, so thought I'd pop by and say hi. That's the thing with technology these days. I've built your website and everything else around it with just a phone conversation and email. Not always a good thing, I don't think, do you?' She held out her hand to him.

Lucas felt himself reddening. He hadn't experienced this kind of immediate attraction since meeting Rosa in the Corner Shop almost three years ago.

'No, it's not and yeah, it's really nice to meet you in the flesh at last.' He held her hand far too long while staring at her button nose. 'It's funny how you imagine people to look from the sound of their voice.'

Carly laughed a sweet tinkling laugh. Lucas thought she could well be a real-life angel. 'I hope it's a pleasant surprise.'

'Yes. You are beautiful.' Lucas was now scarlet. 'Sorry. That just popped out.'

Carly laughed again. 'I bet you say that to all the girls.'

'Say what?' Davina appeared in full police uniform.

'Pop-ups, yes, we were just discussing what to do about them on the website,' Lucas responded smoothly, thankful that he had bothered to get more au fait with technology since taking the hotel on.

'So do introduce me,' Davina said, calling on her best policing skills to try and stop the annoyance showing in her voice.

'This is Carly Jenkins; she has been working on our marketing for us – and doing an excellent job, too. Bookings are flying at the moment,' Lucas directed at the pretty marketer.

'Jessop.' Carly lifted her hand to acknowledge the sour-looking police officer in front of her. 'Carly Jessop.'

'And this is Davina,' Lucas said.

'Hi, Davina.'

'I'm Lucas's girlfriend,' Davina spat through a forced smile.

If awkward was a weather, there would have been a massive

hailstorm falling on top of them all right now. Right in the middle of a strained silence, the front door was pushed open again to reveal Rosa and Hot.

'Okaaay,' Lucas said slowly. 'Hey, Rosa.'

'I'm off to work,' Davina harrumphed.

'Have a good day catching baddies, won't you?' Lucas tried to lighten the heavy atmosphere.

'Beats dating one,' his girlfriend said, supposedly under her breath but they all heard, before stalking out and slamming the door shut.

'I can come back if you're busy,' Rosa said politely.

'No, it's OK.' Luke felt like a thorn between two roses.

'It's just Titch could do with some cover at the shop this afternoon and I wondered if Danny could be spared to help.'

Without any thought, Lucas replied, 'Yes, sure, he's upstairs, go up and see him if you like.' He caught himself up. 'Look at me being so rude. This is Carly, Rosa. She's helping us out with our marketing.'

'Hi, Carly. I see you've been doing a great job. In fact, I might need your help with something too. Have you got a card I could take?'

'I think so.' Carly scrabbled in her bag and pulled one out. 'Oops, excuse the biscuit crumbs. Ever the professional and all that.'

Rosa laughed. 'Don't worry. Now I've got a child, I've been known to pull a dirty nappy out of mine on occasion.'

Carly Jessop smiled and Lucas noticed that his mouth had gone abnormally dry. As for Rosa, she could feel a kindness and warmth emanating from the young woman. A tranquillity. And with the spiritual gift that her mother had subconsciously instilled in her, she also felt that at long last, Lucas Hannafore might have met his real match.

CHAPTER FOURTEEN

'Danny, I'm so grateful you can do this for me. I won't be long.'
Titch went to the back kitchen and pulled on her coat. 'It's just a
midwife check and Ritchie will insist on taking me.'

'It's fine, doll. And there's no need to rush.' Danny grinned at
her. 'Seriously, being here will be like having a break, compared
to all that running around I do at that bleedin' hotel. Anything
you need me to do specifically?'

'If you could put the posh cat food out, that would help –
and there's some pet-themed Christmas crackers that need
to go on the top shelf, over there.' Titch pointed to her newly
arranged festive section on the back wall. 'All the boxes that
need unpacking are in the kitchen. You know how to use the
till, don't you? It's the same one you used when you helped Rosa
out that time. Oh, and if you can push the sparklers, that would
be useful as well, thank you.'

'I'll take a couple of packs myself, if that's OK. It's my lad's
birthday tomorrow and he loves 'em.'

'Have them, Danny. You've done me such a favour here.'

'That's kind. Thanks, little one, I appreciate that.'

Just the way he said *little one* in his Cockney accent made
Titch feel a bit unnecessary. Her fantasy was soon interrupted

by her one true love and husband Ritchie pulling up outside in the fish and chip van and tooting. She was glad to see Theo asleep in his baby seat next to him.

'Just go – go on, clear off.' Danny smiled at the young pregnant girl in front of him. 'And do *not* rush back. I've got this.'

Danny whistled as he worked, and soon had nearly all the jobs done that Titch had wanted. After his stint working at a big DIY supercentre, he realised just how much he enjoyed working in retail and it was good to be behind a till again. However, he wouldn't change his current job for the world. He and Lucas had an understanding. Work hard, play hard. A band of brothers. He'd been right in Rosa asking Lucas if he could help out at the Corner Shop, as his boss would do anything for the feisty London girl. In his eyes, Lucas and Rosa were the perfect couple. He still couldn't understand why she was with Josh. He didn't dislike Josh, but with the bloke's posh public-school upbringing, Danny had never been able to find a level with him. The spark between Lucas and the quirky, lovable Rosa was evident. But as his dear old mum Tina always said, there was naught stranger than folk or their choice of lovers, and she was usually right.

Danny had no right to lay down the law. He hadn't done so well himself on the relationship front. Look at the way he'd got involved with Leah, a woman who became sadly more in love with drugs than life itself, despite the fact that she had someone who adored her – Danny. Yes, the product of their union had been their son Alfie, who was a dear little boy, but if Danny's mum Tina had not taken on a lot of the parenting, Danny would never have been able to cope. He had found it easier not to contact Leah during her rehab. Partly for fear of upsetting her, but mainly because he feared that once she was well again, she might come back and try to get custody of their son. That must not be allowed to happen at any cost. He'd last heard through acquaintances that she was still living with her mother in Wales and was doing OK. He was pleased at that. She was a decent enough girl but they had fallen out of love a long time ago and now he wished her nothing but peace and sobriety, and to keep her distance and not disrupt their lives all over again.

He was neatly arranging the boxes of crackers on the top shelf when the shop bell rang. 'Just a second,' he called down from the stepladder. Then on reaching the ground and turning around, Danny caught his breath.

The woman must have been in her forties, her red hair tied up in a messy bun. She had a tiny beauty spot on her right cheek. The imperfection of a smudge of red lipstick against her alabaster skin tone made her all the more desirable. Her long black coat swung open to reveal a curvaceous figure covered by a smart grey trouser suit. Danny felt like a car that goes from 0-100 mph in a single second. It really was lust at first sight.

'Oh, er. Hi. How can I help you?'

The woman took in the rough diamond in front of her. Then without thinking she reached forward and placed her index finger on the deep scar on his cheek. She pulled away as quickly as she had done it.

'I'm sorry, pal, I know that was weird.' He hadn't expected a thick Scottish accent. 'But how the hell did you get that?'

Even Danny, who had experienced all sorts, including prison life, was taken aback by this woman's directness. He could smell alcohol on her breath.

'It's a long story,' he managed defensively.

'And I've had a long train journey.' She hiccupped. 'Decided to drink two mini-bottles of wine from the catering cart. I'm a bit drunk, to be honest.'

Danny then noticed the wheelie case that she had left just

inside the door. 'Staying down here then?'

'Aye, just for a wee while, like.'

'You're going to miss the fireworks.'

She looked directly into his eyes and ran her tongue around her smudged lipstick. 'Am I?'

Danny felt an immediate stirring in his jeans. 'So, where are you staying?'

'Um. I canna remember the name of it.'

'The Ship?'

'No, that's not it. It's a fishy-type name. I can't bloody remember now.'

'The Lobster Pot?'

The woman giggled like a teenager. 'That's it.'

Phew. Danny felt relief. He couldn't be fraternising with the hotel guests; that was one of Lucas's rules and he kind of understood it.

'I'm Danny.' He held out his hand. She took it in both of hers, looked closely at the top, then randomly turned it over, running her finger along the inside of his palm as she did so.

'And what big hands you've got…Danny,' she murmured.

Stopping himself from saying, 'All the better to ravage you with,' he just said, 'And you are?'

'I'm, um…' the woman stuttered. Then, on noticing the boxes of Lily's Kitchen cat food on the floor at his feet, she quickly replied, 'My name is Lily.'

'That's a pretty name.' Danny was pulling out all the charm stops.

'Flattery will get you everywhere.' She smiled to reveal teeth with a slight gap between the front two. 'Well, I'm pleased to meet you, Danny, or can I call you Daniel?' she purred.

'You can call me whatever you like,' Danny flirted.

'You bad, bad boy.' The woman hiccupped again.

'So are you down here for business or pleasure?' Danny straightened himself up. He must get a grip.

The woman looked directly into the eyes of the stocky, gangster-type character in front of her and licked her lips again.

'Let's just say, *Daniel*, that I have a mind for business…and a body for sin.'

CHAPTER FIFTEEN

'Oi, mate, I'd thought you'd be back before this.' Lucas apprehended Danny as he ran in the back door from a now dark car park and came through to the hotel kitchen, pulling off his jacket as he did so. On realising his T-shirt was on back to front he quickly put on his apron to cover it. He also hoped that neither Jacob nor Raffy had spotted him hot-footing it back down the fire escape of the Lobster Pot.

'Titch left me with a list of jobs. Look, it's a long story,' Danny said truthfully, thinking back to his earlier conversation with Lily, and realising that his life was made up of those. He was knackered but had never felt so satisfied in his whole life – and that was including his encounter with that mad bitch Bergamot a while back, in the kitchen of the Corner Shop. Older women really did do it for him. It was definitely a kink of his. She had been so vague as to why she was down here. In fact, the mystery made it all the sexier; dazed by desire, all the pair knew about each other after their passionate encounter in Lily's bedroom at the Lobster Pot was their first names – and every inch of the other's body.

'Did the single guest arrive already?' he asked, to divert Lucas's attention.

'Yes, but there's no way she looks like a hotel inspector, whatever a hotel inspector should look like. She is far too young – and what's more, she has a visible tattoo. Danny mate, I can't see Alex Polizzi or any of those other snooty hotel inspectors going around with a tattoo. I haven't heard a peep from her since she checked in at four. I went up to my room earlier, and do you know what? It was really weird: she had put the half-bottle of champagne outside her room, unopened.'

'That's odd. Maybe she is the inspector, and they are not allowed to drink on duty or something?' Danny offered. 'Or maybe she's given up drinking and doesn't want the temptation. Lots of people are sober by choice these days. So, what bookings have we got in the restaurant tonight?'

'None, actually. Ms Swift is our only room booking,' Lucas accentuated the Ms, 'and she didn't want to book a table. She's asked for breakfast at eight tomorrow morning though.'

The relief on Danny's face was immense. He could do with an easy night.

'Yeah, I reckon everyone is saving themselves for tomorrow night. It is a bit of an event in the Cockleberry Bay calendar, the fireworks,' Lucas explained.

'Mum's gone home with Alfie, I take it?' Danny went to the chest freezer and opened it.

'Yes, he was crazy excited about his birthday tomorrow.'

'Bless him. OK, I'll get the burgers out to defrost in the fridge for tomorrow and I was going to make some fresh coleslaw. If there are any walk-ins, just shout.'

Lucas went out to the bar, then returned to the kitchen straight away. 'I tell you what, mate, go home and see that lad of yours before he goes to bed. I can manage here tonight. You can do the coleslaw in the morning.'

'If you're sure, that would be amazing.'

'Course I'm sure. He'll never be six again, will he?'

'I'm stoked, mate, thanks.'

'If you don't mind being here to do the woman's breakfast, that would be good though. It's gotta be perfect just in case she is the inspector.'

'Kushti. I'll be here for seven thirty, on the dot. The burger buns are being delivered around then too.' Forgetting his T-shirt was back to front, Danny took off his apron.

Lucas laughed to himself. A long story indeed? But he knew Danny felt like he had been missing out on meeting women since he had moved out of London, so good on him.

Lucas served a couple of locals who had just come in for a quick pint, then tended to the open fire. It had been a funny old day and he was feeling tired. He sighed as he remembered his girlfriend stomping off this morning. Davina was great, a good laugh, and the sex was off the scale, but the honeymoon period was definitely over, and despite them coming up to their one-year dating anniversary, he hadn't once felt the desire to move on with the relationship and ask her to move in with him. He couldn't deny that Carly had really turned his head this morning, but despite him feeling such a huge physical attraction, he sensed that it hadn't been reciprocated; scarred from the trauma of unrequited love he had experienced with Rosa, he wasn't going to put himself through that again.

Realising that he might have upset his girlfriend, he reached into his pocket for his phone and texted her. 'Shit,' he then swore aloud, breaking his own rule of no swearing in the Ship. No wonder she was moody, he'd been so dazzled by Carly he'd forgotten to ask Davina how the interview with the final Father Christmas had gone. He hoped it had been successful, as she had said that all of the others had looked like they would either scare the children or were so old they could well die on the job.

Come to me when you're off shift if you like, Lucas messaged. *I'm closing up at ten, so we have time to eat, rest and play! X*

Her reply was short and most definitely not sealed with a loving kiss. *I'm busy. I'll see you tomorrow for the fireworks.*

CHAPTER SIXTEEN

'Have a good time tonight, wifey,' Josh was saying down the phone line as Rosa pushed the pram up the hill to Seaspray Cottage. Little Ned was sitting propped up and screaming his disapproval of having to come out into the cold November afternoon. Hot, who'd kept hanging back and turning around to go home, was now in the pram too, with his lead looped around the handle. His sensitive ears shivered at the baby's cries and he gave a short bark, which only made Little Ned weep all the louder.

Trying to ignore the din from her two boys, Rosa pushed her earbud tighter into her ear to hear better. 'Your son has been a little bugger today; can you hear him?' She pulled the bud out again for a second and held it to the pram.

'Which son? Do you mean Hot or Little Ned?' Josh joked. Then: 'Mary will sort him out; she always does.'

'I bloody hope so. Remind me when you are home again?'

'I checked the calendar earlier; it's less than six weeks now. Are you sure you're OK for me to keep working away?'

Rosa huffed. 'Please don't ask me that again, Josh. I said I'm fine.'

Josh knew the word 'fine' meant 'shut up', so he did, about

work anyway.

'You're leaving him with your mum early,' he said unwisely.

'Yes, Josh,' Rosa snapped, her voice now full of agitation. 'I want to check that all my charity tins are in place. The Ship, the Residents' Association and the café are going to have a couple out so I'm hoping we will make a few quid tonight.'

'What a good idea. Your great-grandad would have been so proud of you, you know.'

Rosa tutted and went on, 'Plus, the whole thing is starting at five tonight. The tides have been unusually high, so the fireworks will have to be done by six-thirty, then there's just an hour left for eating and drinking before the sea comes up.'

'Are Jacob and Raff going?'

'I think Jacob may pop down. He was moaning about missing out on the action, so the Lobster Pot are providing home-made pasties for the Residents' Association. They are putting their tent up in the pub car park this year, just in case the tide does come right up.'

'The Lobster Pot will be rammed with drinkers later though.'

'Yeah, you know what our friend and drama queen is like. He loves a hissy fit.'

'And we love him for it.' Josh said wistfully, 'I do miss the Bay when I'm away. And you of course, my sweet.'

'Well, you'll be back soon, and I will be handing our little treasure right over to you,' Rosa told him. 'OK, we're here. I'll video call you tomorrow so you can say hello to your son before he forgets what his daddy looks like.'

'Ouch!' Josh replied. 'Catch up tomorrow, darling – oh, and Rosa?'

'What now?'

'I still love you to where the sky touches the sea, you know.' He hung up.

Rosa shook her head. Yes, her husband might be dependable, reliable and kind and yes, she had said that he could go away and work, but if she was honest, it was beginning to annoy her that he didn't seem to appreciate just how much work was involved in caring for a young baby.

Knocking on her mother's front door, she was surprised when Christopher opened it.

'Hello, you,' he greeted his daughter with a beaming smile.

'What are you doing here?' Rosa asked as the tall, white-haired man stooped at the small front door to help her in from the street with the pram. He then lifted Hot out and put him down on the floor, whereupon the keen sausage dog, sniffing food, hurried over to Merlin's food bowl, causing it to clatter on the hearth as he emptied its contents then licked it until it was gleaming while the outraged moggy hunched up and hissed at him from a corner, before going out of the back cat-flap in a huff.

Little Ned then proceeded to start crying at the top of his voice again. Christopher put a hand to his forehead. 'I thought I'd kill two birds with one stone, spend some time with Polly – I mean Mary here – and also our grandson. A bit of co-parenting, or, in this case, co-grandparenting, never goes amiss, does it?' He then grimaced. 'My big mouth. Sorry, Rosa.'

Rosa noticed that her mother had on both mascara and lipstick. It was like looking at a different woman. When she laughed, her face seemed relaxed, prettier even.

'You were never one for tact even all those years ago, were you, Kit Webb?' Mary said, 'but we are very much here for you both now, Rosa. You know that, duck.'

Mary touched her daughter's arm, then lifting Little Ned from the pram, she took off his outer clothes then wrapped him in one of her own crocheted blankets and rested him on her shoulder, walking around the room and rocking him. Soothed and feeling secure, he immediately stopped sobbing. 'You just needed a cuddle, didn't you, my beautiful boy?' she murmured.

Christopher winked at Rosa. It all felt kind of surreal. These two people in the same room as her, were her parents. The little wrapped-up bundle was her son. Feeling suddenly overwhelmed by it all, she walked through to the kitchen to get herself a drink of water. The ever-intuitive Christopher followed.

'Would you like me to leave?' he asked.

'God, no.'

Mary was busy fussing the baby. Hot had been put out of harm's way on Queenie's (Rosa's deceased great-grandmother) old chair. Despite the smell of Merlin and some of his cat hair on the cushion, the small dog was soon lulled by the warmth of the fire and fell fast asleep.

Rosa turned round to face her father. 'It's just a bit weird,' she tried to explain. 'I felt like this when I first met Mum. I am part of you, but I know nothing about you really. It's as if you are a stranger.'

'I understand,' the man replied gently. 'I should have let you know I was going to be here.'

'No, no, not at all, you don't need permission. I'm glad you are here, and I really am looking forward to getting to know you.'

'Good, good.' He sneezed loudly. 'Strangely, I'm allergic to dogs – but not cats. Not that Merlin will give me the time of day. I've just taken an antihistamine but not sure how long it will last. I also brought one of these with me.' He pulled a surgical mask from his pocket and put it on.

Rosa laughed and relaxed. 'You're funny.'

'I prefer peculiar.' His eyes were smiling. He then took her to the side of the kitchen and whispered, 'I also thought I could check on how your mum is – you know, after what you told me the other day.'

'Thank you,' Rosa replied, feeling even more grateful that she shared this truly kind man's genes.

Rosa then went back through to the lounge and removed the huge bag of stuff from under the pram, saying, 'You'd honestly think I was leaving him with you for a week, not a few hours.'

'Don't you worry, duck. When did you last feed him?'

'Just before I left but there are three made-up bottles in there, just in case. Oh, and six nappies.'

'Just in case,' Mary repeated and smiled at her daughter who smiled back and carried on.

'The milk will need warming and my phone will be on, so, honestly, call me if you have any concerns. He does usually go down around seven, but if you can't get him off, don't worry. I reckon I'll be back by eight, latest. Oh, and there's Hot's special bowl in there and I've measured out his biscuits for him. He usually eats about six o'clock. I got so worried about the way he swallows the lot in one gulp that I've started using one of the puzzle bowls that we stock in the shop: they force dogs to slow down and try to get at the biscuits that are all in different places.' At the sound of his name, the little dachshund lifted his head from his comfy chair, then let it flop down again, his eyes closed.

'So you'll be back around eight, you say. The tide will be getting high by then.'

'Yes, Mum. The fun will be over by then, outside anyway.'

An unmasked Christopher bought two cups of tea through and put them on the sideboard. 'Did you want one, Rosa?'

'No, I'm going to get off now, thanks.'

'Make yourself at home, won't you?' Mary directed at the man sarcastically, although she was secretly happy that he was. Then, seeing the yellow teacup and saucer in front of her, the spiritual woman had a sudden flashback. Placing a now-sleeping Little Ned carefully back into his pram and tucking him in, she put a hand on her daughter's shoulder. 'Be careful tonight, won't you, duck?'

'Oh Mum, don't go all weird on me.'

'In fact, hang on, yes, I have something for you.' Mary headed to her messy drawer in the kitchen and returned with a small, polished black crystal. Christopher looked on in bemusement.

'Black tourmaline.' She dropped it into Rosa's coat pocket. 'I love you, daughter. Now go and have some fun and I'll be seeing you later.'

Mary occasionally got things wrong, like thinking that Josh had been involved in a plane crash once, when all that had happened was that he had got stuck in New York because of bad weather. However, Rosa was sure that the peridot stone that she still had in her bedside drawer had helped her with her jealousy and also to move forward in her relationship with Josh. So, she never totally dismissed her mother's motives or visions.

On her way back down the hill to the beach, Rosa hit up Google for more information on the new crystal. She read: *When it comes to protection, the black tourmaline crystal is powerful for more than just your personal energy – it's also a protective shield for your home.*

Rosa was just wondering what on earth it could all mean, when she bumped into Titch, Ritchie and Theo all coming out of the Corner Shop. Theo grinned at her then squealed, 'Hot, Hot.'

'No, he's at Mary's today, Theo darling.' Rosa bent down to his level and took his little gloved hand. 'Exciting about the fireworks though, isn't it?' He started to arch his back to try and free himself from his straps. 'Rosa play. Rosa play.'

'On the beach you can get out, darling,' Titch said, handing him a rice cake, then put her hand to her aching back and sighed.

Ritchie bent down and kissed Rosa on both cheeks. 'I haven't seen you for ages, mate.'

'I know. This baby lark is all-consuming.'

'Yeah, poor Titch, my mum's got full-blown flu now so I'm having to do more shifts in the chippie.'

'Who's got the dogs tonight then?' Rosa asked.

'*My* mum,' Titch piped up. 'She wanted this little man as well, but I think he may be old enough this year to enjoy it, let's see.' She leaned into her husband, who was pushing the stroller. 'We should have left him there for a sleepover, so we can be alone. I need this baby giraffe out now.'

'You've still got nearly two months to go, so you can't be talking like that,' Ritchie said. 'Tell her, Rosa, tell her to behave.' He then confided: 'Despite her womanly wiles I'm ignoring her. This baby can't be popping out too early and I don't want to hurt her. And does that old wives' tale work, anyway?'

'I *am* here,' Titch muttered.

They reached the beach which was already buzzing with people. Nate had done a wonderful job decorating the café and the Ship, too, looked great, with its strings of flashing lights and spotlights. The Residents' Association had made one of their legendary fruit and alcohol punches, which was being ladled out to already stressed parents, and the pasties that Raff had made were laid out above food-warmers on a big long table in front of their white tent in the car park. As usual, a big barbecue was sizzling with burgers in front of the hotel and both Lucas and Danny were manning it, wearing tall white chefs' hats. On seeing the handsome pair, Titch nudged Rosa and winked. Lucas's firework playlist was belting out Katy Perry's 'Firework'.

Leaving Titch and Ritchie to queue for a burger, Rosa walked over to the café. It felt strange being totally on her own but also wonderfully liberating to not have to be Rosa Smith, wife, mother, daughter, sister. She could please herself for a few hours for once.

She was just about to grab herself a hot chocolate from the table out at the front of the café when a small dark-haired boy with a missing front tooth came running up to her. Tina Green was following in hot pursuit.

'Guess what day it is today, Rosa?' the boy cried excitedly.

Rosa got down on her haunches to the lad's level, then went to her bag.

'Hmm, now let me just think.' Rosa handed the little boy a wrapped gift. 'Happy Birthday, Alfie.'

'You knew already!' the boy shouted. 'Can I open it now, Granny Green?' Without waiting for an answer, he ripped open the packaging and dropped it onto the wet sand. Tina Green dutifully picked it up and put it in the bin handily placed next to the table that had been set up for hot dogs outside the café.

'A Lego submarine. *Yesss!* I love it, thank you so much, Rosa. I'm showing Dad.' The boy charged over to the pub.

Tina Green turned to look after him. 'You didn't have to do that, Rosa, but thank you. I'd love to chat, but I'd better go after him.'

Rosa put her arm on the tired grandmother's shoulder. 'We can see him from here. Let's go over in a second. Would you like a hot chocolate?' Nate and Brad, the student, were busy serving hot dogs to the many excitable children waiting for the firework display to start. Rosa jumped behind the table and handed a ready-poured chocolate hot drink to Tina then took one for herself. 'Bless you, it's hard enough at my age, but you must be exhausted doing all this childcare and still working in your sixties.'

'You know how it is, Rosa. My family are my world. I'll take tiredness any day, just to see my boys thriving and content.'

The music stopped abruptly, and the PA system crackled across a clear night sky full of stars. The full moon was also showing her celestial body, lighting a twinkling path across the still, dark waters of the sea.

'Thank you all for coming.' There was a hush as the Chairman of the Residents' Association took to the microphone. 'It has become a firm feature in the Cockleberry Bay calendar to celebrate these fireworks together as a community. We shall count down from ten in just a minute and set off another magnificent sparkly show in the sky, but I would firstly like to thank you all for your contributions for making this event happen. I would also like to thank Rosa Smith wholeheartedly for setting up Ned's Gift, which supports not only our Association but also some other great local charities, including Sea & Save and our amazing lifeboat service. There are tins dotted about on the catering ports, so even if it's a handful of coins from your purse, every little helps. Thank you.'

Unaware that this announcement was coming, Rosa was delighted at the support. Ritchie, with Theo tight in his arms, caught her eye and managed a thumbs-up sign. Titch was stuffing in a burger as fast as her face would allow.

A fanfare of music boomed out from the sound system, then came the shout: 'Ten, nine, eight, seven…' As everyone joined in, their voices reverberated loudly over the Bay, and when they got to '*One!!*' they gasped at the shapes, colours, and joyful explosions of the beautifully crafted firework display lighting the clear Cockleberry Bay night sky.

CHAPTER SEVENTEEN

'It's good to see you again.' Christopher sat at the kitchen table while Mary stirred homemade chicken soup at her old black stove. 'I can't believe where the time has gone.'

Mary turned around to face him. 'I know. Rosa was pregnant the last time we met.' There was a brief silence before she added, 'Thanks for not pushing her.'

'That's not my style.' Christopher said, then sneezed loudly.

'I knew those bloody tablets wouldn't work that you took. Hang on.' Mary went to her messy drawer again. 'Here.' She handed him a little phial of liquid. 'This should help.'

'What is it?'

'Trust me. It's fine. Just sniff it hard up your nose. It's all natural.'

Hot had been taken off Queenie's chair so the grown-ups could sit comfortably and was now snoring gently in Merlin's basket in front of the fire. Little Ned had also been an absolute angel, sleeping soundly. There was no sign of Merlin, who had raced back in and up the stairs the minute the fireworks had started. He was now hiding under Queenie's bed, snuggled inside an old shawl of hers that had fallen down the back and been forgotten.

Christopher did as he was told and sniffed up the potion. 'I don't know, I come round here, you give me drugs – and God knows what's in that pot you're stirring. You'll be trying to seduce me next, Polly Cobb.'

Mary felt herself blushing. She answered, 'I have to say, if I'd known you were going to be a funeral director, I might have married you all those years ago.'

Christopher laughed. 'You and your ghosts and ghouls. Sorry to disappoint you, but in all the years I've been doing this I've never had one body jump out at me in the Chapel of Rest.'

'Nothing out of the ordinary has ever happened to you at all?'

'No. I think everyone in my care remains at peace. I talk to them, you see. I think their souls have long disappeared when they reach me but just in case, out of respect, I have a little chat and make sure they are comfortable and looking the best they can be.'

Mary moved away from the fire and then started fanning herself. 'It's so warm in here, do you mind if I open a window for a second?'

'Of course, let me.' Christopher stood up and then sniffed. 'No sneezing. That's remarkable.'

Mary said nothing. He then added, 'And thanks for doing food.'

'Oh, it's just a bit of soup and homemade bread, that's all, but I have made a blackberry and apple crumble, so we can have some of that later for afters, if you fancy. With custard.'

'I fancy very much. Since I've been on my own, I rarely cook anything decent for myself. My lad has given me a couple of food parcels since I moved in, which is handy.'

'He's a credit to you, your Nate is.'

'Yes, he certainly is. And it's good to see him happy again. It's been a long road.' He looked directly at Mary who had now delivered hot bowls of soup to the table. 'A long road for all of us.'

'So, remind me, how long ago did you split from your partner?' Mary went to the drawer to get spoons then sat down beside him.

'Must be around three years now. It was all very amicable.'

'And how about your ex-wife, Nate's mum – do you still see her?'

'God, no. She was hard work, but she gave me my Nate, so that is the positive I take from meeting her.' Christopher looked sad. 'I failed as a father back then, Mary. Boarding school wasn't for him. He needed love.'

'I failed our Rosa in a much worse way.'

Christopher put his hand on top of hers. His voice was comforting when he said, 'But like I said to you before, we are here now and look at us. Our children seem to like us, despite everything, and that little baby lying in the pram over there, he is our grandson. And we have time to make amends. Our grandson.' Christopher repeated. 'And how good does that feel?'

Mary stood up quickly and went to the oven. She returned to the table with a basket of freshly baked bread and an old-fashioned blue and white butter dish.

'Now what were we talking about?' She had a puzzled look on her face.

'Little Ned, of course.' Christopher smiled.

'Ah, yes.' Mary's face was still slightly blank.

'Since I hit fifty, I'm always forgetting things now too,' Christopher added kindly. 'But we are still young in my eyes and we have so much to look forward to. I can feel it.'

Tears suddenly appeared in the usually stoic woman's eyes. 'Kit. Can I trust you? I want to tell you something. Something I haven't told anyone else.'

CHAPTER EIGHTEEN

As Nate assured Rosa he didn't need any help at the café, she walked over to Jacob, who was standing on the edge of the sea wall near the Ship, oohing and aahing camply at the explosion of colour above him. She went up behind him and pinched his bum gently. He gave a little scream, then as the fireworks display reached its dramatic crescendo, he put his arm around her shoulders and hugged her.

'I forgot how much effort they always make with this. It's fantastic, isn't it, darling? Worth every penny, I say.'

'Have you seen Vicki and her brood yet?'

'No, because the poor little twins have come down with chicken pox; she said to tell you when I saw you.'

'Oh no – that's not good.'

'No, double trouble. How are you, my lovely, anyway?'

'Far from double trouble. I'm child- and dog-free tonight, so I'm feeling bloody marvellous.'

'I don't know how you do it. If Raff ever wavered and said he wanted a child with me, I would have to divorce him. All that crying and having to be at their beck and call day and night. It's bad enough with the Duchess and Ugly and Pongo.'

Jacob then ushered her away out of earshot of Lucas or Danny

117

and tried to whisper above the noise. 'We had the Seaside Star inspector in last night.'

'Really? How do you know it was them? Are you going to tell Lucas?'

'No, I'm not – and please can I trust you not to tell him either?'

Rosa sighed; it was difficult having her loyalties pulled in varying directions. 'Don't be so mean. I want you both to do well.'

'Who says they will send the same person anyway? But OK. It was a woman, on her own. But listen to this: she only brought a man back yesterday afternoon. I couldn't believe it!'

'Hardly professional, was it?' Rosa frowned. 'It can't have been the inspector.'

'Oh, it was. And what's more, she shagged him senseless by the sound of it. We had customers in, too.' Jacob pursed his lips. 'I had to put on Handel's *Zadok the Priest* at full blast to cover the bangs and screams. Even the Duchess started howling. They thought we'd all gone mad.'

Rosa was in hysterics at Jacob's humorous delivery. 'No! Well, if she is who you think she is, a good write-up should be guaranteed.'

'I should say so. She didn't appear for dinner and then this morning, she rang down to order breakfast in bed. I don't think she could face us. She was drunk when she checked in too – and very sheepish when she left.'

'I bet she bloody was, lucky cow.' Rosa was still laughing. 'What did she look like?'

'I shouldn't really tell you, but…red hair, very pale skin. A *hideous* gap in her teeth.' Jacob shuddered exaggeratedly. 'Mid-forties, I'd say. Well-dressed and decidedly haggard – or should I say *shaggard* – when I saw her for the second time.'

Rosa wiped tears of laughter from her face. 'I didn't expect you to say that she looked younger with all that kind of shenanigans going on.'

'Darling, just because we hit forty it doesn't mean we can't still bang like a barn door on a windy night.'

'Stop it,' Rosa pleaded, 'or I'll wet myself! I have zero bladder control since Little Ned used me as a launching pad.'

'Far too much information,' Jacob reproved her while raising his eyebrows. Rosa mock-swiped him but he wasn't finished yet. He carried on with his story. '*Well*, as you can imagine, Raff and I were on *tenterhooks* to see what the man creating such bedroom gymnastics looked like, but we reckon he must have sneaked up and down the fire escape, like some kind of sexual *criminal*. Gutted we were, to miss him!'

'This all sounds so unlikely – so how were you so sure that she was the inspector?'

'Because firstly, when I asked her why she was staying in the Bay, her answer of "needing some sea air" didn't wash with me. Oho no. I was suspicious from the off and then – you'll never guess what – the tick form they must use to evaluate the Seaside Stars was only hanging out of her case. Busted! Bang to rights!'

'Bang being the appropriate word,' Rosa noted. 'Oh my God, she must have been so hungover and embarrassed that everything else went out of the window or rather, down the fire escape.' She crossed her legs. 'Anyway, I'm just going to dash in here for the loo. I'm bursting.'

'And I need to get back behind the bar in the Lobster Pot before this lot start filtering off and hopefully have the good taste to come up into my pub.' He air-kissed Rosa on both cheeks and began his walk up the hill.

Rosa waved to Danny, who was four-deep with burger customers, and made her way swiftly to the hotel toilet. As she sat down to relieve herself, she heard voices coming in through the open window.

'No, Lucas, I'm sick of it.' Rosa recognised Davina's whining voice. 'You always say you're sorry, but I actually don't think you are. Bloody Rosa Smith was only telling me the other day that she has never given you a present before and there she was, bold as brass, handing one over the other day. I saw you both. What was that all about? It wasn't your birthday.'

'For the record, *Constable Hunt*, she hasn't given me a present before and no, you're right, it wasn't my birthday but the anniversary of my mother's death. She gave me a packet of fags and some brandy, not a lock of her fucking hair. It was the kind of thing mates do, Davina.'

'Oh right – I didn't realise.' The woman's voice was sulky.

'Didn't realise? Even though that's when we met! In the police station after your very own idiot DC Clarke thought Rosa was to blame for Mum's fall. It was Halloween, how *could* you forget?'

'I'm so sorry.' Davina's voice softened, but she then couldn't stop herself. 'But I see the way you look at her.'

Lucas sighed. 'I love her, all right. I love the girl's bones. But that doesn't mean I'm gonna be with her. She's married, she's happy with Josh. Our ship sailed before it left the harbour. She's my friend, Davina.'

There was a knock on the toilet door. 'One minute,' Rosa called out, then under her breath she whispered, 'bugger.' She so wanted to hear the rest of the conversation.

'So that means if she wanted to be with you, you would give up everything with…' Davina's voice faltered, '…with us?'

'That's hypothetical bullshit and I'm not answering that.'

'You're a bloody coward, Lucas Hannafore. Why don't you ever say what you are really feeling?'

Rosa felt a white anger rising within her. How dare she talk like that about either of them. Smiling apologetically at the woman who had been waiting patiently outside the loo, Rosa then sneaked into the kitchen to see if she could hear any more, but with the windows closed and the hum of the remaining fireworks crowd, it was impossible.

She was just heading outside to calm herself when Lucas stormed through the back door and bumped right into her. 'Fucking women!' he cursed.

'That bad, eh?'

'Yes. Shame I've already drunk the brandy you gave me!'

Rosa followed him to where one of the barmen, taken on for tonight's event, served him with a large measure of Courvoisier. Then, looking out of the window to see how busy it was outside, Lucas Hannafore downed his drink in one hit, then said, 'I'd better go and help Danny. I do want to talk to you though, bird.'

'OK,' Rosa said. 'I'm home all day tomorrow if you're about.'

'I was hoping more like tonight?' Lucas questioned.

'Er. I'm not sure, Luke. I need to collect Little Ned at eight.' She smiled. 'How about you just call me when you're done.'

Rosa was just on her way back to the café when her phone rang.

'Hi. It's Christopher, Mary said to call. She thinks it makes sense to keep Little Ned all night rather than take him out in the cold again. He's been fed and he's happy and she's just settling him now. I took the pram upstairs and put it next to your mum's bed.'

'Well, I…OK.' Rosa realised she had to trust her mum to look after her grandchild overnight at some stage.

The man could sense his daughter's hesitancy. 'He'll be fine. I said I'd stay in the spare room so nothing's forgotten – I mean, if he does wake with his teeth I can help too. We've planned to have a proper Sunday fry-up for eight o'clock tomorrow morning, so why not join us? Unless you fancy a lie-in, of course?'

'That sounds good. But shouldn't I come and get Hot?'

'He had his dinner at six, as you said, then he wasn't too keen on the fireworks noise so we made a fuss of him. Poor old Merlin's nose is well and truly out of joint. Anyway, the worst of the noise is over now and Hot has been made such a fuss of that he's in doggie heaven at the moment. I'll take him for a short walk soon and then Merlin can have his dinner in peace. Go home and relax, Rosa. You need this tonight.'

'What about your allergy and your sneezing?'

'*Rosa*. Stop worrying. Your mum's given me one of her magic potions and, remarkably, it appears to have worked.'

As he said that, Rosa felt in her pocket for the Black Tourmaline stone that Mary had given her earlier and ran it through her fingers.

Her father went on: 'The only creature not happy in all this is Merlin, but as you know, he's a law unto himself.'

Rosa smiled. 'Thank you so much. That all sounds so wonderful. But do promise me that, whatever time of night it is, if you're concerned about anything you must call me.'

'I promise, my dear.'

'Did you talk to Mum about how she was feeling?' Rosa asked.

Her father's face was now pained at the other end of the phone as he said hastily, 'I think my battery is about to die...'

'How you doing?' Titch enquired, as Rosa appeared at the café. The pregnant girl was scoffing again, this time taking huge bites out of a hot dog; ketchup was smeared all over her chin. Ritchie automatically pulled a wet wipe from the nappy bag and handed it to her. Theo, after his initial surge of energy was already fast asleep over his dad's shoulder.

'Yes. I'm all good.' Rosa's concern waned; she would talk to Christopher tomorrow. Nothing ever seemed as bad in the morning and maybe his battery really had just gone. 'Mum is having Little Ned and Hot for the night. I'm not quite sure what to do with myself.'

'You lucky cow. Maybe I'll come home with you and Ritchie can take our little monster with him.'

'You can if you want,' replied the ever-doting Ritchie. 'I don't mind, honestly.'

'But *I* do,' Rosa laughed. 'I love you, mate, but I'm going to go home alone and have the longest deepest bubble bath and then get into bed and watch all the TV I've been wanting to catch up on for the past four months. Or saying that, I may just sleep.' She let out a big noisy sigh. 'Bliss.'

CHAPTER NINETEEN

It was still only 7.30 p.m. when Rosa made her way along the beach path and back to Gull's Rest. She had always liked the sulphur smell that fireworks created; yellow misty remnants of the show were now hanging over the incoming tide like an eerie fog. She associated that smell with the few happy times she had had in her childhood when the foster-home staff would take a few of the kids to a local display.

In the Bay, the voices of those who'd stayed on for a drink and were gathered in the smoking area of the Ship Hotel carried on the breeze. The peace was soon shattered as, now that the majority of children had made their way home with their weary parents, Luke was blasting out his favourite track from The Weeknd through the big speakers to the side of the burger tables.

Gone were the days when Rosa would party on and drink herself into oblivion. Now, a hot mug of something, a bath and snuggling down to a Netflix series with Josh were her means of relaxation. She was only twenty-eight, but this went with the territory of having small children, she guessed. She had also been lucky in finding someone with whom she found it so easy to do nothing with. Plus, with her choice not to drink any more, partying didn't have the same appeal as it used to. Rosa shivered. She wouldn't want to start drinking again; she had been a bad drunk. An unhappy one. And now that she had worked her demons through there was no need to mask her pain with intoxicating liquor. Most of the emptiness that she used to feel had been replaced with love, happiness – and although she never ever thought she would say it out loud – with the joy of work. Her days running the Corner Shop had been among the happiest of her life and working in the café alongside Sara and Nate had also been such fun. And now she couldn't wait to get her teeth stuck into a new Christmas project.

She was just thinking how she must book Little Ned into the nursery on Tuesday to cover the meeting she had arranged with one of Celia Carlisle's acquaintances, when she noticed the same glowing light she had seen the other night coming from the water. The tide was not quite right up to the wall yet but was high enough for a small boat to be moored about ten metres away. It was from the silhouette of this tiny boat that the light was emanating.

It was reassuring to see that although it did look like someone was trying to put a distress signal out, it was just the way that the waves were rocking the boat on the dark sea that caused the light to flash so frequently. Rosa was comforted that it must have been what she had seen the other night. Not a boat in distress, just a boat bobbing on the water.

Pushing open the front door to Gull's Rest, she shut the curtains to keep the warmth in and went straight to fill and switch on the kettle. Then producing the wrapped hot dog that her brother had given her, she started to eat hungrily while waiting for the water to boil so she could pour it onto the tea bag that she had just thrown into her *I love Dachshunds* mug.

It felt odd for Rosa being in the house alone. Even if Josh

was out working, or Little Ned was at nursery, there was always trusty Hot to keep her company. She knew that neither of them could converse back, but just having two extra little heartbeats in the house was sometimes company enough. The silence was deafening, and it made her think back to Danny's comment that living down here was so quiet you could hear yourself dream. But she wouldn't change that for the world now either. Cockleberry Bay was where her heart lay. And where her whole family now lived. *Her family*. Who'd have thought, just three years ago, she would ever be stringing those two words together?

Removing her coat and kicking off her trainers, she turned all the main lights off and then went upstairs, intending to run a bath. What a treat it would be, to be able to lie in the deep bubbles and even to top up with hot water for as long as she wanted, without either a child, a dog or husband's interruption. However, once she got upstairs, she realised she had forgotten to bring her tea up, so she put the landing light on and went back down to the kitchen. Just as she was checking the snack drawer for some goodies to take up with her for later, she thought she heard a noise in the utility room next to the back door. Her heart fluttered for a second. Wondering what on earth it could be, she stood still – but when straining her ears for the noise this time, she heard nothing. Just put it down to the normal creaks and groans from the house settling that she sometimes heard when she was up feeding Little Ned in the middle of the night.

Turning the lights off to leave the downstairs in darkness again, she went back up to the bathroom and turned on the taps. She was about to get undressed when she heard an almighty crash. Freezing in fear, Rosa's heart fluttered like that of a captured bird. 'Fuck,' she whispered to herself. 'Fuck.' Aware that if she rang the police she could well be dead in her bed before they had even left the station, and having seen Davina drive off from the pub long ago, Rosa's first action was to message Lucas. Then, grabbing the big torch that Josh sensibly insisted they keep under the bed, she tiptoed down the stairs.

CHAPTER TWENTY

Davina Hunt smiled flirtatiously at her bed companion. 'Sorry to come to you so late but I promise I've been a good girl today.'

'And you know what happens to *really* good girls, don't you?'

'You get to slide down their chimneys, of course.'

'Exactly.'

'Ooh, I do love a man in uniform. But I'm not sure if red's your colour and maybe lose the beard next time.'

The couple laughed out loud.

'On a serious note, thanks for giving me the gig,' the man said. 'I've struggled to find work since I got back, and I will soon have a massive vet's bill to pay.'

'It's a win-win then, isn't it?' Davina kissed him on the cheek.

'Trouble is, I've got a bit of history in the Bay. I'm not everyone's favourite person down there.'

'Well, you have the perfect disguise. And like I said, I will arrange your payment in cash, so it will be very much worth *our* while.' Davina ran her finger down the man's chest.

'You're good,' he sighed, his body responding.

'The best.' The blonde leaned forward, brushed her breasts in his face, then started to sing seductively, 'Santa baby, hurry down the chimney tonight . . .'

CHAPTER TWENTY ONE

Switching on the downstairs lights, Rosa ran and opened the front door ready for Luke then cried out, 'Who's there?' Silence. 'What do you want?' Then as if she were re-enacting a scene from the film *Gladiator*, she ran through to the utility room brandishing the large torch in the air. A window was swinging open, the rail of clothes that had been drying out under it had been knocked to the floor. Hurriedly unlocking the back door, she listened and could hear footsteps running at speed, but more hauntingly, through the still, cold air she could also hear the noise of a baby crying.

Within a minute or two, Lucas and Danny had appeared by her side. Handing Luke the torch, a mute Rosa then pointed to the back door, causing both men to charge out there in pursuit, though they returned after a short while. Panting loudly, Luke was the first to speak.

'Shit, bird, what happened?'

'Someone's come through the window – scared the life out of me it did. I'd left it open a crack because of the wet clothes in here.'

'We couldn't see no one,' Danny input. 'It's pitch black and there's a link to the coast path at the back of your garden, ain't there? Whoever it was knew that. We lost 'em. Sorry, Rosa.'

'Don't be silly. Thanks for coming so quickly.'

Lucas was serious. 'Rosa – a message from you saying you're in trouble when I know your old man is away, what do you expect?'

'Anything missing?' Danny asked.

'I haven't had a chance to check.'

A thud, thud, thud noise could then be heard against the metal sink in the utility room, followed by an '*Oh no!*' from Rosa. Lucas's plumber instincts kicking in, he shot through the house and up the stairs, turned off the bathwater, which had already overflowed on to the bathroom floor and was now dripping through the laundry-room ceiling. Danny had already located the fuse box so was able to switch off the electricity in the affected rooms.

Rosa had tears in her eyes when he returned. Danny was now busying himself trying to stem the flow of water that was trickling down the wall after throwing down the towels that Rosa had taken from the airing cupboard.

'Josh is going to kill me. I don't want him to think I can't cope when he's away.' She directed the torch at Danny so he could see what he was doing.

'Rosa, you had a break-in. You didn't just leave a bath running for the fun of it,' Lucas replied.

'I take it you have house insurance?' Danny added.

Rosa managed a smile through her angst. 'I'm married to Josh Smith; come on, we've got insurance on our insurance. But shit, I don't bother faffing with the night alarm when he's not here. We're probably not covered anyway.'

Lucas was reassuring. 'OK. Well, don't worry. I've seen a lot of this in my game and Danny is our man for the building, so we can probably sort it between us, can't we?'

'Yeah, mate, no problem.' Danny looked up to gauge the extent of the ceiling damage. 'It will dry out and need a lick of paint. That's all, I reckon.'

'When's the big man back from the States?' Lucas then asked.

'Not for around five weeks yet.'

'In that case, he won't even know it's happened.'

'Really?'

'Nah. The tank had finished emptying, which is handy. It's not actually that bad,' Lucas soothed. 'And at least you have a tiled floor and not carpet. Just keep the heating on all night for a few days to help dry it out. It will be fine.'

Once Lucas was happy that they had done everything they could to clear up, he turned to Danny. 'Right, mate, you'd better get back to the hotel. Don't forget you need to be up for breakfast in the morning for the guest. I'll be there too but remember to up your game on everything just in case that young bird with the tattoo is the inspector.'

'By the way, did you see her earlier, at all?' Danny double-checked the back door and window to make sure they were both locked securely.

'No. I didn't. She was probably sneaking around with a magnifying glass looking for dust while we were busy with the burgers.'

Danny laughed. 'OK, I'm on it. Don't worry, Rosa. Honestly, we've got this.'

'Drink?' Rosa offered once Danny had left and they had checked that nothing had been stolen.

'Just a cuppa, please. Do you want to call the Old Bill?'

Rosa was still haunted by the baby's cry she had heard soon after the break-in. Her gut spoke for her. 'No. It was an opportunist theft, I reckon, because the fireworks are on. They probably thought I'd be out still. And it's my fault for not putting the alarm on and for leaving the window open. I'm so bloody trusting – or stupid – one of the two. God!' Rosa raked a hand through her curls. 'Josh must never know about this.'

'I told him we didn't kiss that night, so I think I can hold onto this one for you,' Lucas said softly.

Rosa stopped in her tracks. 'You did?' He nodded. 'No wonder Josh forgave me so readily,' she sighed. 'I never knew that. Thank you.' She caught his eye, then coughed. 'I forget, sugar in your tea?'

'Sweet enough, me.' Luke lightened things up. 'But two, please.'

'Throw a log on the burner and we can sit in there in the warm,' Rosa instructed.

They sat next to each other on the sofa, the fire already starting to heat the cosy end of the open-plan lounge.

'It's good that Little Ned slept through it all,' Lucas said.

'He's at Mary's. She's given me a night off.'

'Oh, OK.' Luke took a drink of his tea. 'I'm glad you didn't want the police here. Mind you, Davina's not on duty for a couple of days now.'

'Is she not staying with you tonight then?' Rosa asked innocently, knowing full well the answer.

'We had another row. That's why I was so angry earlier.'

'Ah, really?'

'I don't know what to do, Rosa. I do like the girl.'

'What's the but?'

'She's not you.' Luke smiled. 'But that was said in jest.' Rosa put her hand on his knee knowing full well that it wasn't.

'I know that me and you can't be together and I'm kind of getting used to that now. Me and Davina, well, we have fun, a good laugh a lot of the time, but she's not kind. I mean, I can't believe she hadn't remembered the anniversary of Mum dying.

I would have understood it, if she hadn't been involved in the bloody case surrounding her death.'

'People have busy lives; they forget things.'

'That is pretty important, so don't be sticking up for her. And I'm not sure if I can see a future with her. I know I'm still young, but I do want kids, and like you I want to have them as young as possible. I don't want to be that old dad at the school gates.'

'I don't know if she's that keen on them. She wasn't too complimentary about Alfie or kids in general the other day, to be honest.'

'He can be a handful sometimes though, to be fair,' Luke added. 'But Danny was in the nick, Alfie's mum left and, well, Tina is Tina. Full of love, but she calls a spade a spade. So no wonder he's not the easiest.'

'I love them all though.' Rosa poked the fire.

'Yeah, me too.'

They sat in silence for a second before Lucas went on, 'The reason I don't want to let her go – Davina, that is – is 'cos I don't want to be on my own. She keeps me kind of propped up. Even though I know it's not right, the thought of not getting little messages or having someone to cuddle at night – just an affirmation that I'm not alone – well, I need that.'

Rosa made a little face. 'Alec didn't quite finish his work with you, I don't think.'

'I only met him a couple of times. I don't need a shrink, Rosa.'

'We all want love, that's what makes our world go round. But you've got to love yourself first though, mate. I found out the hard way, but when you do, I tell you – it is a revelation.'

'Josh loves you to infinity and back.'

'Yes, and I love him too, but I am still my own person. I'm going to sound like Mary now, she quoted something so relevant to me from her beloved Kahlil Gibran when I was struggling.'

Rosa reached for her phone and googled what she was looking for. 'Here it is: "let there be spaces in your togetherness and let the winds of the heavens dance between you." In other words, you need to find someone to complement you, not rely on you or you on her.'

'You're so lovely.' Luke smiled at Rosa. 'I fancied you the minute I set eyes on you; you know that.'

'And you were still a bastard to me.'

Luke sighed. 'At the beginning, yes. I was with the wrong bloody woman then too.'

'Carly Jessop is more your type – actually no, she is *a lot* your type, I reckon.'

'OK, I have a confession to make.'

'Oh my God, you haven't already made a move, have you?' Rosa asked.

'I wish. I fancy her and I did feel a rush of something the minute I set eyes on her pretty face.'

'That's brilliant, then.' Rosa became animated.

'It's just – what if she doesn't fancy me? Because I'm not going to mess her around and contact her while I'm with Davina; she seems just too lovely to even consider that. And also, Davina doesn't deserve that either.'

Rosa kept to herself the fact that she disagreed with the second statement, and instead said, 'If you don't take a chance, then you will never know.'

'She's bound to have a boyfriend, she's too gorgeous to still be on the market. How do I play this?'

'I can get Mary to put a love spell on her if you like.' They both laughed. 'I've got a feeling that you two will work it out somehow,' Rosa said. 'I liked her too. She has a good energy. To see you happy would make me so happy, you know.'

'It would?'

Rosa said firmly, 'Of course it would. And what I have learned is, that if it's right, love will find a way. It always does.'

'Rosa, I want to ask you something.'

'Go on.'

'Can you just humour me and say that if Josh hadn't come into your life, we could have maybe made a go of it, the pair of us?'

'I've answered this before.' Rosa took in the man's soulful and brooding hazel eyes. He was so handsome that she couldn't deny that sometimes she still did feel an urge to squeeze his face and plant her lips on his.

'Tell me again.'

'Timing, the timing was wrong, as it so often is in life and love. Maybe we could have made it – who knows for sure? But what I do know is that I do love you, in a deep, caring way. It's obviously less than I feel for Josh, and different from what I feel for my brother, and that's it. If we can keep in this suspended lovely kind of whatever it is, forever, then let's do it. I never want to hurt you, Luke, and I never ever meant to, before.'

Lucas nodded. 'I'll guess I'll have to take that.'

'Well, it's all you're going to get, I'm afraid. Why don't you find out more about Carly, see if she's single? There's no harm in asking.'

'And what should I do about Davina?'

'I can't answer that for you. I'm learning there are no hard and fast rules about motherhood. The same applies with affairs of the heart, or life for that matter. You'll know when it's time to say goodbye and if it's not yet, then there's no right or wrong with that either. People do what they do, Luke. Queenie used to say that. She also used to say, "If you don't know what to do, do nothing, say nothing and the answer will come to you." That mantra has worked for me so many times.'

'Rosa?'

'Yes?'

'What if you do know what you want to do?'

'Just say or do it with honesty, I guess.'

'Then, can I stay with you tonight?'

CHAPTER TWENTY TWO

'Twinkle, twinkle, little star…' Christopher Webb came into the room, lifted the crying baby from his makeshift pram bed in Mary Cobb's bedroom and placed him over his shoulder. Then, realising that he'd forgotten the rest of the old nursery rhyme, the new grandad began to make it up and deliver it in the best way he was able with his limited vocal range.

'WAAAAAH!'

'Shush, little man, it's all OK. There is lots of love for you here and Mummy will be back in the morning.'

'WAAAAAH!' But Little Ned wanted his mummy right now.

Mary reappeared in her bedroom, wearing a new navy velour dressing gown that still had its label in and holding a warmed bottle of milk. Her long black hair had been tidily brushed.

'Here.' She put the milk on the bedside table, then taking the distressed little bundle of warmth and energy, she wrapped him in the crocheted blanket that lived at Seaspray Cottage for whenever he visited.

He stopped crying immediately and instead began to deliver hitching breaths; recovery sounds of contentment at the familiar sound and smells of his grandmother and her home. Mary put her finger to his gums. The baby didn't flinch. 'I don't think it's teeth tonight. I think he must have just woken up and wondered where he was, bless him. What's the time?'

Christopher went through to the spare room and picked his watch off the side. 'It's the devil's hour. Three a.m. to be precise,' he said, coming back into her room.

'Devil's hour? I've never heard that before.' She tested the temperature of the milk on the back of her hand and put the teat to Little Ned's mouth. He started to suck hungrily.

'Yes, when I first started my business, I learned that a lot of deaths happened in the early hours. I checked it out and discovered that our body and immune systems are actually more vulnerable between three and five a.m.'

'That's cheery, isn't it,' Mary said. 'Well, we are all very much alive and kicking in this house and when he's had his bottle and a fresh nappy, I for one need some more sleep – if I can get off again, that is.' She shivered. 'The heating should kick in in a minute.'

Once he'd finished and been burped, Mary changed Little Ned's nappy on a towel on the bed, patted some cream on his sore bottom, buttoned up his Babygro and swaddled him in the blanket again. Then she tucked him into the crook of her arm, sensing that he wasn't quite ready to go back to sleep yet.

'If there is something wrong with me and I am losing my marbles, Kit, you will look after Rosa, won't you?' she whispered.

'Oh Polly. I'm sure you're not, but of course, without question.' He paused. 'And I would look after you too.'

Mary felt herself well up. 'You would?'

The man didn't answer. 'To be fair, she doesn't seem to need a lot of looking after, that one.'

'You know what I mean.'

'Of course I do.'

'And I don't want a huge send-off. I like to keep myself to

myself. And I must tell Rosa that I want to be buried in with my mother and Queenie.' Mary paused. 'My mother died while she was having me.' Her voice tailed off at the end.

'That is so sad.'

'Yes, it is. I don't tell many people that.'

'I know,' was Christopher's reply as he joined the fragile woman on the edge of the bed.

They sat in silence. Thighs touching. Hearts knowing. The contented snuffling noises coming from their grandson were slightly hypnotic. After what seemed like only a few minutes, Mary jolted slightly as if she was dropping off to sleep. Then, just like he had done with his Nathaniel all those years ago, Christopher took Little Ned from her and tucked him back in the pram. The baby did not stir. He then did the same to Mary. Coaxing her to get back into bed, he tucked her in and leaned over to kiss her cheek, then pulled up the embroidered bedspread that was resting by her feet. Leaving the two sleeping, he went back into the spare bedroom and was soon fast asleep himself.

CHAPTER TWENTY THREE

Lucas bounded down the stairs of the Ship to find Danny dancing around to Slade and 'Merry Christmas Everybody' on the radio. Sausages were grilling and he had made some hash browns.

'I overslept. Sorry, mate.' Lucas nicked one of the hash browns off the side, then finding it was very hot, quickly dropped it with an *ouch!* 'Good work on making these yourself.'

'Late one, was it?' Danny took a slurp of his coffee. 'I thought you might stay at Gull's Rest, considering what had happened.'

'Er no. You know what Rosa's like, nothing fazes her.'

He didn't want to explain that while waiting for a reply to his question about staying the night, Josh had phoned, and Rosa had mouthed to Lucas that she was fine and would see him tomorrow. In his dreams he had thought maybe they could just lie together until the sun came up, chatting and laughing. Despite him knowing perfectly well that Rosa would never hurt Josh, he often had fantasies like this. There was always a glimmer of hope, that maybe she would turn around and say that it was him she had wanted all along and they would run off into the sunset together and live happily ever after. But he had grown up to realise that there were very few happy ever afters in real life. And that she had only kissed him before because she had been blind drunk and thought that her husband had cheated on her. He needed to stop watching so many bloody romcoms on Netflix.

'Oh sod it!' Danny said into the ether, forgetting about the no swearing ban, then to Lucas, who was making sure the breakfast table was up to scratch: 'Mate, if *Ms* Swift' – he too emphasised the Ms – 'comes down, take her order, will ya? I just need to run over to Nate and get some ketchup off him. Looks like we are clean out after the burgers last night.'

Danny was back as quickly as he had left. He shivered as he came in out of the cold. Wiping his hands on his apron, he hurried back into the kitchen, put the ketchup in a small bowl and added a teaspoon. As he went through to put it on the restaurant table, he noticed a woman sitting with her back to him.

'Good morning, madam,' he said politely. 'I do hope you slept well. How can I tempt you to have your eggs this morning?'

The woman turned around, causing Danny's mouth and eyes to spring open in disbelief. 'If I were a joker, I would say fertilised,' she replied calmly, with a slight smirk on her face.

'Leah? What the fuck are you doing here?'

The woman then stood up and put her hand flat out as if in surrender. 'Dan, please don't panic. All is good and I promise not to upset anyone. I'm completely sober. Don't worry.'

'*Ms* bleeding Swift? What's that all about? – Or have you got married and forgotten to tell me or summink?'

'I was listening to Taylor Swift when I made the booking. Didn't want to give my real name as I thought you might try to stop me coming.'

'Come in here.' He ushered her into the kitchen, not wanting Lucas to overhear their conversation. Looking right at her, he

141

softened. 'I have to say, you look fantastic.' The young woman's eyes were bright and clear. Her skin glowing. Her once bleached blonde hair, a natural ash colour. She had an air of confidence about her that Danny had never seen before.

She was forthright in her delivery. 'I never thought I'd ever say this, but I bloody love being sober. I've cracked it – not even any booze now.'

Leah's ex-partner's reaction was as she had predicted. 'So now you're sober you've come to make a claim on our Alfie. I get it.' Danny's voice was calm but concerned. But inside he was shaking. Then on seeing Leah's face fall, he hugged her, saying, 'I knew you were strong enough. Well done. God, it's good to see you.' She broke away.

'So, *are* you here for Alfie?' Danny asked, noticing the pretty butterfly tattoo just above her thumb and remembering back to the lovely day they had spent together in Brighton when she had decided to have it done.

'I found out that you and your mum were down here now and I wanted to see how you were getting on. I waited until I knew you were both away from here before I checked in. I had my hat pulled down and some glasses on, and I sneaked out among the fireworks crowd last night. I saw your mum with Alfie; he looked so happy and well. You've done a great job.' Leah exhaled deeply, tears welling in her eyes. 'How could I have left him? Left you? So bloody selfish. But that's what addicts are. Selfish liars. I'm so sorry, Danny. About everything.'

'You were ill,' he said with rough kindness.

'Nah. I was high. There's a difference.'

'But look at you now,' Danny boosted.

'The last thing I want to do is come into your lives and confuse Alfie. That's not my intention. I have got a birthday present for him upstairs though. Say it's from you, if you like. I was hoping that maybe we could introduce me back into his life gradually. Through my therapy, I've found out how we do it properly, so as not to disrupt him.'

Danny hesitated. 'Do I have to say yes right now?'

'Oh, Danny, of course not. It's a big decision, I realise that, but I come with love and would never take him away from you.'

He was confused. 'So, are you thinking of moving down here then?'

'No, not at all. I've got a job I really enjoy in London and, well, I have met someone else – through my rehab. I call him my sober saint.' She smiled warmly, thinking of the man who had helped her to live again. Then went on, sounding worried: 'You didn't expect that when you saw me, did you? For us to get back together?'

'Not at all. We had some good times, Leah, but we were never right for each other, sober or not. Having time right away from you and our old lives has made me accept that.'

Leah was impressed and relieved at the emotional intelligence of the man with a huge heart standing in front of her.

'Maybe if it works out, and it's what our son wants, we can share him at school holidays or one weekend a month. It's all about Alfie now.'

'It always was for me,' Danny said quietly. 'Let's see, shall we? It's a long way from here to London.'

'Yes, it is. But we've come a long way too, Dan. Let's see what we can work out, eh? For our son.'

Lucas, wondering why the breakfast table was still empty, walked into the kitchen. 'Ah, I got ya,' he said to Danny, beaming. 'Is this "the long story"?'

'One of 'em.' Danny couldn't help but smile at his boss's astute observation. 'This is Leah, Alfie's mum, aka Ms Swift.'

'Ah, hello. We met already,' Lucas said, shaking her hand.

'You're not a hotel inspector then? That's a relief.'

'For you maybe. It would have been easier for me if she had been.' Danny sighed.

Leah grinned up at Danny. 'Come on, Dan, I'm starving. Show me what breakfast delights you have on offer here.'

Wishing he hadn't hit the brandy quite so hard when he had got back from Rosa's, Lucas yawned loudly. 'Tell you what, mate, plate three up, extra hash browns for me, and go and join Leah. I'm sure you've got a lot to catch up on. Then it's all hands on deck to clear up the mess from last night.'

'Especially now we know I'm not the real inspector,' Leah added. 'Or am I?'

'Not even funny,' Lucas told her. 'Now go and eat, the pair of ya.'

CHAPTER TWENTY FOUR

Little Ned was having great fun bouncing up and down in the rocker chair that Rosa had placed next to her in the kitchen while she got them both ready for the day. Rattling the teething toys she had put across it, he shrieked in delight as Hot ran around him in circles, the crazy hound not wanting to miss out on a piece of the action. Hot loved babies – unless they cried, of course.

Rosa had decided that she didn't need to come clean to Josh about flooding the bathroom. He could do nothing while in New York so why worry him? – and she trusted that Lucas and Danny would put things to rights for her. For some reason she didn't feel any fear about the break-in either, but for the sake of her neighbours she had decided that she ought to report it; just not today. For today she was off to meet Janie, the person whose email the late Celia Carlisle had written in the front of her folder next to the word *Contact*. And if she were to report it, once she rang DC Clarke at the police station, she knew from past dealings she had had with the bumbling officer about a theft at the Corner Shop, that it would not only cost at least an hour of time, but also half a tin of biscuits. Nor could she face the thought of having to converse civilly with Davina if he sent the hard-faced WPC to investigate instead.

'Right,' Rosa said aloud, turning the radio down so that she could concentrate on what she was doing. 'Folder, phone, purse, keys, pen, notebook. OK. That's my stuff, now your bag, Master Smith.' She looked down to her son who was now chewing on one of the hanging teething toys. 'Look at you, you handsome soldier. You're with Gladys today – that'll be nice, won't it?' She went through to the utility room to fetch some nappies and milk formula. On opening the door, she screwed up her face. Just a half packet of nappies and one tin of formula stared back at her. How odd. She had done a big online shop before Josh had left. Firstly, so that he could help her unpack it all, as it was her least favourite thing to do, and secondly, so she didn't have the bother of doing it every week while he was away. Granted, she was quite often so tired that she walked around in a daze, but surely it wasn't logistically possible to have already used the two big packs of nappies they had bought. Maybe she'd put some upstairs in the bedroom and not remembered.

Making a mental note to check later, she settled Little Ned in his pram, then loaded up everything he needed for the day. She had always thought parents were making a fuss when they said how long it took for them to get out of the door with a small child and, in parrot fashion, claimed, 'It looks like I've packed for a small army, but I'm only going out for three hours.' Now, she understood. Gone were the days of just grabbing her coat and Hot's lead and gaily shutting the door behind her. Such simple things that she had taken for granted. Nowadays, merely leaving the house was like a military operation. And if there wasn't an emergency nappy or clothes change required just before leaving base, she felt like she was winning.

Nate came out of the café as he saw her walking past. 'Morning, sis, how you doing?'

'Good, ta. I've got a meeting today.'

'The events stuff?' Nate leaned in to look at his nephew, who, full of milk, just contentedly stared back at him with a cheeky smile. Hot, tied to the pram with the lead, barked his disapproval at having to stop.

'Yeah. Looking forward to using my brain, to be honest.'

'I'm going to get the last of the Christmas decorations up today.' Nate uncurled his finger from the little lad's. 'I figure if the Grotty Grotto is starting at the pub on December the first, we'd better be in the game at the same time, as, hopefully, it will bring some business our way too.'

'Good idea. Are you coping OK without Sara?'

'I think I could do with an extra pair of hands leading up to the holidays. Brad is great but he can only do weekends until his uni breaks for Christmas.'

'Let's have another chat about that when I'm not so busy.'

'No rush. Where's your meeting?'

'Polhampton Sands Café.'

'You interloper! Steal a menu, can you?' Nate suggested. 'It's always good to see what the competition are up to and get some new ideas.'

'Like peas in a pod, we are. I've already thought about it,' Rosa laughed, and did a high five with her brother.

After seeing Little Ned settled at the crèche, Rosa got on the bus to Polhampton, alighted at the town hall and made her way down to the beach. She had wanted to combine her meeting with seeing Vicki for a coffee, but the vet was due to operate on a Great Dane today and that would take up most of her morning.

Rosa was feeling pleased with life. It was so comforting to know that Little Ned was happy and safe in the confines of Little Devils. Gladys Moore had proved her worth – and some. Rosa had also had a lovely conversation with Josh the night before. She had unburdened some of her worries and realised that he did fully support and understand, and now she knew that if she had asked him to come back earlier, he would have done his best to do so. Even Hot was in his element, as he was having a play date at the Lobster Pot with his girlfriend, the Duchess, and Ugly and Pongo, the excitable pugs.

Polhampton Sands Café was busier than she had expected it to be. A group of mums with pushchairs having a catch-up over coffee and cake, and workers from a local building site munching on scrumptious-looking bacon and egg baguettes, made up the majority of the clientele on this winter morning. Their animated chat and the steam from the kitchen had caused the windows to mist over, hiding the glorious view of the expansive Polhampton Sands. Tourists were few and far between down here in wintertime, and although this wasn't good for her own business back in Cockleberry, it suited Rosa when she was out and about as she wasn't one for queuing, especially for food.

Rosa had no idea how this meeting would pan out. Wasn't sure if this Janie would be able to advise her. She hadn't even been able to find a surname for her, so that she could check her out online. The email that she had received confirming the meeting had just signed off with a single J, and despite Rosa asking for a phone number this had not been given either. Rosa had jokingly written *I'll be wearing a red carnation.* Then realising that maybe she should be slightly more business-like, had added: and *I have curly brown hair and a lightning-shaped scar on my left cheek.*

Rosa got to the café counter and looked around to see if there were any single women sitting on their own. She assumed that, as Celia had been in her sixties, then maybe this was another retired friend of hers, who was helping out. She would find out soon. Just as she was shoving a menu in her bag, a deep voice behind her said, 'Are you Rosa? Rosa Smith?'

She turned around to see a man in his late twenties, with blond surfer-dude-type hair, strong lion-like features and a wide perfect smile, worthy of any Hollywood actor. He was dressed casually in jeans, work boots and a thick black hoody with *JW Gardening Services* branded in white on his left pec.

'Oh. I thought...' Rosa was perplexed.

'That I was a woman?' Jamie grinned. His face was friendly, his demeanour approachable. 'I am J – but Jamie Ward, to be exact. Pleased to meet you, Rosa.' He held out his hand. 'Now, let me get you a drink, food, cake – whatever you'd like – and I can explain everything.'

CHAPTER TWENTY FIVE

Thank you so much Mrs Treborick.' Titch opened the Corner Shop door for the white-haired lady who owned the wool shop down the road. 'Mum says she's popping in to you later as she's promised me a merino wool jumper for Christmas. Said you've just the colour she's after.'

Titch then went back through to the little rear kitchen and put the kettle on. Saveloy and Mr Chips, her sausage dogs, oblivious to the cold were playing together noisily in the back yard. She made herself a decaf tea and hoisted herself onto the stool behind the counter. Looking at her phone she counted down the days again to when her baby was due. It was less than seven weeks until Christmas Day. That wasn't so bad. If she broke it down into just seven more Saturdays, even more doable.

Titch dunked a custard cream biscuit in her tea, put it in her mouth, then shut her eyes for a second. Remembering back to the years that she had worked here with Rosa, she had learned from experience that there would be a slight lull in the shop now until the Christmas rush started. The October half term and Halloween always brought with it an influx of tourists and locals, and Fireworks Night always caused a flurry of sales. Then it was time to restock for Christmas, with all the work that entailed to get the shop looking truly festive.

Ritchie had promised her that as soon as his mother was fully recovered from the dragging after-effects of the flu, he would only work the evening shifts at the chippie in the run-up to Christmas. He had already booked January off so that he could be fully on duty when the baby came. Ideally, Titch didn't want him to work at the chippie at all, but she had to be realistic. As it was being handed over to him by his parents when they retired in the not-so-distant future, he needed to play his part. They would then have both businesses to their name and the opportunity was just too good to miss out on. She had always been used to hard work anyway, holding down many part-time jobs before she had got herself pregnant during a mad one-night stand with junior doctor Ben Burton, who turned out to be counsellor Alec Burton's son. A grafter, that's what Titch Whittaker's mum called her.

As if Edie Rogers knew that her daughter-in-law was thinking about her, the shop bell rang and in she strode – tall and thin with a face that reminded Titch of a rat. The girl found it hard to believe that Ritchie, her kind, warm and funny husband, had come from the loins of the woman who now stood in front of her. Titch put her hand to her stomach and grimaced.

'Are you feeling all right, Patricia?' Only Titch's deceased father had ever called her by her full name before she had met Ritchie. Edie Rogers coughed, then dug out a tissue from her bag and blew her nose loudly.

'Braxton Hicks, that's all,' Titch replied, with difficulty. 'Had the same with Theo from about this time. Ooh.' She held her tummy again.

'Stop making a fuss, girl; you're pregnant, not ill. I'm the one who's been suffering.' Titch was sure that the woman had Munchausen Syndrome. 'Flu, like nobody's business, I tell you.

Now you know I'm not one for being under the doctor – not like some I could mention – but even I had to go today.' Inwardly screeching with mirth about 'under the doctor' and so glad that Rosa wasn't there to make her laugh, Titch put on a false look of sympathy as Edie rasped, 'My throat is that sore. Blisters all over the back of it. Terrible!'

'Oh dear, that's no good, but please keep it to yourself, Edie. I can't afford to be ill with a toddler, a baby on board, two dogs and a shop to run.'

The shop bell went, and Titch acknowledged a customer with a smile. The middle-aged woman went straight to the back of the shop and started looking at the Lily's Kitchen cat food.

'There's an offer on today,' Titch alerted her, causing the woman to turn around and listen. 'Buy any two products and you get a free flea comb.' Again, she struggled with the desire to laugh out loud.

Edie then lowered her voice. 'You know that I'm not one to gossip either.' Titch nearly fell off her stool. Edie Rogers was and always had been, lead stoker of the Cockleberry Bay gossip train. 'You'll never guess who I saw coming out of the doctor's as I was going in.'

'No, I'll never guess, but I'm sure you're going to tell me,' Titch replied.

'Mary Cobb and that new funeral director in town she claims is Rosa and Nate's father.' The rodent-like face smiled gleefully at the imparting of this information. Titch sincerely hoped the features would not be inherited by her new baby. 'Mary looked very sombre too.'

'Well, everyone has to go to the doctor's sometimes. This isn't actually front-page news, is it, Edie?' There was sarcasm in the young girl's tone.

Edie ignored her. 'He stayed over the other night, so I hear.

Disgraceful. No wonder STDs are rife in middle-aged women.' She added pruriently, 'I wouldn't be surprised if they've both got the clap.'

Titch's eyebrows shot up. She looked nervously at the other customer, who was still busy at the cat food. 'Edie, how would you feel if somebody were talking about you in this way?'

Edie drew herself up. 'I would quote to you the wise words of Oscar Wilde, notorious homo-sexualist though he might have been, and say that there is only one thing in life worse than being talked about and that is *not* being talked about at all.'

Then, seeing the only other customer turn round and look at her in disbelief, Edie Rogers cleared her throat loudly and carried on: 'Now, did you get those Koi Carp pellets in for me, like a good girl?'

CHAPTER TWENTY SIX

'I understand now. So *you're* the gardener.' Rosa sat opposite Jamie Ward nursing a large mug of hot chocolate. 'I had the pleasure, if that's the right word, of meeting Felix Carlisle, who, I'm afraid, explained in detail how his mother died.'

'Oh. That's awkward.'

'Not at all. I think it's brilliant. Well, not exactly, but you know what I mean. I am sorry for your loss though, of course.'

Rosa could sense a wave of sadness sweep over the man in front of her and immediately pushed Celia's famous last words out of her mind. This was neither the time nor the place to regurgitate those facts, nor indeed to look at his crotch to see if Mrs Carlisle's last words were really true.

'I know everyone will be laughing, but I loved her.' Jamie took a deep breath. 'I met her and just saw a vibrant, intelligent, fun-loving woman. Her drive and passion were infectious. Her charm, captivating. Age never came into it. The circumstances of her death were traumatic and unfortunately became public, or our love affair would never have been outed and shamed. I miss her dreadfully.'

Rosa put her hand on top of his. 'Tough stuff.'

'Yes. Thanks for not being judgmental. You're the first

not to be.'

'Blimey, Jamie, I was brought up in foster homes, I've lived on the street. I have craved and looked for love in all the wrong places. So, if you find something in someone, like you say you did, I don't blame you for grabbing on to it good and hard with both hands. I don't judge anyone, me.'

He noticed her wedding ring. 'You found it in the end then. Love, I mean?'

'Yes. I did. Josh is an amazing husband and father.'

'Oh wow, a kid too. You didn't hang about.'

Rosa smiled. 'All the more reason I want to help out with the charity stuff if I can. Escape reality for a bit. I love my boys dearly, but isn't Happy Families just a card game from the nineteenth century?'

Jamie laughed and took a drink from his coffee mug. 'So where did you meet the delightful Felix then?'

'My dad is the funeral director in Cockleberry Bay. He is dealing with your…with Celia's funeral arrangements.'

'Your father seemed like such a lovely guy when I spoke to him,' Jamie said. 'In fact, do you see him much?'

'Yes, the bus I take to come here goes from outside his place so I may even see him later. Why do you ask?'

'I want to put something in Celia's coffin with her. Mr Webb kindly agreed and said the family need never know.'

Rosa knew how to keep the confidence of her father. 'That's nice.'

'Yes, jasmine. A sprig of jasmine. You're probably thinking why not a red rose or another traditional symbol of love. But as you know I tended to Celia's garden as well as her other needs, and she loved jasmine. It really was her favourite. So unbeknown to her, for her birthday last year I planted a jasmine bush underneath her bedroom window to allow the fragrance to drift up and in on the summer night air.'

'That is so romantic.'

'Yes.' The young man's voice was so quiet she could barely hear him. He made a visible effort to control his grief. 'I have a big cutting of it in my van. Remind me to hand it over to you before you leave.'

'Are you going to her funeral?'

'God, no, I couldn't bear the pointing fingers.'

'If she had died in a different way, would you have gone?'

'Yes, of course. The plain "gardener", rather than "Lady Chatterley's Lover" label would have been acceptable to all and sundry.' He sat upright in his chair and pushed his long blond hair back from his face.

'I will do anything to help that I can. And I am truly sorry.' Rosa tutted sympathetically, then pulled the blue folder from her bag. 'Right, now let's see if we can get this Christmas show on the road.'

'Ah, there it is,' Jamie said. 'Her Nativity Bible, she used to call it.'

'So why is your name in the folder?'

Jamie took it from Rosa. 'Let me see. She took down my email address the other day, telling me she wanted to send me something – a surprise. Her handwriting always was appalling …here it is, see. That says Jamie, not Janie. She'd just scribbled down *Contact Jamie* to remind herself to email me, probably. She was so sporadic and disorganised; never had a notebook handy. When you contacted me, I played along with it as I was so happy to get the folder back. The Christmas concert was very important to her.' Jamie rubbed a hand over his face before confiding, 'I don't trust her family, Rosa. I didn't think for one moment that they would do the decent thing and hand the running of it over to someone like you. It makes me feel all the more guilty, in fact.'

'Guilty, why? Because you were sleeping with Celia?'

'No.' Jamie gulped. 'Because the surprise she was emailing me about was that she's left me everything in her bloody will.'

Rosa tried not to laugh but couldn't help herself.

'I wasn't after a single penny of hers, I swear,' the gardener managed, but began to laugh, seeing the funny side of it too.

'You can't kid a kidder,' Rosa managed to blurt out.

'You are so right. And then when what happened, happened – well, I thought I'd be arrested for bloody manslaughter. Miss Marple and *Murder at the Vicarage* kind of thing.'

Rosa had to apologise. 'Sorry for saying that – the kidder bit, I mean. It's just, well, you read about these things happening and here you are, living proof that they really do. Do you think she knew she was going to die then?'

'God no! She was nearly killing me in that bedroom before she had the sudden heart attack. I think it was just a glorious coincidence for me, that she got it all tied up when she did.'

'Too much information.' Rosa shook her head.

'She hated her family,' Jamie said grimly. 'Felix only ever showed his face and came to see her when he wanted something.'

'He seemed distraught when I saw him.'

'Probably because he had to put his hand in his pocket to bury her.'

'So, do the family know yet about you getting the money?'

'God no! I spoke with the solicitor, pleaded for him to arrange the official reading to take place on the day *after* the funeral. The same day I fly out to Ibiza.'

'Ooh nice, how long for?' Rosa piped up.

'Forever,' Jamie Ward replied confidently.

Rosa was just making her way to the bus stop when she noticed a familiar-looking figure walking towards her accompanied by a Great Dane on a lead. Attractive in a geeky sort of way, the man had short fair hair and was still wearing the same horn-rimmed glasses that he had when she first set eyes on him in the Lobster Pot. Their affair, pre-Josh, had been full-blown but one-sided, because unbeknown to her, he had three kids and his wife was expecting another one.

'If it isn't Joe Fox,' Rosa said curtly. The sneaky one had a beard or was trying to grow one, at least. It didn't suit him. 'I heard you were back.'

'Of course you did,' Joe said nonchalantly. 'You only have to take a shit down here and a klaxon goes off.' His Mancunian accent seemed stronger somehow.

Yuk. Then she noticed a bandage on the dog's foot. 'Poor Suggs.'

'Yeah, he's OK, had to have a lump removed from his paw. Note to self: get insurance in future.'

'Ah, here's my bus now.' Rosa reached for her purse. 'Well, I hope he gets better soon.'

'Marriage suits you. You're looking good, Rosa,' he shouted after her as the doors were about to close.

'And you're still a cock,' Rosa said under her breath.

CHAPTER TWENTY SEVEN

Christopher wasn't home when Rosa arrived back in the Bay, so she put the sprig of jasmine under the wheel arch of the hearse that was parked outside the back entrance to his office and then messaged him to explain what she had done. Checking her watch to see how much time was left before she had to collect Little Ned, she walked down the hill and stopped at the Co-op to see if Mary was working. On seeing that she wasn't, she knocked on the door of Seaspray Cottage. No answer – that was strange too. Her mum rarely left the Bay.

Needing the loo, Rosa let herself in. Fires were burning, she saw, in both the lounge and kitchen grates. There was a half-finished bottle of Zero-alcohol champagne on the kitchen table and a Meerschaum pipe lying right next to it. And then, oh man alive, right there, coming from upstairs in her mother's bedroom, were the sounds of joyful and rampant lovemaking. Even Merlin was just sat mute in his basket, his yellow fog-lamp eyes staring, big pointy ears up.

Reversing on tiptoe as if she was in some crazy sitcom, Rosa silently shut the front door behind her and, in total shock at what she had stumbled upon, headed straight to the Corner Shop.

'You look like you've seen a ghost,' Titch remarked, rubbing her aching back.

'It would have caused less anguish if I had, to be honest.'

'Oh no, what's happened?'

'It's Mary.'

Titch ran round the counter to her friend's side. 'Oh no! Dearest mother-in-law said she saw her coming out of the doctor's earlier. What's going on?'

'Doctors?' Rosa queried. 'That's odd; she sounded fine to me. In fact, she appeared to be having a rather large injection of the sausage kind.'

'What? Do you mean... Oh my God!' Titch burst into laughter.

'I popped in to say hi on my way back from Polhampton and they were at it upstairs.'

'Do you think it was Christopher?'

At this, Rosa laughed until she nearly wet herself. 'Mate, my mum hasn't had sex since the Boer War – *of course* it was Christopher. I need the loo!' Racing off into the back kitchen to the toilet, she called out, 'Now I know what people mean about not wanting to think of their parents doing it. Put the kettle on, Titch.'

The girls sat next to each other at the shop counter as they had done many times before. The biscuit tin nearly empty, the conversation was flowing. 'So, about Edie's sighting of Mary at the doctor's, tell me about that,' Rosa asked. Then light dawned. 'Shit, her memory stuff. What am I like? I forgot about that.'

They both laughed again.

'Yes, well, Edie saw both your mum *and* Christopher leaving the surgery together. Her diagnosis: they both have gonorrhoea.'

Rosa was set off again, crying with laughter. But underneath she was cross. 'That spiteful woman! I mean, how can someone even get to that conclusion? She really is something else.'

'I just ignore her now and keep thankful that Ritchie is more like his dad.'

'Well, from what I heard just now at Seaspray Cottage, there's not much wrong with my mum,' Rosa said brightly. 'Unless they were doing the "life's too short bit".'

'No, of course not.' Titch made a face and started massaging her bump.

'Well, whatever it is, I can't very well ask her now. And she must never know that I heard them *in flagrante* – she would be absolutely mortified and I doubt I could look Kit in the face. Although, I don't think I will ever *un*hear it.' Rosa cringed. 'I will arrange to see her tomorrow when I've dropped his lordship off at Little Devils.'

Titch sighed contentedly. 'This is nice, isn't it? Me and you having a bit of peace. I don't mind that the shop is quiet this week. I've been getting more of those fake contractions, and it scares me a bit if I'm honest.'

'Yes, you don't want the baby giraffe coming before he or she is cooked. If you get worried though, get on to your midwife.'

'I will, of course. How was your meeting anyway?'

'Good. Another funny story actually, but...' Rosa checked her watch, '...Shit, is that the time? Do you want me to fetch Theo too?'

'No, Ritchie is doing it – and then he's taking over from me, thank goodness. I can have a lie-down upstairs – bit like your mum and dad.' Titch giggled. 'You go. Let's catch up soon, mate, and as for your mum, good on her, I say. She's getting more of her fair share than the pair of us, by the sound of it.'

Rosa arrived home at Gull's Rest, glad to kick off her shoes and sit in her favourite place: the window-seat. The house was warm and peaceful. Worn out from chasing the eager pugs Pongo and

Ugly, and his dachshund 'wife' the Duchess at the Lobster Pot pub, Hot was already snoozing beneath his stinky green blanket in his basket in front of the log-burner. Little Ned was also tired after an exciting session at the nursery and was having a nap in his pram. Both of her boys thereby allowing their mum to take a few minutes to make sense of her day.

Every day, the view from the front bay window gave Rosa great pleasure. The tide was making its way in. Seagulls were cawing their delight at a wrapped-up couple sitting on the bench down the path eating chips from cones. The pair were chatting so animatedly they were oblivious to the feathery thieves waiting to swoop at an opportune moment for a carb-laden afternoon snack. The sharp line of the horizon was marred by the low cloud of the November day, and the café, now lit with Christmas lights and chimney smoke weaving into the cold air, made for a picture postcard scene.

Her mind began to clear. It had been a bizarre day. Jamie had seemed so sincere about his love for Celia Carlisle and the jasmine story had seemed so believable and sweet, but a tiny part of her suspected that he knew damn well whose name would be on that last will and testament. But with the way her own childhood had gone, Rosa trusted no one – and in most cases it did indeed turn out that people were guilty until proven innocent. Jamie was undeniably a handsome man and had given the deceased woman great pleasure, so did it matter? To Celia's family, yes, but in Rosa's eyes nobody deserved anything from anyone else. Inheritance. It wasn't a right. Just a tradition.

She thought back to her selfless great-grandfather Ned Myers, who had set out to find her and leave her his beloved Corner Shop. And how both Mary and her great-grandmother Queenie had relinquished their claim on it, in order to make sure that Rosa was set on the path to a decent future. Life worked in such mysterious ways and there was not one day when she was not grateful for how hers was turning out. Maybe that was it about life: if you never expected anything, you were never disappointed – and then when something good did happen, you appreciated it all the more. Her existence had gone from dead-end jobs and drunken one-night stands to a happy, fulfilling life full of love and financial security – and it had happened almost overnight. And for this she would be eternally grateful to her son's namesake, her great-grandfather.

Maybe it was her turn now to do some good for someone who hadn't had the chance to fulfil their wishes. She reached in her bag for the blue folder. When she and Jamie had looked at it properly in the café, inside were just a few coloured Post-it notes with scribbles on them and one A4 printed sheet. Between them they had managed to glean that Celia had been midway through arranging a carol concert for the smaller of the two churches in Polhampton, in order to raise money for its new roof.

There were no names of people who had agreed to take part, no date, no timings. However, clearly typed on the A4 sheet was the list of celebrities she wanted to approach to open it. All of them were very handsome A-list male Hollywood stars. And, as much as Rosa would have loved to book Idris Elba for the gig, she guessed that he had something far better to do with his time than be a compère for a charity in a small Devon seaside town. Rosa laughed to herself. Felix was under the impression that his mother had been working hard on her beloved charity work, when quite clearly she was talking the talk to disguise the fact that she was walking the walk with her young and handsome hired help.

Thinking of mysterious ways, Rosa thought that if her father hadn't moved to Cockleberry Bay and set up business, she would never have overhead the conversation with Felix, which had now given her the perfect idea for her Christmas charity event.

A log shifted in the burner and brought her back to reality. Little Ned would soon be awake and wanting his supper, playtime, bath and bed. And despite having all that free time today, she had forgotten one key thing: to buy some more nappies. Rosa could have kicked herself. It was too cold and late for them to be going out again. This was exactly when she could do with Josh being here. If she had still been living up in the centre of town in the Corner Shop flat, the Co-op was literally two minutes up the road, but she wasn't, and she would have to manage. She had two left, that would just have to be OK and if not, she would make use of one of the huge sanitary towels she had worn after giving birth.

Leaving her two boys still asleep, she was just going upstairs to check if she had maybe left some nappies up there somewhere, when she heard a light tapping noise coming from the utility room. Freezing on the bottom stair, she prayed that Hot wouldn't wake up and start barking. Not even daring to breathe, she stood completely still before hearing the sound of footsteps running away and a baby crying that wasn't her own. Brandishing a rolling pin from the kitchen drawer, Rosa ran out to the utility room and feverishly unlocked and opened the back door. Not wanting to leave Little Ned in the house alone, that was where she stopped in her tracks. There was no one to be seen as she peered into the gloaming; however, her attention was drawn to the porch step. Looking down she was amazed to see two packs of nappies, a plastic tub of formula milk and a handmade paper heart with just a single X on it.

'Who are you?' Rosa bravely shouted out. Her reply was a loud thud at the end of the garden, followed by the cries of not just a baby this time, but a young woman clearly in distress.

CHAPTER TWENTY EIGHT

'Nice arse,' Davina Hunt commented as Lucas bent down to put some lagers on the bottom shelf of the hotel bar fridge.

'You've forgiven me then.' Lucas stood up and smirked at his girlfriend, who immediately walked behind the bar and slid her arms around his waist.

'Forgiven you? I was the one who forgot something so important to you. I'm really sorry, Lucas. Are you working tonight?'

'Only until eight. We've only got four dinner bookings and Danny said he can deal with that. We've taken on a couple of new bar and waiting staff to get ready for the Christmas rush and help with the grotto. So, I will have more time for fun.' Lucas winked at Davina. 'Drink?'

'Yeah, I'll have a gin and tonic, please. Make it a large one.' Davina winked back, before adding casually, 'Actually, I'm glad you mentioned the grotto because I've found our Father Christmas. Seeing as I took on the big, bearded man myself, I'm also happy to sort the financial side of stuff if you like. You are going to be so busy running the hotel and I'm on a four-on-four-off shift pattern through December, so I will have plenty of time to help. I've sourced a reindeer too! Just one though, but that's better than nothing. He's very placid, evidently, and you'll never guess his name: he's called Rudolph – how imaginative.'

'The kids will think that's magical.'

'Yes, so could I have four hundred pounds upfront for Rudolph, please? That covers the four December weekends we can have him.'

Lucas frowned. 'That seems a lot, but I guess it's not, at fifty quid a day. OK. Is that with a keeper too?'

'Er no, I am going to look after him.'

'You're not just a pretty face, are you? You can add *Reindeer Keeper* to your CV after this.' Lucas then went serious. 'We *are* going to make some money out of this, aren't we?'

'Of course, or I wouldn't have organised it. There's been so much interest. It's all everyone is talking about at the moment.'

Lucas wasn't sure what kind of chill pill Davina had been prescribed but he was liking this change of attitude very much. 'You have taken the pressure off already, thank you.' He kissed her on the forehead. 'We are fully booked from December the first so yes, if you're sure you can fit it all in, what with you being Mrs Plod an' all, that will be such a help.'

'Come here.' Davina checked the bar was empty, pulled Lucas towards her and then rubbed herself against him, whispering in his ear, 'I've been thinking about this all day.'

'Have you now?' Lucas could feel himself quickly hardening to her touch.

Just then, his mobile rang on the side of the bar. Davina was next to it, and on seeing Rosa's name flashing up, she quickly pressed decline and switched it off. 'They hung up; it can't have been that important,' she lied. 'Certainly not more important than me taking you upstairs for a quickie to show you just how sorry I am.'

Rosa's heart was beating fast as she walked down to the bottom of the garden, big torch in hand, baby monitor in her pocket so as not to miss even a murmur from her son. Hot, at her heels, eager to follow, could not be deemed any kind of guard dog but she was happy to have him with her, nonetheless. She stood still for a second to see if she could locate any noise. The light crash of waves on the shore and a lone caw of a seagull making its way through the misty November skies were now the only sounds she could hear. She waited, holding her breath. Then, hearing a slight rustle in the hedge that surrounded the fence, Rosa shouted, 'Who's there?' Nothing, but then the muffled cries of a baby became audible. Barking, Hot scampered over to where the noise was coming from. Quivering, Rosa shone the torch into the hedge – right into the terrified eyes of a brown-eyed woman holding a baby so tightly to her chest in a hand-made papoose that Rosa was worried she might smother it.

'It's OK,' Rosa said gently, her fear now completely gone. 'There's nothing to be afraid of.'

The woman began to whimper like a puppy. Rosa could see that her jeans were ripped, and her knee was bleeding.

'I'm so sorry,' the woman sobbed.

Rosa could detect an accent but had no idea where from. 'It's fine,' she soothed again. 'I'm Rosa and this is Hot.' She pointed to her little sausage companion and smiled warmly.

'Amira.'

'That's a pretty name.' The woman must have been in her late twenties, but at this moment all Rosa could see in front of her was a frightened child. 'Can you walk, do you think?'

The woman nodded.

'What I'm going to do is take your baby from you and you follow me into the house, OK?'

CHAPTER TWENTY NINE

'There is a never a dull moment in your life, Rosa Smith.' Titch reached for a fig roll from the biscuit tin, dipped it into her tea until it went soggy then slurped it into her mouth. 'Mmm, luvverly. Did you see Theo when you dropped Little Ned off?' she asked indistinctly.

'Yes, he was just about to poke a bread-stick up Pablo Escobar's arse until Gladys stopped him.'

'That's my boy.' Titch laughed and sprayed bits of fig seed.

'As for *never a dull moment*, I think I may have to correct you there.' Rosa sat down next to Titch at the shop counter. 'It hasn't exactly been show tunes and jazz hands for at least a year since I got pregnant and became a slave to love and the laundry basket.'

Titch nearly choked. 'You know what I mean,' she managed. 'Anyway tell me the whole story, I want to know all the details. Then I really must tidy up Christmas Corner. The second-homers will be descending on us soon and I want to be ready.'

'Basically, the person who broke in was a woman called Amira – it means Princess in her language, so she told me. She is the sweetest person. She managed to escape from Syria on her own and got to England. You'd think that would be the hardest bit. Anyway, she ended up in Stanley's Point – you know, the bay on from Polhampton Sands. Met a guy down here, who promised her the world. They had a baby. But unfortunately he turned out to be a drunk and a bully. One night he beat her so badly that she stole his boat and has been living on it ever since.'

'No!'

'Yes, that was how she got into the Bay. She saw from my window that I had Little Ned and was so desperate that she broke in purely for milk and nappies.'

'Oh my God.' Titch shivered. 'That's terrible – and in this weather too.'

'I know.' Rosa blew out a breath. 'I am so relieved now that I didn't call the police, especially as she stole his boat.'

'Are you angry with her?'

'Titch, mother to mother, I'd do the bloody same if my baby needed food.'

'She could always get a job, sort out benefits?'

'She probably can't until she gets her stay finalised officially. She didn't know where to turn for help.'

'Please don't tell me you've taken her in, Rose.'

'Like I did for you, all those years ago when you were pregnant, you mean? Come on, Titch. Yes, I am going to help her get everything sorted.'

Titch bit her lip. 'Sorry, what am I like? I have been there too. Shit. How far we have both come.'

'So all the more reason for me to want to support someone else in need. Especially this close to Christmas. However, I can't have her living with me. Josh wouldn't have it.'

'I don't understand. If she has no money, how did she get the nappies and milk for you?'

'She stole them from somewhere else. She was on a cycle of sadness and despair. I can't let her get caught. She's a grown-up so is responsible for her own actions and their consequences, but what would happen to the baby? It's too awful to contemplate.'

'How old is he – or she?'

'It's another little boy, Zaki. He's the same age as my boy.'

'Aw. So what's happening with her now then?'

'I gave her twenty quid to go to the café with Zaki and get something hot to eat and drink. I've arranged to meet her there in an hour or so. After I've been to see Mum, I'm going to get Lucas to call his brother and see if it is OK if Amira gets her stuff from the boat and goes to stay in the big house with Tina, Danny, and Alfie until she sorts herself out. It's huge up there and I know that they don't even use the attic room and bathroom up the top. She should be safe there, and with luck that bloke she was with will never find out where she and his son are.'

'You're so sweet.'

'Sweet and me? I'm not sure about that combination.'

'What about the boat?'

'I will also get Lucas to speak to one of the fishermen in the Ship to see if they can sail it round to Stanley's Point Harbour and leave it one night maybe. The last thing we want is some crazed woman-beater turning up in the Bay.' Rosa sighed. 'God.'

'What is it, mate?'

'So much going on. Mum summoned me to Seaspray this morning. I reckon it's about her news from the doctor. I kind of don't want to know in case it is serious.'

'Oh, Rose.' Titch hugged her with her bump in the way. 'Well, I'm always here for you, you know that.'

'I know – thanks, mate.' Rosa clutched her head. 'Oh, shit – and I forgot to tell you about Carol-oke!'

'Carol who?'

Rosa laughed out loud. 'That's what I've decided to do for the charities. "The Cockleberry Bay Christmas Carol-oke Concert, in aid of Ned's Gift and the new roof fund for St Michael and All Angels Church in Polhampton".'

'Oh my God, that's a mouthful but sounds hilarious. So how does it work?'

'Basically, teams from each of the charities get sponsored to compete and there is a prize at the end for the best group. I want to make it a real community Christmassy event for all ages. People will pay to come to watch and pay to vote for their favourite on the night.'

'So they are choirs then, really?'

'Yes, but they won't all be the best singers. Hence the "oke" bit. They have to choose a carol or Christmas song to sing.'

'I love it. It will be so festive.'

'Yes, there will also be a prize for the best Christmas jumper in the audience, a big Christmas raffle, and I need to speak to Nate about providing pasties, mince pies and mulled wine maybe. All profits from the food and drink will be going to the charities too. It's just a bit of fun for the community and I think will make a tidy sum for all the charities.'

'Not like you to go religious though,' Titch said, wrinkling her tiny nose. 'What's all that with the church roof?'

'Celia Carlisle – you know, the lady who died on the job with the handsome gardener, whom I've since met – that's what she was working towards. I kind of stole her idea and I did promise her son I would take on her project.'

'When are you doing it?'

'It's got to be Christmas Eve, I reckon. If the church hall is free.'

'Count us in to give you a raffle prize.'

'Thanks, mate.'

'So, is the Bay going to have a team then?'

'Of course. Under the umbrella of Ned's Gift, we have to,

really. I am going to see who wants to join. Rehearsals to start in the church hall on Sunday evening.'

'I've got our song already.' Titch laughed to herself then started to sing badly: 'It's reindeer men, Hallelujah, it's reindeer men.'

'Mum? Mary?' Rosa shouted up the stairs. Perish the thought she was up there again with Christopher.

'I'm here, duck.' Mary appeared through the front door, a pint of milk in hand. 'I'd run out of semi-skimmed and you always moan about me only having the full-fat version.'

They sat opposite each other at the kitchen table.

'Are you all right, Rosa? Something's happened. You needed the black tourmaline, didn't you? I saw.'

Merlin squeezed himself through the back cat-flap and sauntered past them, giving Rosa a dark look from his orb-like eyes; he'd never forgiven her for bringing Hot into 'his' house. He then started to crunch hungrily on his dry cat food.

'Yes, you were right to give it to me,' Rosa said over the noise. 'I will explain, but more importantly, how are you?'

'It's the bloody menopause. Well, bloody isn't really an appropriate word in this case, is it?'

'Thank God.' A waterfall of relief rushed through Rosa's body. 'I thought you were losing your marbles.'

'No. Just my womanhood. It seems I have months of a dry fanny and sweaty bedsheets to look forward to.' Mary made Rosa laugh. She went on, 'The forgetfulness, the hot flushes obviously, the mood swings – they are all part of the process of my womb giving up the ghost. Strange, I didn't suspect it for one moment. My periods were never regular, but it's a joy they've stopped completely now.'

Rosa shied away from thinking too hard about why this

should be such a joy. 'Have you got a natural remedy that could help?'

'Of course I have,' her mother nodded. She beamed. 'In fact, I feel younger and better already.'

'Maybe that's down to a certain someone, perhaps?'

Mary's cheeks reddened. 'I actually have something else to tell you.'

'Blimey, you're not moving in together already, are you?'

'Not quite. But we are getting on very well.'

'That's great news. Kit – well, he seems so decent.'

'He is, and guess what?' Mary looked excited. 'He's only asked me if I can help him out at Webb & Son as an assistant. Not full-time, but as and when he needs me until business picks up.'

'That's your ideal job, isn't it?'

'Yes, it is.' Mary's beautiful eyes twinkled. 'Dead easy too, some might say.'

They both laughed.

'So, have you got time for a cuppa?'

'Of course I have – and Mum?' Their matching green eyes met across the table. 'I'm so happy you're well and so happy you're happy.'

Mary leaned over and gripped her daughter's hand. 'Thank you for letting me in, Rosa, when many would have left me out in the cold.'

Feeling her eyes welling with tears, Rosa coughed and stood up. 'Please tell me you've made some fresh cookies to go with this tea, although I mustn't stay long.'

'Of course. Now come here and tell me all about who disturbed your peace the other night.'

CHAPTER THIRTY

'Could I have chocolate sprinkles on there too? Thanks, Amira.' Rosa directed. Then added, 'How are you getting on?'

'I love it here.' Amira straightened up her Christmas hat, retied her apron strings and looked around Rosa's with a huge smile on her face. 'As I said, I used to work in a restaurant back in my hometown near Damascus before it got bombed nearly three years ago, so this is like a dream for me to be here. I will be thanking you every day of my life, Rosa. For this and for sorting everything so quickly.'

'We all need a little leg up, sometimes.' Rosa smiled. 'How is Zaki?'

'Leg up? I do not understand.'

'A little help. We all need a little help sometimes.'

'Ah, I will remember that one now. And my Zaki, he loves Gladys. I mean, who would not? She says she has the bingo wings. I don't understand that either. I say "No, Mrs Moore, you have the angel wings".'

Amira turned to serve the next two customers in the queue while Nate came out from behind the counter and gave his sister a quick hug. Hot whined and did his cute little dachshund dance up and down, nudging at his legs. 'OK, OK.' Nate reached for some chopped cucumber behind the bar and the little dog trotted after the two humans to the back of the café. 'Ready, sis? I thought we could just sit here to chat.'

Rosa took off Hot's lead and he sat under the table to attack his healthy treat. She spoke quietly. 'I'm so glad it's worked out. I wasn't sure if it was the right thing to do at all.'

'Amira is such a hard worker. She's so good with the food and with the customers. And I trust her to work alone at quieter times so I can catch up with admin in the back and at last I'll be able to have the odd whole day off now without worrying.'

'Good – but Nate, you must have more time off than just an odd day here and there or you'll burn out. Running this place solo is a big responsibility.'

'I'm fine. There's enough time for a good rest in January. We all go into hibernation then down here; you know that.'

'And I haven't seen Danny or Tina yet to ask how Amira is getting on in the house. Is that OK too, do you know?'

'I haven't heard otherwise. I think Danny quite fancies her.'

'I think Danny fancies anyone at the moment.'

'True.' Nate relit the candle that had gone out in its holder. 'Have you been in Tom's place before? It's a huge house and the attic room is on its own level, so I reckon it'll be fine.'

'No women in your life at the moment then?'

'Er. No. I…there's no time for women. I want to make a great success of this place for you and for me. I still can't believe you are giving me a profit share. It's so kind.'

'Like I've said before, we're family, Nate.' There was a silence. Then: 'Nate, why did you take the summerhouse option then, if there's so much room in the main one?'

'That's what Tom offered me,' Nate explained, and he laughed. 'But I love it in there. It means I'm nearer the beach and, as much as I love them, I could do without being surrounded by noisy kids when I do have my downtime.'

'I'm with you there, bro.' She cleared her throat. 'The Grotty Grotto opens in the Ship car park today, remember.'

'I know, hence our own festive hats. Is Father Christmas coming on his sleigh down this hill? Joking aside, I have got supplies in. Lucas did the decent thing and agreed as part of the ticket price to offer a Rosa's Café mince pie and hot chocolate for all kids, so I expect we will be busy as long as the adults do eat and drink too when they are here.'

'Is he not doing food too then?'

'Yeah, the usual pub grub, but not everyone will want that, and they may not have enough space at busy times, he reckons.'

'It's good you're working together,' Rosa said quietly.

'Yeah. Makes for an easier life, that's for sure. Hey, sis, Josh must be due back soon, surely?'

'Couple of weeks – it's flying by now. I'll be so excited to see him.' Rosa licked the hot-chocolate moustache from her top lip.

'I saw you advertised your Carol-oke Concert. Genius, but what else would I expect from my clever sister?'

'I'm still looking for members for my singing team.'

'Well, don't be looking at me with "Good King Wenceslas" in mind. My backside plays better tunes than anything that comes out of my mouth.'

Rosa laughed out loud. 'I wonder if that's where the saying "bum note" comes from.'

'Don't give up the day job.' Nate grinned. 'Oh, you already did.'

'Right, that's it, you're lead vocal after that comment.'

Rosa stood up as Amira approached and said shyly, 'If Zaki can come with me, I'd like to sing with you, please. It brings joy to hearts, I think. The singing.'

Rosa smiled at the dark-eyed, dark-haired beauty in front of her. 'Then joy to hearts we will bring, Amira.'

CHAPTER THIRTY ONE

Lucas groaned as his alarm went off at 7 a.m. He knew he shouldn't have sat up drinking at the bar with Danny last night, but Davina was on the last of her night shifts and it had been a good laugh and much-needed lads' time. As he came to, he heard the sound of a lorry engine vibrating right under his window. Looking outside he was shocked to see a low-based trailer which had had to reverse its way right down the hill. He was even more shocked to see the size of the Christmas tree which was being unloaded into the pub car park. Throwing on some joggers and a sweatshirt, he ran downstairs.

'You just need to sign here mate, please.' The driver shoved a clipboard in front of him just as Tina appeared to start her cleaning.

'What size tree did you order for the grotto entrance?' Lucas shouted across the car park to her.

'Five metres, like you said.'

Lucas was more amused than cross. 'I said feet, not bleeding metres.'

The driver laughed too. 'Look mate, I can't take it back as the gaffer would find it hard to sell another one of this size.'

'We'd better keep Santa busy to pay for it then, hadn't we?'

Luke signed the form.

'And a second mortgage for the lights,' the driver replied, tooting loudly as he made his way back up the hill.

Rosa, who was walking Hot on the beach with Little Ned held close to her in his papoose, wandered over to see what the commotion was all about. She looked at the tree, then at Lucas, who was smoking a cigarette, and put a hand to her mouth in mock horror.

'What the fuck?' she asked, pointing to the colossal tree.

'Tina thought I said five metres.'

Rosa burst out laughing. 'You wait until Jacob sees it; he'll definitely be coming out in hives with erection competition of this kind.'

'Ho, ho, ho.' Father Christmas waved awkwardly to the group of children who had already gathered along the sea wall. There wasn't a sleigh in sight, or a reindeer, just him in his hired red and white outfit with a wide black belt and his horn-rimmed glasses perched on the end of his nose above his long white beard. He was swinging a brass bell, a sack stuffed with a pillow over his shoulder, and another one up his tunic to make a big, round jovial tummy.

Davina had persuaded him to make this kind of entrance, much to Joe Fox's acute embarrassment. She then ushered him under the ribbon that was strung between the car park gates and into the signposted *Santa's Grotto*, and locked the door behind them. Two huge sacks of presents that she and Tina had spent hours wrapping were placed behind the comfy armchair that Lucas had hired in specially. A fan-heater was blasting out much-needed heat.

'Well, *hello*, Santa.' Davina put her hand on the man's chest and pushed him back into the armchair.

Joe ran his hand up her wool shift dress to find lacy stocking tops. 'You are such a minx,' he murmured. 'The show opens in fifteen minutes.'

'Plenty of time. Now you just sit quietly and let me see what goodies Santa has for me in here, shall we?' She trailed her fingers down past his huge tummy. 'Amazing what goes on in *Cock*leberry Bay, isn't it?' Licking her lips, she knelt and stared up into his eyes. 'And no one likes to go to work on a full sack now, do they?'

'Fuck it!'

'That's a nice greeting.' Carly walked into the hotel bar to find Lucas searching frantically for something to cut the ribbon and officially open the grotto. He looked up and felt himself reddening immediately. 'Oh hi, Carly, sorry for my language. I'm looking for a pair of scissors. Santa's little helper, also known as my bird Davina, is just settling him into his cabin, and I think she may have taken them with her.'

'Here.' Carly pulled a pair out of her bag. 'You can tell I was a Girl Guide.'

Lucas felt funny again. What was it with this woman? It was like she put him under a spell every time she saw him.

'So,' she went on, 'South Cliffs Radio are here to do the live broadcast, and the *Gazette* is covering it too. Are you still OK to have a little chat with them?'

'It so puts me out of my comfort zone,' Lucas fretted. 'I should have got Tom to do it. He's much better at all this stuff.'

'I'm surprised we got both the radio and the local rag on a Saturday, so let's make the most of it.'

'Are you joking? A grotto coming to town – this is big news for Cockleberry Bay.'

Carly laughed. 'Good. Now, Lucas, please calm down. You'll

be fine. I'll be holding your hand all the way. I've even written a few lines of what would be good to say. Key facts that the *Gazette* will hang onto and use. Reporters love it when it's all done for them if possible. Here.' She handed him a typewritten A4 sheet.

'Thank you. You're amazing.'

It was Carly's turn to redden now. She cleared her throat. 'Just remember, PR doesn't stand for Public Relations at all, but Perjury Rules. Big it up and bring it on, Mr Hannafore. Oh, and here.' She handed him an envelope. Lucas tore it open to reveal a card with a four-leaf clover on the front.

'Aw, that's so sweet. I don't think I've ever received a Good Luck card before.'

'Not that you need it, but I know this is kind of a big deal for you, especially as you mentioned about taking over from your mum and stuff.'

Lucas gulped and came round the other side of the bar. Just as he was giving Carly a spontaneous kiss on the cheek to thank her, a flushed Davina came charging in. Ignoring the pretty marketer and what she had just witnessed, she snarled, 'So there you are. Are you coming out or not? It's a minute to ten.'

Danny, who had only just finished stringing up the lights on the monster Christmas tree in the nick of time, gave a thumbs-up to Lucas as he passed the kitchen. Tina, all wrapped up, with Alfie by her side wearing an elf's hat, was sitting at a table ready to take ticket money from those who had not purchased them in advance. As Lucas appeared in the car park, the gabbling of excited children died down, their parents shushing them in anticipation of the grand opening.

A big, fluffy grey Outside Broadcast microphone was pushed under Lucas's nose. Rosa, running at speed along the beach path with Little Ned strapped to her chest and Hot trotting along beside her, made it just in time to give her friend a big grin of encouragement.

'Welcome to the Cockleberry Bay Ship Hotel Christmas Grotto,' he announced. 'It's fortunate I have my good teeth in, as that's not easy to say.' The crowd laughed. 'For those of you who don't know already, I'm Lucas Hannafore and I'm the proud owner of this place, along with my brother Tom, who's over there.' He pointed over people's heads. Children were already getting jittery. Carly, standing right next to him, whispered like a ventriloquist through her closed mouth, 'Bit faster.'

'We hope you have a lovely day. Santa has allocated slots, but there's a present for everyone – and if you want to write him a letter so that he can take it back to the North Pole with him, if you've been a good boy or girl this year you may get another present on Christmas Day.' A few of the waiting kids cheered.

'Mums and dads, we have mulled wine heating on the bar and of course we have a full menu of snacks on offer too.' Rosa caught his eye and looked at him meaningfully. 'And don't forget to use your mince pie and hot chocolate vouchers over at Rosa's Café, where they also sell an array of tasty snacks. Plus, they are offering take-out teas and coffees today, I believe.' He looked at Rosa again, who nodded at him.

'Where are the reindeers?' a little lad shouted out from the front row of children. Lucas looked at Davina, who mouthed, 'Later' to him.

'They…er…Mrs Christmas is just feeding them at the moment. They will be down shortly.'

Carly handed him the scissors, at which point a photographer from the *Gazette* came rushing forward, saying, 'Just hold still there, mate, so I can get a good shot. Maybe you could get in there too, love.' Carly awkwardly put her hands on top of Lucas's as the photographer clicked away at the pivotal opening scene.

181

'Before I let you in, we are here until December the twenty-third, the day before Christmas Eve, so tell all your friends, aunties, uncles, grandparents et cetera, won't you, children? Everybody is very welcome.' Lucas smiled, then went forward with Carly to cut the red ribbon that was holding back the crowd. 'I now declare the Cockleberry Bay Ship Hotel Christmas Grotto well and truly open!'

Screams of excitable children and the voices of adults eager to get a mulled wine filled the chilly December air. Rosa, who seemed to be able to control her bladder less these days, left the pram and Hot with Raff, who had been instructed to see what all the fuss was about by Jacob, and rushed in the back door to the toilet.

As she did so, she looked through to the reception area to see a red-headed woman with alabaster skin and a beauty spot on her right cheek, pulling a wheelie suitcase awkwardly over the step of the front door. On seeing that nobody was there to greet her, she held her hand down on the reception bell and didn't let it go.

Rosa quickly removed her coat, brushed her top down, fixed on a smile and went through to the reception.

'Good morning, madam. I am so sorry to keep you waiting. You can see we have an awful lot going on here today.'

'I want to check in,' the Glaswegian said abruptly.

'That's fine.' Rosa was relieved to see an old school diary open at today's date on the desk. 'Anna Wallace?'

'That's me.'

'Er. Check-in is usually at two. You are booked into the *Titanic* room. Let me just check with a colleague to see if your room is ready. Hold on one second, please.'

Knowing the upstairs of the pub well, having stayed there herself when she had first arrived in the Bay, Rosa, now bursting for the toilet, ran upstairs, found the *Titanic* room with the key in the door, rushed in, checked it had been cleaned, then ran down again, only to bump into Davina who was coming through from the bar.

'What the hell are you doing?' Davina looked furious.

'Guest,' Rosa said breathlessly. 'Important guest.' She winked.

'Ah. OK. Well, I can take over from here.'

'I told her I'd see if her room was ready as she's early for check-in. She's in *Titanic*. Here's the key.' Rosa nearly threw it at her then raced into the toilet.

Looking after her contemptuously, Davina stalked into the reception area. She planted a fake smile on her face as she said, 'Oh hi, Anna Wallace, isn't it?'

'Yes, that's me.'

'Do follow me.'

'I will be wanting dinner – and what time is breakfast?'

'I was just coming to that, madam.'

Anna struggled with her case up the old staircase, wondering why the snooty blonde hadn't offered to help. It was not a good start.

'Oh, and before I forget,' Anna told her, 'could you warn your chef I am allergic to prawns. Even a minute amount makes me sick as a dog.'

Downstairs, Danny came through from the kitchen to make sure the extra bar staff and waitress knew exactly what was being served from the menu and how the day had been planned to run. As he did so he saw a phone on the bar that had just flashed up with a text. Looking to see whose phone it was, he couldn't help himself from being nosy. *I'll need more than a BJ after a day of dealing with all these little fuckers. Love Santa x*

Davina came running back downstairs and, recognising her phone cover in his hand, grabbed it off him. A few parents were already queuing for a drink. 'I wondered where I'd left that.' She then took Danny to the side. 'Rosa is on good authority and goodness knows how, that the hotel inspector has arrived. I'm just going to tell Lucas and Tina that she's already upstairs in the *Titanic*.'

Pushing to the back of his mind what he had just read, he replied, 'OK. So what does she look like?'

'Bit tarty,' Davina sniffed. 'Mutton dressed as lamb, red hair, gappy teeth, goes in and out in all the right places. You won't miss her, she's got a Scottish accent too.'

Danny poured a shot of neat gin into a glass and drank it down in one.

CHAPTER THIRTY TWO

With Little Ned in a papoose, a cosy hat pulled over his ears, Rosa pushed open the café door to find Nate cooing over Zaki in his pram in the kitchen while Amira prepared a tray with a pot of tea and a plate with two scones, jam and cream. She let Hot off the lead to go to his basket behind the counter. He trotted his way over, his tail sailing from side to side, got in and burrowed under the blanket there and began rhythmically licking a ragged cat which had long since had its stuffing pulled out by his sharp teeth.

'Cream tea at this time, Mrs Treen?' Rosa teased the customer, one of her favourite ladies, who was waiting for her order at the counter.

'Now if I were drinking a whisky at eleven a.m., young Rosa Smith, I would expect that kind of comment,' the eighty-three-year-old replied with spirit. 'At my age, a little bit of what I fancy does me good.'

Rosa smiled. 'And I don't blame you. I would have clotted cream with everything if I could.'

The old lady licked her top lip in anticipation. 'Everything in moderation, dear. That's how I've got to this ripe old age. Oh, and having a sherry with my breakfast, of course.' She grinned to reveal a missing tooth, then leaning heavily on her stick she negotiated her way over to her seat.

Nate came through to the front of the café. 'Take the C off chips and what have you got?'

'Very funny, you killjoy. Luckily I am tiny and don't have to worry about these things.' Rosa placed her hand over her stomach.

'You are pregnant,' the pretty Syrian directed at Rosa as she carried the tray with the cream tea over to Mrs Treen's favourite window-seat and unloaded it. The sea was still today, a greyish blue against the dull winter sky.

'Is that a question or a statement, Amira?' Rosa was shocked but trying not to show it.

'You *are* pregnant, Rosa: I can see it in your face.'

'No, I can't be – and I was so sick with Little Ned. I feel fine.'

'We shall see.' The woman nodded wisely and went back behind the counter.

'You don't mind Zaki being in his pram out the back, do you, Rosa?' Nate wiped down a couple of tables with spray and a clean cloth.

'Of course not, if you don't.'

He peeped at a sleeping Little Ned, whispering, 'Hello, little nephew.' He straightened up. 'I asked Amira if she'd mind coming in for a few hours this morning – just thought it might be crazy today with the grand opening of the Christmas Grotto, and Brad can't turn up until midday.'

'You're the manager, Nate. It's OK. You do what you think is right.'

'Thanks, sis. How's it going over there anyway?'

'It's busy and Lucas did announce the hot chocolate offer and that you were doing take-out teas and coffees. I reckon people are more likely to drift over before and after their Santa slot.

186

You've got a month of it to come, so enjoy this bit of peace.'

'Did I see Tom and his brood over there too?'

'Yes, they just came down for the day to support Lucas.'

'That was nice.'

'Yes, Tom's a good bloke and Lucas loves his nieces and nephew. They call him Uncle Louie, so cute.'

'How's your Carol-oke thing going? Amira tells me you're starting rehearsals tomorrow.'

'Yes, all good. The charities were well up for it, so we have six competing teams. Our team Ned's Gift, and the Carrot Footprint, Lifeboats, Polhampton Paws, Sea & Save and the gang from St Michael and All Angels Church in Polhampton. No doubt the churchy lot will include proper choir members and will be brilliant, but it's just a bit of fun and it's all about the most entertaining group, not about the singing in my view.'

'So, who's going to judge it?'

'We have a whole panel of judges, I'll have you know. I've asked Kit, as I thought it would be a good bit of advertising for Webb & Son, as it's going to be live on the radio.'

'I don't suppose Simon Cowell could make it?' Nate asked, straight-faced.

'About as available as Idris Elba, so they'll both just have to miss out.' Rosa shifted Little Ned, who was heavy on her chest, deep in his mid-morning nap. 'But we do have the equally charismatic Mr Gunter, the verger from Cockleberry Bay Church. He was delighted to agree, said it would warm him up for Midnight Mass, and to add the female touch, we have Madeline Baker from St Michael's, who I have met on a Zoom call and is like a real-life Vicar of Dibley. She assures me she is going to remain impartial, and I guess if you can't trust a vicar, then who can you trust?'

'You've done well, sis – it's going to be great. Foodwise that night, what do you reckon? What time is it that people are arriving?' Nate opened his notebook.

'It's four till six, so hot and cold snacks will be fine, I reckon.'

'Let's keep it simple then. The church hall kitchen is not the biggest or best, and rather than take money on the night, why don't we include the food in the ticket price?'

'Genius – and quicker too.'

Nate went on, 'Raff's pasties were amazing the other night. How about those, along with mince pies, slices of chocolate log and teas and coffees? And rather than muck about with mulled wine, let's get Jacob to do the bar. It'll be safer with kids running around too.'

'Look at you with all the good ideas. Yes, Jacob loves to be involved and it's up at his end of the street too, so that'll make him happy.' Rosa sighed. 'I suppose we'd better keep the Carrot Footprint mob happy and ask Amira to make some vegan cheese and onion pasties too, and a mince pie with no naughty stuff.'

'Is that even possible?' They both laughed. Nate shut his pad. 'Sorted. You can give me an idea of numbers nearer the time.'

Little Ned let out a little cry, followed by a full-blown wail. 'That's my signal to get home and feed my son.' Rosa pulled up the baby's blanket and tucked her coat around him, ready to face the elements. 'Shush now, bubba, Mumma's taking you home.'

Nate went off to saddle up Hot, who was very reluctant to leave the bliss of his cosy basket, just as the door opened letting in a rush of cold beach air and a couple with three excitable boys, all under five by the look of it, crowding their way to the counter.

'Here we go.' Nate squeezed Rosa's arm lovingly. 'Happy Christmas, sister.'

CHAPTER THIRTY THREE

Danny, why are you wearing shades in the kitchen?' Davina asked as he filled yet another fryer load of chips.

'I er…I got a bit of fat in my eye. It's sore, that's all.'

'That's another three cheeseburgers and chips, please, and two tuna steaks with sweet potato fries and lemon sauce.'

'What time is old Saint Nicholas here until? This is crazy.'

'The last kid's in there now, so I reckon it will quieten down soon. There's no one in the letter-writing hut now either.'

'Thank fuck for that. I've never known it so busy.'

'Good though, isn't it? A great success all round, I reckon,' Lucas said, walking into the kitchen. 'Do you need a hand, mate?'

'Nah, not if it's slowing down, I'll be fine. Is Alfie all right?'

'He's happy. He got cold so went upstairs to watch a film. I put your mum on cashing up for me as I want Davina out the front tonight.' Lucas walked out and then back in again. 'Anna – the hotel inspector, according to Rosa – is booked for dinner at seven. I've briefed Davina to take her order. She will come in and tell you what she wants, so make it tip-top, won't you?'

'Course I will, boss.' Danny took off his sunglasses and rubbed his eyes. He couldn't believe his ears earlier when Davina had described the hotel inspector. It just had to be that Glaswegian sex-bomb, Lily. Maybe if an inspector visited in the same town, they had to give a different name in case anyone sussed it was them. Also, how on earth did Rosa know it was her? Anyway, he wasn't allowed to fraternise with the guests and he really didn't want her to know he was working here as it could well jeopardise the 3-Star Seaside rating – a sure-fire sackable offence; of that he was sure. The sex had been mind-blowing, but that's what it had been – just sex – and he'd had his fill from her to last him a good few weeks now. No, he would lie low and do the best job he could to make Lucas proud.

Davina caught Lucas checking the bookings for the next few days. He looked up and smiled. 'Hey you, everything OK?' he asked.

'Apart from seeing you kiss Carly and finding Rosa upstairs, yeah, great.'

'Don't be silly. Rosa did us a massive favour sussing out that Alex Polizzi had arrived when she did, and as for Carly, she gave me a Good Luck card and I was just thanking her.'

Davina sighed. 'I suppose you hate me now for not sending you one.'

Lucas shook his head. 'For God's sake, we are not fifteen.' He put on a childish voice. 'Hate me, like me.'

'I'm not even sure if you do like me any more,' Davina huffed. 'It feels like there are now four of us in this relationship. It was bad enough with just Rosa "she gets me" bloody Smith, let alone Miss Prissy Marketing Pants on the scene now.'

'Quit the dramatics, love, we're fully booked and need to make sure everything is prepped for tomorrow.'

'OK, well, I can take on the cashing up from now on, all right? Tina doesn't want to be worried with that. She has enough to do with looking after Alfie.'

'See? You can be thoughtful.'

'Wanker,' Davina said under her breath as she sashayed back out to the grotto to say goodbye to Santa.

Lucas went back in to Danny. 'So, dinner-wise, inspector at seven, and the two couples in HMS *Victory* and the *Mary Rose* are both booked in for eight-fifteen. The *Golden Hind* have gone into Polhampton for food.'

'OK. Look, mate.' Danny paused. 'This isn't easy to say, but I don't think Davina is the woman for you.'

'What? Why do you say that?'

'There's summink about her I don't trust.' Not wanting to appear like a snooper, Danny felt uneasy. 'Just…um…a feeling I've got. That she may be cheating on you.'

'Dan, you stick to your cooking and if you come up with some proof and not just "feelings"' – Lucas made quotation marks with his fingers at the word – 'then I might act on it.'

'I'm saying listen to me, mate,' Danny tried.

At this, Lucas lost it. 'And I'm saying get on with what you're good at and mind your own fucking business. This really isn't the best time.' With that he stormed back outside.

Danny swiped a glass bowl to the floor and ripped off his apron just as Tina was popping her head round the door. She knew that expression on her son's face only too well.

'Don't you dare,' she said through gritted teeth. 'You take a deep breath right now, my boy. You need this job, and we need that house. What's happened?'

'Lucas is such a dick sometimes.'

'He's busy and stressed about the hotel inspector, that's all.'

'He won't bleeding believe me that that bitch of a girlfriend of his is cheating – with old Santa Claus out there. I saw a message.'

'Shush your language in here. And if she is, you have warned him. He will take that in, and it is his business, Danny – not yours – not ours. *His* business,' she repeated. 'You'd think you'd have learned that with all our years living where we did before, especially where relationships are concerned. You keep your nose out of it. If their relationship needs to run its course, it will. The truth will out.'

Danny punched his fist into the palm of his other hand, then bent down to retrieve his apron. All the while, Tina Green picked up the big bits of glass from the floor then swept it deftly with a dustpan and brush.

'Now, I'm going upstairs to fetch Alfie and take him home,' she told her son. 'You make sure you cook a feast fit for a queen for that woman, you hear me?'

Danny breathed out then forced himself to get a grip and pulled his apron back over his head just as Joe Fox was pulling off his beard as Davina entered the hut and shut the door.

'You did good, Santa.' Davina kissed him on the cheek. 'Lucas has no idea it's you. He's still so protective over his darling Rosa that if he finds out, you'll be kicked off the grotto before you can say pigs in blankets.' She sniggered. 'Anyway, I've thought up a plan to keep them all side-tracked with something else. We're going to cash in, I tell you.'

'We haven't delivered any reindeers yet, either.'

'I have a little idea about that too.' Davina grinned.

'Full of 'em, aren't you, blondie?' Joe ran his hand up her dress to reach her stocking tops again.

She moved it away and stepped back, saying, 'No – too dangerous tonight. Maybe tomorrow. Right, I've got to go. See you soon, Santa. Oh, and I'll message you later about the reindeer.'

CHAPTER THIRTY FOUR

Rosa bathed and fed Little Ned and settled him in his cot. She was tired. It had been a long day but a fun one, with the opening of the grotto and spending some time with her brother.

What a good job that Jacob had given her a heads-up on the hotel inspector, or they would probably have just lost the rating by the woman having to wait to check in. Thank God they had got the room prepped and ready in advance too. She so hoped Lucas got the accolade he deserved after all the hard work he had put into the newly revamped Ship. It would give him a much-needed boost. She would tell Jacob that she had shared the information about the hotel inspector. In her eyes competition was healthy. And there were plenty of rooms at both inns to service this busy seaside town.

How lovely that now she was home with the heating cranked up, she could have a nice bath herself and relax. And then watch her guilty pleasure, *Strictly Come Dancing*, without Josh interrupting. Just one more weekend after this one and he would be home.

It would feel strange having him back but so, so good to be able to share not only the bed but their precious son with him again. Luckily, Danny had managed to squeeze in some time to make good the damage to the kitchen ceiling with a lick of paint, so that was another tick off her list. And a tiny lower tooth was showing now, giving Little Ned respite from his painful gums and allowing for more sleep for the pair of them until the next one came through. Maybe it was getting easier.

Deciding a milky coffee would make a nice bath accompaniment, she went into the kitchen and spooned coffee granules into her favourite mug, but as she began to pour the hot milk in, the strong aroma hit her and she only just made it to the downstairs toilet in time before being sick. After throwing up her hot chocolate and mince pie from earlier she sat on the closed toilet lid and put her hand inside her bra. She'd been trying to ignore the fact that her boobs were feeling not only a little bit bigger, but decidedly sore. Adding Amira's astute remark of earlier to her bout of nausea, all bets were off that the Smith family might well be growing from a family of three to four.

Hot came waddling in and lay down across her feet. 'Oh Hot, what have we done again?' She put her hand on her tummy and smiled with happiness. Yes, she'd been finding motherhood hard, but the couple had always discussed having more than just one child. A *lot* more, if Josh had his way. And now that another miracle could well be growing inside her, rather than feeling agitated at having to go through all the trials of motherhood again so soon, she felt a weird sense of peace. Feeling, somehow, that it was meant to be.

She gently moved Hot, then washed her face and rinsed her mouth. Feeling better, she went back to the kitchen to look at the wall calendar and started counting the weeks. She knew the exact date of conception as they had only had sex once in the three months – just before Josh had left for the States. She thought they had been careful – as careful as the rhythm method ever allows. If her deductions were right, then baby number two would be due on the ninth of July, exactly the same day as their precious Little Ned.

Rosa leaned down and tickled her furry companion behind his ears. 'Looks like we may need to make more room at this inn too, eh Hot Dog?'

CHAPTER THIRTY FIVE

'OK, are you ready?' Davina rushed into the kitchen. The evening tide had brought with it a brisk wind, so much so that Lucas was outside in the car park trying to secure the Christmas tree to a pole with a rope to prevent it from blowing over and crashing into the Christmas huts – or worse still, onto a customer, or the roof of the hotel. 'She wants pâté on toast to start and the pan-seared tuna for main.'

'Which sauce?'

'Lemon and caper. She's already on her second large glass of Sauvignon, so that's good. She may not even taste the food.' Davina laughed spitefully.

Danny opened the fridge – and promptly turned a matching shade of pale. 'I sold the last tuna steak to that family earlier. Fuck it! I should have taken it off the menu. That's so not a good start.'

At which point Lucas walked in, his face red from the cold and wind. 'What's not a good start?'

'Mate, I need to come clean. She wants tuna and we've run out.'

'That's all we need! OK – think, Hannafore, *think!*' Lucas said aloud. 'I know – let me call Rosa. She can call Jacob; he will have some, I'm sure, even if it's frozen. We've got none in the freezer, no?'

'I'm so sorry, I didn't expect it to go so crazy today.'

Lucas could see how pained Danny's face was. 'We've got this, don't worry. Be slow but not too slow with her starter. Davina, offer her a glass of wine on the house, say that's what we do for all first-time guests.'

'It's happened to us all,' Jacob replied to Rosa's urgent plea down the phone. 'Tell him not to worry but send someone up here to the back-kitchen door and Raff will have a couple of our tuna steaks ready for them.'

'Jacob, thank you so much. Luke would help you in a situation like this, I know he would.'

The publican harrumphed down the end of the phone. 'I can't believe you told them you knew it was her anyway.'

'You are both my friends. I want you both to be successful, which *you* clearly are already, so give the poor bloke a chance. He's just starting out and it was only a year ago he lost his mother. It's such a help to know who the inspector is.'

'Oh, very well.' Jacob heaved a put-upon sigh, although of course he would never let his friend Rosa down. 'I hope it goes well for them.'

'Phew! Done!' Danny put the perfectly cooked tuna steak down on the side counter, then adding the zingy sauce, he motioned for Davina to come in and collect it. 'Can you just wipe that little bit of sauce off the side with a bit of kitchen roll? After that stress, I need a bloody drink.' He made his way to the back of the bar to get the barman's attention.

'Of course,' Davina said calmly, punching the air in her mind. The moment Danny was out of sight, she did as she was told, then, with a smug expression, the devious diva made her way out to the restaurant and put the fragrant fishy dish carefully down in front of the redhead, to whom she had given the best seat in the restaurant.

CHAPTER THIRTY SIX

Rosa manoeuvred the pram up the Corner Shop steps and pushed open the door. Titch was singing along to 'Do They Know It's Christmas?' while arranging tinsel among the new designer doggie coats she had got in ready for the festive rush.

'I need a wee. Watch the bairn for me, can you, for a sec?' Rosa shouted. Instead of using the loo by the back kitchen, she wanted privacy. She ran up the steep stairs, then sat down on the toilet, ripping open the pregnancy test she'd bought on the way as she did so.

Titch looked up from cooing over the sleeping baby. 'You took your time. What's the matter – the downstairs loo no longer good enough for you?' she said casually when Rosa appeared a whole ten minutes later, unable to keep the grin off her face.

'What is the matter with you this morning?' Titch frowned. 'You're behaving oddly. Anyway, it's your turn to put the kettle on.'

The two sat side by side at the Corner Shop counter. When Titch spied Rosa's ginger tea, she knew immediately. 'Oh my God, are you saying what I think you're not saying?'

Rosa tried to keep the secret but her eyes were dancing and then her smile lit up the whole of her face. 'I haven't told a soul, not even Josh yet, so mum's the word, all right? It's the early hours in New York still and I just couldn't wait. We've shared this baby journey so it seemed only right I was with you when I found out.'

'Blimey though, Rose. Little Ned will only just be one, won't he?'

'Don't even go there. I know. It's because Josh went away a similar time last year, didn't he? We must have shagged before he left then too. I like the idea of summer birthdays though, and together it will be fun.'

'When do you reckon you are due?'

'Around July the ninth, same day as Little Ned. If it works out that way, I shall be so thrilled. One birthday party only!'

'A very small silver lining.' Titch laughed. 'You seem so happy. I thought you were set on having just the one?'

'I know, I'm surprised at my own reaction. Vicki said when the time was right, I would want another one. But is the time ever right to be a mum? I don't actually think so.' The two girls hugged, and Rosa said, 'Where are your boys this morning? Ritchie usually works on a Sunday, doesn't he?'

'I told him to lie in as he didn't get in from the chippie till late and Mum had Theo overnight, which was lovely. We are going up there for a Sunday roast when we've done here.'

'Mum's doing roast beef today too, with Kit and Nate, so that will be nice. If Nate's not too busy in the café, that is.'

'He can run up for an hour surely? But I guess it's busy in there because of the grotto. We may wander down there and have a look after lunch.'

'Yeah, they've done a good job of it. The Christmas tree can be seen from France probably. Tina ordered a five-metre one, instead of a five-foot one.'

'That's bloody hilarious.'

'Isn't it? That reminds me, I will pop in before I go home and see how they got on with the hotel inspector. Lucas rang me in a panic last night and asked me to see if Jacob could give them a tuna steak as they had run out and, sod's law, that's what she'd ordered.'

'Sounds like *Fawlty Towers* down there.'

'Ha.' Rosa grinned. 'It is a bit. Mary loves that programme.'

'My mum does too. The oldies are always the goodies, she often says.'

Rosa got up and started to look through the doggie coats. 'Only three more Sunday mornings to work and it will be Christmas.'

'I can't wait. When the new baby comes, we are not opening on a Sunday and Monday in January, as you know how quiet it is down here then.'

'I don't blame you. The café is always quieter too.'

Titch then exclaimed, 'Both your babies will be so close to this one in age, now that *is* exciting.' She caressed her tummy. 'These Braxton Hicks contractions are getting stronger each day. And he or she is such a little wriggler. I don't think there's much more room in here for them to grow, to be honest.'

'I can't wait to meet him or her.' Rosa took a slurp from her mug.

'I wanted them to be early but I'm now not so keen to give birth just yet. I haven't got all of Theo's presents and nothing for my Ritchie.'

'Oh my God,' Rosa suddenly said, putting her hand over her mouth and running through to the back kitchen toilet. 'Not again.'

She reappeared five minutes later with a glass of water, and smiling through watery eyes, began to sing, '*Deck the halls with pools of vomit, tra la la la la, la la la la.*'

CHAPTER THIRTY SEVEN

'I think she might have carked it, mate.' Danny Green's face was as puce as that of the smartly dressed, curvaceous woman who was currently lying spread-eagled and lifeless on top of the sumptuous blue velvet throw.

Lucas Hannafore put a hand to his forehead. 'Shit. If this wasn't so serious, it would be hilarious. I can just see the headline in the *Gazette* now: *Hotel Inspector Found Dead in the Titanic*.'

Danny gulped. 'What the hell are we going to do?' He had a flashback to the very same redhead bouncing on top of him, her huge breasts almost suffocating him. Both enjoying such a sexy and spontaneous encounter. And now here she was, lifeless with a pile of sick on the floor next to the bed. It seemed somehow surreal.

Seeing how badly the woman had been staggering as she left the bar last night, and knowing how much wine she had consumed, Lucas had not been too concerned about her not showing for breakfast, but when it had got to check-out time and she was still absent, he felt concerned and thought he had better call in on her. When there had been no reply to his knocks, he had opened the door a crack – only to see the grisly sight that was now before them. She was even still wearing her high-heeled shoes.

Tina came up behind them and grimaced at the stench coming from the room. 'I told you not to put her in the *Titanic*, didn't I?' She stalked in and put the back of her hand to the woman's mouth. 'Panic over. No one's going down with this Ship 'cos she ain't bleeding dead. Food poisoning, I reckon, by the colour of that puke.'

'She's so white though.' Lucas's voice was full of panic.

'That's her natural colour,' Danny added without thinking, just stopping himself from adding, 'all over.'

The woman then started to regain consciousness; she murmured something, causing both men to swear and bolt for the door, with Tina hastening after them. She closed the door behind them as quickly as possible before the ailing guest fully came round and saw them.

Shooing the boys down the stairs, Tina turned back to the Titanic room and knocked briskly on the door. 'Housekeeping!' she sang out.

Anna Wallace groaned. 'You'd better come in,' she said in a weak voice. Tina held her breath and entered as the woman hot-footed it to the bathroom and began to loudly retch.

As Tina began opening windows to let some icy-cold fresh air in, the woman reappeared with a wet stain on her dress where she had attempted to wash some dried sick off. She was carrying a glass of water.

'That's it now,' she managed. 'It's all gone and I should start feeling better soon.' She managed a grim smile. 'I'm Scottish. I can drink ten barrels more than that and no' be sick.' The strong Glaswegian accent had a croak to it. 'That was a prawn, I'm telling ya. Only one of those pishy little pink things makes me as ill as this.'

'I thought you had our tuna dish,' Tina offered.

'I categorically told that woman who checked me in, that *I was allergic to prawns*.'

'And I know for a fact that there are *no* shellfish in that tuna dish. We have a full list of allergy warnings listed on the menu, too.'

But knowing that her words were falling on deaf ears, Tina saw not only the Ship Hotel's third Seaside Star but also its whole reputation fly over her head, out of the window and deep into the English Channel. 'Here.' She handed the woman a key. 'I've just serviced the *Mary Rose*, why don't you take your things and get yourself ready in there. Would you like me to wash your dress for you too?'

With the woman now safely stowed in the other room, Tina looked out of the window to the already busy grotto below. Davina was smiling sweetly, taking money and bookings for Father Christmas, and from a distance, without her specs on, it looked to Tina as if there could even be a reindeer lying down in the pen too. Fetching her cleaning kit from the upstairs kitchen, she lugged it into the *Titanic*, pulled out her rubber gloves and filled her bucket with hot water under the bath taps. Then she squirted in some magic cleaner, swished it around and began to furiously tackle the pungent mess before her, employing her full and fruity range of swear words as she did so.

CHAPTER THIRTY EIGHT

'I can't see what it is.' Josh was peering close to his computer screen to try and make out what the white stick was that Rosa was holding up. 'Is it a pen?'

'Joshua Smith, no, it's not a pen. Guess again?'

'Mary's magic wand.' He laughed at his own joke.

'No husband, it's a pregnancy test.'

'Oh my God!' Josh jumped up so she couldn't see his face and did a little dance. He sat back down abruptly. 'How did that happen?'

'I'm not drawing you a picture,' Rosa teased. 'Queenie warned me about men like you. A friend of Ned's had seven kids, and his wife used to say that he only had to hang his shirt on the bedpost and she would get pregnant.'

'Solid sperm, that's what I have. Competing for swimming in the next Olympics. We've barely had sex since Little Ned was born though.'

'I know, and I'm sorry.'

'Don't be silly. We've both been knackered. But bingo! He shoots, he scores!'

'Do you have to be so coarse?'

'Yes, I do. And I think we need to make up for this lack of

lurve-making over Christmas. I'm gagging here.'

'Don't talk about gagging, the sickness has already started.'

'Poor you.' Josh stuck out his bottom lip. 'So, when are you due?'

'Get this, the same date as Little Ned, I reckon.'

'And he'll be two, right?'

'One! I'm not an elephant, Josh, it's just the usual nine months' gestation.'

Josh laughed out loud. 'Amazing! OK, that's going to be a challenge.'

'We'll be fine between us.'

'Yeah, we will. I'll make sure I fully play my part this time. When did you find out?'

'This morning – it's such early days. I will call the doctor tomorrow and get my appointments sorted.'

'I'm so happy, Rosa.'

'So am I, surprisingly. I can't wait to see you.'

'Me too. Where's my son?'

'He's napping and I don't want to wake him. I took a video of him last night playing and shrieking in the bath, I will send it to you after.'

'Bless him.'

'He has two teeth come through now.'

'That's early, isn't it?'

'Your baby knowledge is exemplary, Daddy Smith. Well, apart from the basic fundamental of how long they are carried for.'

He laughed. 'Any other news?'

'Mum and Kit seem to be going from strength to strength, and Mum is going to be working for him at the funeral directors.'

'Her dream job,' Josh said in a silly voice. 'Yeah, right – and rehearsals are going well for the Carol-oke, are they?'

'They start tonight. I think it will be hilarious. And you, dear husband, are obviously earmarked to sing in my group.'

Josh groaned. 'You know I'm tone deaf. I was thinking more of being a wise man and offering to look after Little Ned.'

'Ha! Very good and OK, that's a deal. Ritchie is minding Theo and Stuart has all the Cliss kids, so you can have a drink with them and watch.'

'Sounds far more civilised.'

'By the way, the Grotty Grotto as I call it has opened at the Ship. It's lovely actually – so Christmassy. This'll make you laugh: Tina only went and ordered a five-metre Christmas tree instead of a five foot one. It's massive and kind of swings in the breeze.'

'Ha! Brilliant! I bet the beach is buzzing too.'

'It really is. And Amira is getting on so well in the café. Nate needed the support, with Sara going away.'

'It's all going on then.'

'Yup, and the hotel inspector was in the Ship last night. I was going to pop in earlier and get the rundown but the little one was hungry, so I came back here.'

'How did they suss out it was the inspector? I thought you weren't supposed to know.'

'Jacob had realised it was her when she went to them and he described her to me. I couldn't not fess up that I knew.'

'Ah! I hope Lucas gets the extra star; he's worked so hard.'

'Yes, so do I. It wasn't a good start though, as she ordered the tuna dish and they had to go and get some from the Lobster Pot, as they had sold out.'

'Oops!'

'Right, I need to sort the boy out. We are going to Mary's for lunch.'

Josh yawned. 'And I need some breakfast. We are working

again today, but as soon as we are finished, we can get away from here. Carlton is wanting to get back early now too. I will keep you posted.'

Rosa waved down the screen to him, then pulled down her top to give him a quick flash and shake of her growing boobs.

'I forgot how big they get. Oh the joy, it's a win, win for me, your pregnancy.'

'You won't be saying that when I'm demanding boiled eggs dipped in horseradish at midnight.' Rosa blew him a kiss. 'Love you to where the sky touches the sea.'

'You beat me to it. Love you too and take care of you and Bump *and* our precious boy, won't you?' As if not to be left out, Hot suddenly let out a little bark. Josh laughed. 'And you too, my other best boy.'

CHAPTER THIRTY NINE

Davina came through into the bar from the grotto. She was shivering. 'Brrr, it's freezing out there today. I need a coffee to warm me up.'

Tina Green came down the stairs and confronted her. '*You* greeted the inspector, didn't you? And she categorically said that she had told the person who had checked her in that she was allergic to prawns.'

Davina screwed her face up. 'I've no idea what you are on about, Tina. She must have told Rosa, as it was she who checked her in. I just showed her to her room.'

Lucas then appeared and went through to the kitchen where Danny was cleaning down after breakfast, ready to prep for the lunch rush.

'I know you were angry with me, mate,' Lucas said tightly, 'but this takes it to a new level.'

'What – you think I'd do that on purpose? And how she can prove she even had food poisoning, let alone pinpoint it to a bloody prawn? Prawns are only on the lunch menu; they are in a plastic box in the fridge.'

'That's not the point. She thinks she did and that's it – we are fucking ruined.'

'Nothing to do with her being so pissed that she could have puked up then?' Danny's face was getting redder by the minute. 'Maybe Jacob gave us an old piece of tuna. Did you not think of that, or were you too busy trying to scapegoat me?'

Lucas raised his voice. 'Whatever has happened, it's come out of our kitchen and I don't think I can—' He stopped.

'Have me work for you any more?' Danny said slowly. He felt his temper rising. Pulling on all the memory points from the anger management course he had done in prison he took a deep breath. His own strength frightened him sometimes. Tapping his wrist as he'd been taught, he inhaled slowly again, then slowly and deliberately took off his apron and walked out of the hotel and on to the beach, where he stood staring at the sea and trying to cope with his emotions. Lucas went to follow but Tina put her hand on his shoulder to stay him.

'Let him calm down, love. You're both angry. I know my boy and he has the utmost respect for you. What's more, he doesn't bear grudges.'

Tina was still trying to pacify Lucas in the kitchen when she saw Danny sneak in the back door. He had changed into a smart top and jeans. He put a finger to his lips to shush her and made his way quietly up the stairs.

'I can't believe Rosa didn't think to tell us that the woman had a bloody prawn allergy!' Lucas banged his hand down on the metal kitchen counter. 'For fuck's sake. How could *she* let me down like that too!' He sighed loudly. 'We are definitely ruined. When this gets out, no one will want to eat here, let alone stay here, as she's sure not going to keep this quiet.' He ran his hands through his hair. 'What's happening with her upstairs now anyway?'

'Last seen sorting herself out in the *Mary Rose*.'

'I see. Thanks, Tina. Well, don't let her leave without me

210

speaking to her, OK? The least I can do is not charge her for her stay.'

'A terrible mistake, you say,' Alabaster Anna repeated breathily, as the rugged Londoner tenderly sucked each of her nipples. Then after delivering delicate butterfly kisses all around her full breasts, he slowly and deliberately moved down the wanton woman, using his hands and mouth to caress her in every which way. As he reached her sweet spot and pushed her legs gently apart, he found his head being shoved forcefully down by the now fully aroused hotel inspector.

'Mary Rose, Mother of God,' the woman moaned. 'One orgasm per star, you say?' She then gasped, sounding even more Scottish than before, 'Is tha' a promise?' Without waiting for a reply, she arched her back and between animalistic growls of ecstasy, cried out, 'Oh, Daniel. You bad, bad boy. Can't you make it four?'

CHAPTER FORTY

'It's reindeer men, Hallelujah, it's reindeer men,' Titch sang as she entered the church hall for Carol-oke rehearsals then carried on singing while dancing on the spot, her pregnant belly moving up and down with her. 'Ooh.' She held her tummy.

'Are you all right?' Rosa asked, with concern in her voice.

'Yeah. Just a twinge. Baby Rogers obviously doesn't like my singing. And I still don't know why we can't sing the reindeer song. I think it will be funny.'

'We are doing "Jingle Bells" and that's it. It's easy for us non-singers and everyone knows it. I mean, what's not to like about the joys of dashing through snow-covered fields while riding on a one-horse open sleigh?'

Titch laughed. 'Hark at you, getting all romantic.' She went through to the kitchen to turn on the hot-water urn and put some milk in the fridge as the church hall door opened. It was Amira, with Zaki, who was sound asleep in his pram. She kissed Rosa on both cheeks.

'I hope he will be OK here. I've just fed him, and he sleeps all through the night now.'

'Bloody hell, what's in the milk? – Whisky? I can't remember the last time I had a whole night's sleep.' Rosa smiled at the young woman. 'Next week, if you like, I can ask my mum if she will babysit. She's got Little Ned and she and Kit would enjoy it. The babies might like it too.'

Amira blushed. 'You have been too kind already.'

'There is no such thing as too kind.' Rosa squeezed the girl's arm. 'There are drinks and mince pies out the back if you fancy something.' She so wanted to tell Amira that she'd been right – that she was pregnant – but she hadn't even told her mum, Nate or Kit yet and it was still such early days that she wanted to keep it to herself for just a little bit longer.

Rosa looked around the hall. It had been decorated beautifully for Christmas. Cut-outs heavy with glitter that the older, pre-school children had made hung all around the walls, put up with Blu tack and drawing pins. Various Christmas-themed paintings done by the toddlers were stuck to one of the windows. The church had also put a splendid six-foot Christmas tree in the far corner of the hall. So all that would be needed for the Carol-oke concert was to bring the stage out to the front and get the chairs out of the back-storage area. Easy!

As Rosa was thinking this, the hall door swung open and in strode a rotund man wearing a smart winter coat and a brown felt Fedora.

'Oh, hello Rosa, dear girl. I hope you don't mind my joining you.' Felix Carlisle's deep voice reverberated around the hall. 'Marvellous, marvellous. Let's try a bit of *Rigoletto*.' He puffed out his chest and sang a few bars then looked up at the ceiling. 'Listen to that – these acoustics will work so well with my vibrato.'

By now, Tina and Amira were peering through the hatch, wondering who on earth the loud, self-important voice belonged to.

Controlling herself, Rosa said faintly, 'I don't understand.

213

Why are you here, Felix, and why have you chosen to join this group?'

'Oh, didn't you hear?' Felix made a dramatic gesture. 'Mother left *everything* to that blessed gardener. Well, I say everything. He got the cash, the pensions, and the holiday home in Ibiza. The house was in my name, thank the Lord, so he couldn't get his muddy paws on *that*.' He winked at Rosa. 'Mummy and I did that a while back to try and avoid the old taxman.'

'Ah, so are you here to organise the house sale?'

'No.' Felix gave a large sigh and took off his hat. 'I realised when I came down to take care of poor Mummy's funeral how simply lovely it is in this part of the world. I'm utterly *sick* of London,' he snapped, 'and once I sell up in Chelsea for *vast* amounts of money, that will give me the freedom and finance to semi-retire. I can perform when I want to, enjoy the beautiful scenery and *immerse* myself in the community down here, just like my dear mother did.'

'Oh, does it work like that with your singing then?'

'I'm a singing waiter, darling,' Felix informed her gaily. 'I can go where the work is. Restaurants, bar mitzvahs, hen parties – you name it.' He tapped his nose knowingly. 'And I have discovered that an *awful* lot of weddings happen at this end of the country. I may just set up my own business; hire in some more singers. The Devonshire Divas – how does that sound?' His stomach moved up and down as he guffawed.

Rosa tried not to laugh out loud. When she had first met the bumptious Felix, she had had visions of him starring at the Royal Opera House. Not of him going around various different venues bursting into song and deafening unsuspecting event guests. Although meeting him again now, she realised that this kind of career suited him far better, with his exuberant personality. She looked at him closely as he went to hang his hat and coat on one of the hooks at the back of the big room. Yes, he was a little tubby, but his face was handsome, his thick brown hair shiny and well cut.

The door opened again and in walked Nate. She saw Felix look her brother up and down then sashay over towards him. 'Indian bells, darling?' he said, and handed him the two little bells held together with a short piece of cord – an instrument Rosa remembered using at school in many a Christmas production. 'You can ring my bell any time,' Felix added archly.

Unfazed, Nate replied cheekily, 'Maybe you'll have to show me how. I'm Nate, by the way, Rosa's brother.'

'Felix Carlisle.'

'I can't believe you're here, Nate, not after our bum note conversation,' Rosa told her brother.

'Oh, there will be bum notes a-plenty, sis, I can promise you that.'

'I have a whole *box* of Indian bells, Rosa,' Felix boomed. 'And have you chosen a song yet? I shall offer myself as the choir master.'

'Don't get too excited,' she warned him. 'We are only doing "Jingle Bells".'

'Oh.' Then he cheered up. 'Well, I suppose the Indian bells will fit with that nicely, at least.'

'They will have to, Felix, as I am the choir master,' Rosa informed him. 'Ned's Gift is my baby, you see, and that is our song. Why are you not with the Polhampton St Michael's lot, anyway?'

'Oh Rosa, I told you why. I couldn't even bear the embarrassment of burying Mother at her church because of the way she died.'

'I think you need to get over it,' Rosa said in her abrupt London-born manner. 'Look at it this way: your mum was

215

happy and having fun. It wasn't your money; it was hers to give away.'

Not used to someone standing up to him, Felix went quiet. But only for a moment. 'Hmm. When you put it like that… Now,' he too became brisk and professional, since music was his life, 'who else is coming along tonight?'

The door opened and Vicki walked in. She smiled at the others then went straight over to Rosa, took one look and whispered, 'Congratulations. When is it due?'

Rosa shook her head in disbelief that yet another mum had sussed her. She gave her friend a secret little wink, then lifted the wooden spoon she intended to use as a baton and brandished it in the air.

Addressing all those gathered there, she called out, 'Hello, the Ned's Gift Cockleberry Bay Choir, let's get ready to massacre "Jingle Bells", shall we?'

'Hardly, dear, not with *moi* here as a *member*,' Felix said, catching Nate's eye, and giving him what he thought was a seductive gaze.

CHAPTER FORTY ONE

As all the punters had left and the room guests gone up to bed, Lucas was not only surprised but also slightly annoyed to see the door of the hotel bar open and somebody walk in just as he had instructed the barman to close up for the night. His attitude soon changed, however, when he recognised who it was.

'Room for a little one?' Carly Jessop took off her coat, hung it on a peg under the bar, then went and sat herself on a stool next to Lucas who was relaxing with a pint of cloudy cider in front of him. The fire was still giving off a cosy heat, the remnants of a large log glowing warmly, and the off-white Christmas tree lights made for a romantic setting. Checking the clock in front of him, he glanced at the pretty young woman. Her dark hair was tied back in a loose ponytail, her tight jeans and cream roll-neck jumper emphasising her trim figure.

'Hello, what a pleasant surprise. What are you doing here at this time?' Lucas looked behind to see if anyone was following her in. He then noticed that she had been crying. He was surprised at how sad that made him feel. The cider loosened his lips. 'Aw. Sweet girl. What can I get you?'

'A dark rum and Coke, please?'

'Large?'

'Larger than large, please.'

Lucas signalled to the barman who was already putting ice in a glass, then said carefully, 'Tell me to mind my own business if you like, Carly, but do you want to talk about it?'

Carly took a large slug of the ice-laden drink that had just been put down in front of her. 'It's boring really.'

'I'm sure it's not and I've got all night.'

'I'm embarrassed to talk about it, to tell the truth. It's like this: I've been seeing someone down here in the Bay. Well, I say "seeing" but he's never been very attentive. I just ended it this evening. It's OK though; it wasn't right.' She sighed deeply.

'But that doesn't make it any easier, does it? You've had that connection.'

'Yes.' Carly got a tissue out of her bag to blow her nose. 'The kind of stupid connection that has a mind of its own.'

'Do you want me to go and sort him out?' Lucas put his fists in the air and pretended to punch.

Carly managed a smile. 'No, he wasn't a bad man, just wanted different things to me.'

'Like what?' Lucas said, then groaned. 'None of my business, sorry.'

'It's fine.' Carly took in the handsome man in front of her and felt her tummy do a little rushy thing. 'You see, I wanted something more permanent.'

'Like marriage and kids, you mean?'

'Er, yes. Which I know is a red flag to many men but I'm not going to lie about it. I'm twenty-nine; I want the full package.'

'So, was he The One then, do you think?'

'That's the thing. I was trying to make a square peg fit into a round hole. So no, he wasn't. I kept thinking that maybe things would change. But they didn't – *he* didn't. It's been a good wake-up call.'

Lucas's hand brushed her knee as he went to move his stool. 'Sorry, sorry.'

Carly blushed, then took another sip of her drink, which was already working its magic. 'I'll get there,' she said more cheerfully. 'It's all one big learning curve, this life and love thing, isn't it?'

'With no handbook or rule book, so how is anyone expected to do it right?' Lucas agreed.

'No girlfriend tonight then?'

'No. Father Christmas and the reindeer needed a lift back to Polhampton earlier. His car wouldn't start or something. Anyway, Davina lives near him and said she might as well stay at her place tonight.'

'The reindeer too?'

'Don't ask, he has a crate that went into her boot, I think.'

'That's mad.'

'This whole grotto idea is mad. I will rethink for next year for sure. I'm wrung out already and we've only just started.'

'You don't live with your girlfriend then.'

'God no! Uh oh, I know that makes me sound like a red-flag man but I'm not, honestly.'

'You just don't want to live with her then?' Carly said baldly.

'It's complicated.' Lucas wasn't ready to lay bare his fears of being alone to this beautiful woman in front of him who had already shown him more kindness with her support at the grand opening than Davina ever had.

'You've certainly given me food for thought now though,' he mused.

Carly put down her drink, stood up and announced abruptly, 'I must go.'

'Oh. But you've only just got here.' Lucas was disappointed. 'Can't you stay for a bit longer and finish your drink?'

'No, I'm driving. I'm going to head home. I came in here with the intention to drown my sorrows – but what good would that do? And, well, now I know you want to get married and have kids too we might as well just set the date.'

Her face remained deadpan until Lucas laughed out loud. 'Well, now you mention it, I've always liked the idea of a summer wedding, if that works for you?'

Carly beamed at him. 'That's settled then.' She turned to leave, then remembered: 'Oh, yeah. Have you got time to discuss the website one day this week? I need to start planning ahead for spring packages, menus, et cetera.'

Lucas got off his stool and faced her. 'For you, I will make time.' He stared right at her with his brooding hazel eyes. She had never noticed his long lashes before and the butterflies in her tummy started to do the hokey-cokey all over again.

'I'll check my diary and message you tomorrow.' Carly scrabbled in her bag to find her car keys. 'Hang on, I need to pay you.'

'For three sips?' Lucas held his hand up. 'On me. And let's meet in Rosa's Café. I feel I need to get away from this place, even if it is just for an hour.'

'Sure thing. And Lucas? Tonight has made me realise that I'd rather be single and happy – even single and miserable – than in a relationship and miserable.' As Carly got to the door she turned around and smiled. 'And look at you, you won't be single for long.'

Lucas sat back at the bar and drank the rest of his cider down in one. When he had first met Davina, it had been a relationship purely based on sex and not mutual affection. If he was honest, it wasn't any different now, although even the sex had been waning of late. He was biding time. Wasting time. But now she was helping with the grotto he couldn't be finishing with her;

it didn't seem right. She had been so keen to help and she was being extremely useful looking after the finances and managing Father Christmas.

But what if she was cheating? It would piss him off but not upset him, he didn't think. His heart obviously wasn't in it any more. Not like it had been with Rosa when the torment of unrequited love had hit home. Once he learned that she was pregnant he had realised that she would never leave Josh. It was game over. No hope left. At that point he had experienced a despair equal to that of losing his mother, so intense were his feelings for the feisty fellow Londoner.

The last day or so had been so busy and messed up with the Prawngate incident and the hotel inspector that he hadn't even had time to think about what Danny had said about Davina cheating. If he had genuinely cared, he would have tackled her there and then. Or maybe if he knew, then the decision had already been made for him and he would find himself back on his own again. Lucas felt guilty. He had acted so harshly in accusing Danny before he had any true facts. No wonder the bloke had stormed off; he had every right to have done that. Good old Tina had stepped up to the plate, not having a go at him but taking Alfie home to be with his dad while she donned the whites and did the cooking and cleaning for the day. God, that woman was a brick, as was Danny. He liked him too. Liked him a lot.

'Fuck,' Lucas said aloud. He must text him tonight, arrange to talk to him civilly and calmly tomorrow. Apologise for being such a twat. Yes, the two of them had had a row, but Danny was only warning him about Davina in order to protect him. What's more, if Lucas thought about it logically, why on earth would Danny want to give the hotel a bad rep? He loved his new life; his family were stable and young Alfie was safe and happy.

And if the Ship only had two stars, what did it really matter? Two was better than none. They were still doing OK. And what if Alabaster Anna did write them a bad review? Maybe Carly might be able to get it taken it down – so really when he thought about it, it wasn't the end of the world. Cockleberry Bay would forever be a beautiful place to visit and he would always make a good living from the restaurant and bar alone if need be.

Feeling so much better, Lucas turned his thoughts to Carly. She was not only incredibly pretty but she was also sexy, kind – and now he knew she shared a common vision of the future, with marriage and kids – even more desirable. But had she been flirting with him just then? Or just being her usual funny self? He decided that he would go and talk to Rosa tomorrow; OK, it seemed fucked up to go to the woman with whom he had been so deeply in love to ask for relationship advice, but Rosa would set him straight. He also had to have the difficult conversation with her about Prawngate.

'Do you want me to turn the alarm on, on my way out?' the barman asked as he turned off the glass washer.

'No, you're all right, mate, I'll do it,' Lucas replied. 'And thanks so much for your hard work today. It's been a busy one.'

Lucas let out a big burp as he made his way to check the alarms. He also had a quick look at the cameras that pointed out onto the car park, plus into the kitchen and the bar area. He laughed as he caught sight of the huge Christmas tree swaying around in the breeze with enough lights on its branches to power an electric car. His van was sat in the corner, alongside a couple of other cars belonging to the few who'd had too much mulled wine that afternoon and were sensibly leaving their vehicles there. For some reason, the screen on the second camera, the one that pointed to the two Christmas huts and the table where Davina sat to take the tickets and money, was black.

He turned on the outside light and went out of the back door to check what was going on with it. The camera was still in place, but a cable had obviously come loose. With the wind hitting his face and waves crashing on the beach, he jumped up on the table and pushed it back in place. Just as he was hurrying back into the warm, a message beeped in on his phone.

Thank you for making me smile again tonight. Carly x

Lucas felt his heart smile. She never usually left a kiss on her messages. Not sure exactly what to reply, he put his phone in his pocket and climbed wearily up to bed. He needed his beauty sleep. Tomorrow was a new day – to make amends and big decisions.

CHAPTER FORTY TWO

Tina Green made a small supper of a cheese and onion toastie and a mug of milky coffee with two sugars, then walked upstairs and knocked on her son's bedroom door.

'Come in.' Danny was lying on his bed in T-shirt and boxers browsing through his phone. When his mother handed him the plate and mug, he looked amused and said, 'This is what you used to bring me when you'd shouted at me for summink when I was a kid.'

'You're not too old to be shouted at now neither.' Tina sat at the end of the bed. 'It wasn't your fault, lad.'

'Maybe it was. I didn't smell the tuna before I cooked it, so it could have been off.'

'Nah. The silly bitch was pissed, and of course you would have noticed if that fish was bad – you're not daft, son. And like you say, how could a prawn get anywhere near it? – And that's what she was allergic to.' Tina fanned herself. 'Bloody hell, that room took some cleaning – ugh. It'll take time for that smell to go.'

Spotting that her son was looking queasy at the memory, she quickly added, 'And Lucas will have calmed down by now. You are so like brothers, you two, in temperament and relationship.'

'He's asked to meet me tomorrow on the bench up on the West Cliffs path at ten-fifteen.'

'Maybe he's going to push you over the edge?' Tina laughed.

'Oh yeah? Him and whose army?' Danny smirked.

'But that's a weird place to meet, innit? Are you going?' Tina began to straighten the curtains that Danny had closed awkwardly.

'Course I am. We need these jobs, Ma. I'm not uprooting again, not now Alfie loves his school and his new friends down 'ere. It's a safe place for us all.'

'I'm proud of you for controlling your temper and seeing the bigger picture, really I am,' his mother said.

'It's taken me a long time to get this far.'

'I know, but you're getting there and that's what matters.' Tina yawned. 'Have you thought any more about Leah?'

'I've thought a lot about it, of course I have. But like I said, I want to get Christmas out of the way first. And it's got to be right for our Alfie.'

'OK, son. I think that's a good idea. But if it works out, it will free up some time for you too, you know. We all need a bit of that.'

'And more importantly for you, Ma. I do realise how much you do for us, and I am so grateful. You go above and beyond, always.'

'That's my job, ain't it?' Tina Green rubbed her eyes and through another noisy yawn managed, 'What's all this about Davina cheating, then? What proof have you got of that?'

'I saw a text from someone signing off as Santa, insinuating they were at it. I'm assuming it was from the narky northerner in the grotto.'

'He's northern?'

'Mum. Get real. He sounds more like Noel Gallagher than

Noel Gallagher does. For some reason he's putting on a southern accent. I heard him on his phone in the bog. I don't fucking trust him either.'

'So, did you tell Lucas you saw a text?'

'No, I didn't want him to think I was snooping at his bird's phone.'

'What a mess.' Tina sat back down, deep in thought. 'But I will get this sorted.'

'Mum, I don't want you getting involved. I can fight my own battles.' Danny picked up his now cold sandwich and took a bite.

Tina ignored him and stood up. 'Lucas needs us as much as we need him. He won't ditch us. But if I have to clear the Green name, I will. I've done it before. You bloody know that.'

Danny shook his head. 'I'd rather get in the ring with Tyson Fury than you, Mum.'

Tina smiled. 'Just keep chatting to him up those cliffs as long as you can tomorrow, mind.'

'Why, what you up to?'

'Just trust your old mum to do right by us, that's all.'

With that she kissed her son on the cheek, stepped quietly down the corridor to check on Alfie, then getting into her own bed and taking the weight off her feet, let out a massive sigh of relief.

CHAPTER FORTY THREE

'Not too early, is it?' Lucas pushed open the door to Gull's Rest and followed Rosa through to the open-plan kitchen, stopping to thoroughly make a fuss of Hot Dog, who rolled on his back and made his special creaking sound when Lucas knelt down and blew raspberries into his tummy.

'Nine-thirty, early? Are you having a laugh? I'm usually awake before the bloody gulls start their screeching. Do you want a coffee?'

'Nah, thanks, I'm not stopping long.'

'What brings you here anyway? Surely you should be checking people out.'

'I have staff for that.' Then Lucas corrected himself. 'Well, I have Tina this morning, anyway. Me and Danny had a fall-out.'

'Oh, shit.' Rosa carried on loading the dishwasher.

'He thinks Davina is cheating.'

'Oh, double shit.'

'He's got no evidence, just thinks so.'

'Danny's no fool. He's cut from the same cloth as me. He wouldn't stir up a storm if there's wasn't some truth in it. But how do you feel about it?'

'I'm fine,' Lucas replied resolutely.

'Why didn't you just have it out with him there and then and find out why he thought that?'

'Because we were just about to start service and the bloody hotel inspector was there. It's been a nightmare, Rosa. I honestly thought she was dead from food poisoning.'

'*What?*'

'She didn't come down for breakfast, didn't answer when we knocked, so then we went in and found her next to a pile of sick, fully clothed on the bed – and she was so white I honestly thought she was a goner.'

Rosa laughed. 'She's pale as a ghost anyway.'

'I know that now!' He paused and took a deep breath. 'Why didn't you tell me she was allergic to prawns, Rosa?' he asked awkwardly.

'What? What do you mean? I didn't know.'

'Davina said you checked her in, and you must have forgotten.'

'Did she now? Well, Davina is going to get a piece of my mind when I see her for being a complete and utter lying bitch.'

'Oi. That's a bit strong.'

'No. The lying cow. I got as far as running up and getting the key out of the door of the *Titanic*, that's all. By the time I got back downstairs to reception, Davina had just arrived and carried on checking the woman in and showing her to her room. There was no mention whatsoever of prawns.'

'Hmm.'

'Luke, you do believe me, don't you?'

He looked directly into Rosa's pretty green eyes. 'I trust you with my life.'

'Good, because you should.' Then without even thinking, the words, 'I love you, Luke Hannafore,' shot out of her mouth into his ears and wrapped around his heart like clingfilm.

Tears formed in the man's eyes. 'I love you, too,' he replied softly.

'In the way we discussed the other night, I mean,' Rosa quickly added.

'I knew what you meant.' Lucas cleared his throat.

'So, you don't think it was the tuna, do you? Fuck! This is just the worst thing to happen.'

'Yeah, thanks for that – and yes, it had actually crossed my mind that Jacob may have given us an old bit of fish.'

'Come on – Jacob is hot on his fresh stuff, and he may be a drama queen sometimes but he would never in a million years stitch you up like that. It must have been a prawn.'

'But there were no prawns in her dish. It is a bit of a mystery; she was really drunk though.'

'Well, that's it then, she probably just had too much to drink.'

'She's blaming the food, and Tina did say the colour of her puke looked like it could be food poisoning. So we are fucked whatever way.'

'Shit. I'm sorry.' Rosa started to make up bottles of baby milk.

'It's fine. It's just a star.'

'A big pulsating Seaside Star.' Rosa then laughed.

Lucas grinned back. 'And we already have two of those.'

'But two's not three.' Rosa then decided, 'OK, this is awful, but I think this is one for "chuck it in the fuck it bucket and move on", don't you?'

Lucas started laughing. 'The inspector woman, she was dead glamorous in an older woman kind of way, dead loud though, and the drunker she got, the more she swore.'

'Maybe she was so hungover, she will just forget all about it.'

'Rosa, you're talking to me. I don't think so.'

'On a positive, no one will know you were going for the third star unless you tell someone. You may get a bad review – so what? Happens to everyone. In fact, you know how I like my reading? Well, before I download a book that I fancy, I always check out the bad reviews before the good ones because they are usually codswallop with spelling mistakes and make me laugh. It's so obvious that people write them out of malice and because they've got nothing better to do.'

'Jacob will know though,' Lucas said moodily.

'Don't worry, he won't spread it around. He's too decent for that, and he knows he's got a good business going on up there. I've said it before and it's true, there is plenty room enough for the both of you in this town.'

'Actually, can you find out if he knows when we are likely to hear about whether we've got one or not?'

Rosa opened her eyes wide. 'Why? You don't honestly think you will get a star after this, do you? Actually, can they take them away from you?'

'You're such a bitch.' Lucas threw a tea towel at her.

'But yeah, let me find out so you can avoid Jacob boasting about his.' Rosa filled the kettle and turned it on. As she was hunting for mugs she said casually, 'You don't seem terribly upset about Davina and the situation.'

'If I'm honest, I feel a bit relieved, especially after last night.'

'How come?'

'I saw Carly.' Luke couldn't stop the grin spreading across his face. 'She popped into the bar late last night.'

'Ooh, go on.'

'She's just split from someone, actually, had just dumped him last night. He evidently wasn't looking for the same thing as her.'

'Which is?'

'Marriage and kids.'

'Shut the front door!' Rosa rubbed her hands together. 'You're made for each other, honestly.'

'She's got your eyes.'

'Well, as long as she protects your heart, I don't care what else she has.'

'She rushed off, then texted me. I don't know if she likes me or not.'

'Show me.' Rosa read it out loud. '*Thank you for making me smile again tonight. Carly* – and a kiss! Of course she likes you. There's the evidence right in front of your eyes. Does she need to spell it out?'

'I don't know, because when she left she said that I wouldn't be single for long.'

'That's another good thing.'

'Is it?' Luke looked perplexed.

'Anyway, what did you reply?'

'Nothing. Thought I'd think about it.'

'Oh Luke, she probably sat awake waiting for a reply from that message.'

'There wasn't a question mark!'

Rosa bashed her forehead with her hand. 'Men! Reply now, something nice.'

'I'm still seeing Davina.'

'I don't want to be cynical, but by the sound of things I don't think she'd care.'

Lucas started typing. He read out: '*Glad I made you feel better. Thursday at 4 in the café for our meeting? Kiss. PS: Will you marry me?* Smiley face. How about that?'

Rosa laughed. 'The last bit is a joke, right?'

'It's our standing joke.'

'Whoa, well don't scare her off.'

'I give up.' Lucas scratched his head and pressed send. 'You can't win with women.'

Little Ned started crying upstairs. 'I'd better go and get the main man,' Rosa said.

'I need to leave anyway. I want to walk up the cliffs to clear my head before I meet my main man, Danny.'

'OK. Good luck and I want to be kept posted on everything – and I mean everything. All right?'

CHAPTER FORTY FOUR

Satisfied that she had cleaned all of the rooms ready for new arrivals later, Tina Green ripped off her pink rubber gloves, put them in the upstairs cleaning cupboard then made her way back into the *Mary Rose* – the room with the best view of the back car park of the Ship. Thanks to the magic carpet cleaner, a great deal of elbow grease and ditto fresh air, the *Titanic* was now good as new.

Tina took a minute to peer outside. She hadn't expected a Monday morning to be busy at the grotto but, surprisingly, there was a steady flow of mums and toddlers – nothing like the queues of the weekend, but a good little gathering nonetheless. Davina, wearing a Santa's hat and taking money at the table, smiled sweetly and made polite conversation. Opening the window a crack to get some air, the savvy Londoner trained her ears to pick up the conversation below.

'I'm ever so sorry but the card machine isn't working today, so if you've got cash, that would be great. If you need change, I have loads here, and if you have none on you, there is a machine inside Bercow's the newsagents, just up the hill on the right.'

Tina's jaw dropped in disbelief. The card machine was working just fine, she had been using it herself for check-outs earlier. Glancing at her watch, she was happy to see she still had plenty of time. Time that she would bide until she had gathered enough evidence to ensure Santa's Little Helper was sent packing, reindeer and all, back to Liarland and beyond.

CHAPTER FORTY FIVE

Lucas walked slowly up the West Cliffs path, taking in the beauty of the scenery around him. Seagulls and other coastal birds whipped around in the light breeze, shouting their appreciation at such a glorious day. Despite the bright sunshine that lit up the sea to a topaz blue way below, he shivered. Winter had most definitely reached Cockleberry Bay. Taking in a big breath of sea air he slowly blew it out, causing misty plumes to multiply, as if he were smoking an expensive Cuban cigar. The view from where he was standing – the sea, the horizon and the magnificent rolling sky – put everything into perspective. His problems, he realised, were just small blips in a humungous universe.

Despite the bench glistening with traces of the morning frost, Lucas sat down. As he watched a solitary fishing boat heading through the waves, he became almost hypnotised by the sight and fell deep into thought. The last time he had been on this bench, he had felt like that boat, but with no anchor. He had been in a desperate state. His mother had just died. He knew he could never be with Rosa. He felt that he didn't belong anywhere. It had seemed a strange coincidence that Alec Burton, the counsellor, had been up here on that very day and said a few wise words to him that had hit home. He couldn't even remember what they were now; that's how good a counsellor he was. But whatever the big man had said, Lucas had felt so much better when he walked back down the hill. At last he felt as if he had a reason to live, to be. The conversation, Lucas recalled, had kind of led him into Davina's arms, which, to be fair, hadn't been such a bad thing at the time. A welcome distraction from the many raw emotions that had come hand-in-hand with his grief.

After a few moments, Lucas looked down the path to see the stocky figure of Danny Green jogging up the hill.

'All right?' Danny said tentatively, tearing off his Wet Ham beanie hat. 'Jesus, I need to get fitter. I'm sweating my bollocks off here. Do you fancy a fag?'

Lucas took one that Danny had already pre-rolled. As they sat side by side smoking on the bench, Lucas broke the silence.

'No bullshit required here, Dan. I'm sorry, mate.' He let out a big sigh, then took an even bigger drag on his cigarette.

'About what, me trying to kill the inspector or me insinuating your bird is cheating?'

'Both.' Lucas laughed. 'We should write a bloody sitcom.'

'Would be easier than running a hotel, I reckon.' Danny blew out a stream of smoke. 'Look, it could have been the fish, but I guess we will never know. I would never have done it on purpose, mate; you know that.'

'It could have been worse; she actually could have died.'

Danny laughed. 'She was a big girl – quite a challenge to drag down the stairs and bury on the beach, I'd say.' He then had a fleeting vision of 'Lily' bouncing on top of him, nearly suffocating him with her voluptuous bosoms.

'Fuck me – can you imagine?' Lucas said.

Danny was imagining a lot and suddenly felt bad about

talking about the woman in that disrespectful way. They had satisfied each other's needs, that was all. So, what harm? For a second Danny toyed with the idea of telling Lucas what he had done, but knowing he was on sticky ground already, thought better of it. Sleeping with a guest was a sackable offence. If he confessed that he'd shagged her not once, but twice, and (despite his good intentions the second time), who could predict how Lucas would react? Also, there was no guarantee it would go in their favour. Anna Wallace owed them nothing and a lie from her could quite possibly put her own job on the line.

'So, I'm not sacked then?' Danny asked nonchalantly.

'Mate, the Ship would go down without you and your mum. I was angry. Sorry again. You'd better tell me what you know about Davina as well.'

'Ah, her. Well, I don't like to be the bringer of bad news, but I saw a text on her phone from Santa.'

'Our Santa?'

'I assume so, and they were talking about giving each other presents of a different kind. I'm sorry, mate.'

'How did you get to see it?'

'She left her phone for a short while on the bar. I wasn't snooping, honest – it just flashed up and then she came down and grabbed it. I kind of sensed there could be something going on with her and northern boy.'

'Northern?'

'Yeah, he's a cocky cunt; avoids me like the plague, but I overheard him talking in the bog the other day. Sounds like he's from Manchester.'

'OK,' Luke said slowly, 'now my blood is beginning to boil. There's only one person who would need to hide their accent down here.'

'I don't get it, mate.' Danny trod on his cigarette, then picked it up and put the dead butt in his pocket.

'You don't need to get anything. Dan. All you need to know is that he hurt Rosa.'

'Our Rosa?' Danny asked.

Lucas nodded. 'Yeah. Our Rosa. He's a cheating scumbag.'

Danny stood up and wrapped his scarf back around his neck. His voice was level. 'Then all you need to do is turn off the outside cameras as soon as you get back.'

CHAPTER FORTY SIX

'Jingle Bells, jingle bells, jingle all the...'

The second Ned's Gift Cockleberry Bay Christmas Carol-oke concert rehearsal was in full swing, with Gladys manfully thumping out the tune on the upright piano in the hall. Rosa had changed rehearsals to a Monday night this week; people hadn't been that happy with having to come out in the cold on a Sunday night, as it broke up their weekends.

'Mrs Treborick, you know you don't bring in your Indian bells until the second chorus,' Felix Carlisle boomed, causing everyone to stop mid-verse. Titch and Rosa – who had quickly handed over the job of choir master to him – burst out laughing. 'And you two need to concentrate,' he said sternly, looking in their direction. 'It's like teaching at a kindergarten,' he directed at the pair, who started to ring their instruments in fast succession to annoy him further. 'We are so not going to win at this rate,' he huffed, then added in a stage whisper, 'and I am doing this for free!'

'Ow.' Titch put her hand to her stomach.

'What's up?' Rosa asked, on the alert.

'I'm fine, it's just I've been having those silly little contractions all day. Baby Rogers wants to get out and show everyone how to do it, I reckon.'

Mrs Treborick, who was also now sniggering nervously, went to the kitchen to check whether Mr Ping-Pong (no relation to Jacob and Raffy's pug Pongo), her ancient Pekinese, named after a character in the *Rupert the Bear* books, was behaving himself with Hot. She returned to report to Rosa that both animals were lying down, contentedly chewing on either end of an old dog toy, and that Zaki was sleeping soundly in his pram. Amira, not wanting to put upon Mary and Kit, had decided to take her chances and bring her baby son with her again.

Nate, who'd been persuaded by Rosa to join them to make up the male numbers, was the only one there who seemed to be taking the concert seriously. 'Listen everyone, Felix is right,' he said. 'It would be good to win. After all, Ned's Gift is the reason we are doing this, and it would so make sense to promote the charity efforts further.'

'Hear, hear, darling boy,' Felix affirmed, blowing an exaggerated kiss at him.

'The radio is covering it, aren't they?' Nate added.

'They sure are,' Rosa replied.

'Good! We can plug the café too,' her brother said. Then: 'Actually, that's a point. If I'm singing, someone will need to cover the food for our bit.'

'We'll sort it out nearer the time. It'll be fine,' Rosa pacified him.

'Yes, we do not wish to lose your fine tenor voice, dear boy,' Felix announced, causing Nate to look shy.

'The only tenner you're going to lose is if you bet on us winning,' Vicki quipped humorously. 'It's supposed to be a bit of fun too, you know.'

Felix carried on regardless. 'And we mustn't forget the whole evening is for the church roof fund, must we? My dear mother

Celia would turn in her grave if we made a mockery of it.'

Hearing this, Rosa had a sudden vision of Jamie tanning his perfect body on a sun-lounger in the Ibiza sunshine. Wherever Celia Carlisle was looking down from, she was sure that an old church roof would be the last thing on her mind. Nonetheless, to keep the peace she agreed. He needed her support.

'We are with you, Felix. Come on, everyone,' she urged.

The singer dramatically lifted the wooden spoon baton in the air. 'Very well, everyone. We'll take it from the top, Gladys dear. Amira, remember to breathe ready for your solo this time please, if it's not too much trouble.'

'Peace at last,' Rosa whispered to Titch, who had now started washing up the teacups in the back kitchen. 'It's bloody funny though, isn't it? I nearly wet myself when Gladys fell asleep at the piano. I thought Felix was going to explode like Monsieur Creosote.'

Titch laughed. 'I'm loving it, and it's so nice to be doing something for us without the kids too.' She had reckoned without Hot, who had woken up and came running around to them. He gave an 'I need to pee,' kind of bark.

'You told Josh then?' Titch asked.

'Yes, he's so excited. I am too. I feel…well, I can't really explain how I feel.' Rosa bent down to tie on Hot's warm tartan coat and harness before putting her own coat on and lifting her bag over her head, messenger-style.

Titch said, 'We will both have two little monsters each to grumble about now. Anyway, you go off, Rose. I'll finish up here. I'm meeting Ritchie at the chippie straight after. He's gonna drive us up the hill when he's done. What's the time? I only went and left my phone in his van earlier.'

'Nearly nine. If you're sure, thank you. I can relieve Mum of

Little Ned then. Just pull the door to behind you and I'll put the key in the key safe for Gladys tomorrow. Her Frank wanted to get her home.'

'Brilliant. Thanks, mate.'

'Jingle Bells, jingle bells…' With jazz hands aloft, Rosa began to sing on her way out, causing both of them to laugh out loud and Hot to run around his mistress's legs with frantic barks that meant: 'Stop that! I need to get out and cock my leg against the vicar's yew hedge right this minute.'

CHAPTER FORTY SEVEN

'I know that expression,' Tina Green said to her son as he walked back into the hotel kitchen. 'You talk to me before you act on it.'

Ignoring her, he went to the fridge, fetched some carrots and began to chop them furiously.

Lucas locked the car park gates that blocked off the grotto area, then calmly apprehended Davina as she walked through the back door to the reception.

'Have you got a minute?'

'Um. Well, I need to cash up for you out there and then I said I'd give Father Christmas a lift home.'

'It won't take long.'

Davina frowned. 'Look, I've one more day off then I'm back on shift at the station, so I want to make sure everything is in order before Tina takes over.'

Lucas felt slightly sick at what he was about to do. 'Has Father Christmas not got a real name?'

'I'm trying to keep in the spirit of Christmas – for the kids, you know.'

'You are so good.' Lucas then growled, 'What's his fucking name?'

'It's um…Jon, Jon Badger.'

'Badger, that's an interesting name for a fucking fox. I think we need to talk, don't you?'

'Can't it wait until tomorrow? Er, Jon needs to get back and the reindeer is hungry.'

'Upstairs now!' Lucas was trying to suppress the white-hot anger that was pulsing through him.

'You can't tell me what to do.'

Lucas took the woman's arm and dragged her to his bedroom. His laptop was open on his desk.

'Sit down.' The fair cop, realising this could well be a fair cop, sighed deeply as Lucas looked her in the face and said, 'Strangely, I can kind of deal with you cheating on me. We are over, of course, but it's the rest I'm struggling with.'

'I don't know what you're on about.' Davina stood up and went to push past him.

'Been screwing him since the interview, or did you know him before that?'

Davina held up her hands as if in surrender 'OK, OK, I've done wrong. But me and you, we weren't getting on anyway.'

'So rather than communicate that like an adult and talk it through, you thought you'd shag the first guy who came along and then wave him in front of my eyes on a daily basis, right? It is Joe Fox, isn't it?'

'Yes, all right, it is!' Davina spat. 'And you're not angry about me and you, you're only angry because he did the dirty on your precious Rosa.'

'I'm angry because he's a shyster. And that you – my girlfriend, someone who I should be able to trust implicitly – have not only been cheating on me but stealing from me too. I don't want him on my premises. I don't want to be giving him money – my hard-earned cash. But most of all, I don't want to ever see you again.'

'Well, don't worry, you won't have to see either of us again now, will you?'

'Good riddance. You bloody deserve each other.'

With that she got up and went to the door, but Danny and Tina were blocking her path.

'No rush to give Father Christmas a lift; he's long gone,' Danny said, rubbing his knuckles, his face like thunder.

'As for you thinking we didn't realise that Rudolph the red-nosed reindeer was just a big dog with antlers on, give us some bloody credit,' Lucas added. 'We thought it was quite funny at first. The younger kids didn't realise, and the parents thought it a hoot, but that's four hundred quid I want back off you.' He looked Davina up and down with scorn on his face. 'It all makes sense now. I remember Rosa telling me that creep had a Great Dane. I can't believe I didn't realise what you were up to.'

Davina opened her cross-over bag and pulled out a wodge of cash. She thrust it at him. 'Here! There's your money. That's it, I'm going now.'

'And the rest, you lousy thief,' Tina said. 'I've been watching you, milady, saying you could only take cash and then putting "one for the money tin, one for me" as you loaded as many notes as you could in there.' The tough East Ender pointed to the policewoman's bag.

'That's a lie,' Davina hissed, fronting up to her. 'Bloody prove it.'

Lucas began to play the video that Tina had taken earlier from her viewpoint in the Mary Rose. 'I think in your game that's called strong evidence, isn't it, WPC Hunt? And this was just from today. Maybe it would have been cleverer to cut the camera's wire, rather than just pull it out, eh? Call yourself a detective,' he sneered.

Davina angrily emptied her handbag of notes and threw

them down on to the desk. 'I don't want your bloody money.'

Lucas laughed sarcastically. 'Of course you don't, not now you've been rumbled.' He shook his head. 'Money makes the world go round and I can see why, aided and abetted by that scumbag Fox, you thought you'd make a fast buck for Christmas – but why sabotage my chance with the Seaside Stars too? I just don't get it.'

'Now you really are going mad. That woman was pissed, she made all that up. You know she didn't have prawns, she just wanted to cause a fuss.'

'The thing is, officer – or should I say "former officer", since your career will be well and truly over when word gets round – as it will. You see, we've got proof of you putting the prawn in her food too. As you coppers say, we've got you bang to rights. You could have killed her – did you think of that?'

As he spoke, Lucas saw the blood draining from Davina's (to him now ugly) face.

'I was never one for security cameras until Rosa got done over last year in the Corner Shop,' Lucas carried on. 'So in every room downstairs, including of course the kitchen, I put a hidden one which links directly to the computer up here. Once Tina told me that you were stealing on the main cameras, I thought I'd have a little look on here too.'

Danny, praying that his boss hadn't secretly put them in the bedrooms too, looked intently at the screen. Lucas set the footage on his computer screen running, and there for all to see, clear as daylight, was Danny at the back of the bar getting the attention of a barman and Davina opening the fridge, taking a prawn from the plastic box in there, cutting a tiny piece off and pushing it under the tuna steak, mixing it in the sauce with her finger as she did so. Then wiping the sides of the plate as Danny had asked, she smugly took it out to Alabaster Anna.

'I don't know what to say,' Davina said quietly. Her face was now a deathly white.

Danny's mouth nearly dropped to the floor. 'Sorry could be a starter for ten, you rotten bitch!' he roared. 'I could have lost my job because of you – my family could have lost their home!'

Tina, seething with fury, and longing to get the horrible woman by the hair and slap her face hard, nearly had to walk out of the room at that point for fear of what she might say or do.

'That's enough, now,' Lucas interjected. 'Tina and Danny, you've been great and I can never thank you enough, but you two can go back downstairs now. We've got a hotel to run and I need to ask WPC Charlatan here just one more important question.'

CHAPTER FORTY EIGHT

Christopher opened the door to Seaspray Cottage with a beaming smile.

'Hello, girl. How was the rehearsal?'

Rosa started to laugh. 'Honestly, it's like a farce. Felix Carlisle has taken over and I don't mind really. He has got the best voice – although I'm not sure that whoever wrote "Jingle Bells" had in mind an operatic version.'

'He is a one, isn't he? Well, at least it's fun, and that's what we all need a bit of in this life.'

'Shut that door and stop that cold coming in!' Mary shouted from the kitchen.

'I was saying fun, that's what we all need, isn't it, Mary?' he repeated, walking back into the kitchen and smacking her bottom.

'That's enough of that,' Mary chided him as Hot in his usual routine scampered over to Merlin's metal food bowl and thoroughly licked it, chasing the bowl over the kitchen tiles.

'Get a room, you two,' Rosa said and wished she hadn't as it immediately brought back the sounds that she could never unhear from the other day.

'Your hair looks amazing, Mum,' she added quickly. Mary

had had it cut to just over shoulder length, which suited her so much better than having it just heavy and long down to her waist. 'You had it tied back earlier so I didn't notice.'

'She looks ten years younger, I reckon,' Kit said. 'You always were a beauty, Polly Cobb, you just never realised it.'

Mary blushed, giving a look to the tall, white-haired man in front of her that said more than any words ever could. Rosa felt warm inside. Mary Cobb had found her peace, at last. Just like Rosa herself had when, helped by others, she had come to realise her own worth. This, in turn, had allowed her to let Josh in and continue on an equal footing in the relationship they had with each other.

Rosa peered into the pram at her sleeping child. 'Has he been good?'

'When your mother actually let him go to sleep, he has,' Kit grassed on her.

Rosa grinned. 'Well, thank you both, so much. Right, I'd better get him home, it's late for all of us on a school night.'

Mary packed everything back in the baby bag. 'There's some banana bread in there for you too, duck. Good for your energy.' She then suddenly clutched her stomach, doubled over and made a moaning noise.

Christopher jumped to her side. 'Polly, oh God, what's the matter, my love?'

'What is it, Mum?' Rosa, used to her mother's sixth sense, stayed calm.

Mary was upright again in seconds. 'I can see Titch. How was she when you left her?'

CHAPTER FORTY NINE

When they were left alone, Lucas asked Davina to follow him downstairs to the office. 'Why did you do it?' he wanted to know. His anger had died away and was replaced with a tinge of sadness. 'I've been nothing but good to you,' he added, sighing deeply.

'It was all Joe's idea,' Davina Hunt's lies continued. Her face then contorted. 'OK, I'll tell you why. Because from the minute I met you, it's been Rosa this and Rosa that. I never, ever was good enough, was I, compared to wonderful her. Face it, Lucas, you're still in love with the girl. And then I saw you take the present from her, and then rush around to her house when she had a break-in. It's all about her, her, her.' Her voice rose. 'And then to top it off, I see you with Miss Prissy Pants Marketing and think, Oh, OK, if he's not going to get it on with Rosa – which, sorry to piss on your firework, but you never will – then he'll have a go with dear sweet little, butter-won't-melt, fucking Carly. Who, by the way, looks just like a dark-haired version of your beloved Rosa, so in my eyes, case closed.' She finished disgustedly, 'You're obsessed with the bloody woman!'

'Just get out,' Lucas told her, conscious of not raising his voice, as he could hear Tina checking a couple into HMS *Victory* in the reception area next door.

'Don't worry, I'm on my way. You're pathetic,' Davina Hunt uttered as she swung her way out of his life and out of Cockleberry Bay for ever.

Lucas went upstairs and slumped down on his bed. He had met Davina when he was going through the deepest grief and loss. Had clung onto her when he felt so alone, with no one to give him the affection he craved. She had made him smile, and he had enjoyed their physical connection – but in the cold light of day and faced with just how badly she had betrayed him, it made him realise what a big mistake their union had been. Their moral compasses couldn't be further apart. Her empathy and kindness gene were missing. On a positive, at least now, with her doing him such wrong, he would not dither and hold on to her, even mentally, just for the sake of not being alone. Carly was right. It was better to be single and happy – or even single and unhappy – than in a relationship that was going nowhere.

CHAPTER FIFTY

'Damn,' Rosa said aloud, checking that Little Ned's hat was pulled tight over his ears to stop any of the cold December night air getting to him. He was snug as a bug in a rug inside his soft blankets. Hot was dutifully trotting along beside the pram. 'Come on, Hotty, get those short legs of yours going; we need to go back to the church hall. I forgot to put the key in the key safe for Gladys tomorrow.'

There were still no streetlights in the main roads of Cockleberry so, holding her torch as well as directing the pram, Rosa reached the church hall and tied Hot to the handle so she could see to dealing with the key. Despite it only being nine-thirty, it seemed eerily quiet. She was just bending down to tap in the code, when she heard a familiar voice shouting for help. As fast as she was able, she unlocked the door, pushed the pram over the step and shooed Hot in before closing the big door behind them.

Titch was in the kitchen where Rosa had left her. She was kneeling on the cold floor, one hand on her back, her underclothing strewn around. Her waters had obviously broken. 'Rose, oh my God, Rose, I am so happy to see you,' she wept. 'Call Ritchie, please.'

Immediately dialling 999, Rosa ripped off her coat, laid it on the floor and asked her friend to lie down.

'Stay on the phone the whole time,' the operator instructed, once Rosa had relayed what was happening and had given her the address.

'I'm sorry, the signal is so bad in here,' Rosa explained, trying to keep her panic at bay.

'OK, Rosa, are you a mum yourself? Have you given birth naturally before?'

'Yes, yes,' Rosa replied.

'Good. If you lose me, just try to keep your friend calm, talk her through the contractions, and if the baby does come, just place him or her on Mum and don't do anything with the cord, all right? And make sure that both of them are warm – that is very important.'

'Yes, I've got that.' Rosa made a little scared noise.

'We will be with you in twenty minutes. Stay on the line.'

'I will.' Rosa put the phone on loudspeaker, propped it up on the kitchen side and then got down on the floor with Titch, taking her hand and saying, 'It's all going to be fine. I'm here and the ambulance is on its way.' Then, realising she couldn't call Ritchie with the operator on the line, she silently mouthed, 'Shit!'

As Titch tensed through another long contraction, crying out in pain, the operator was advising Rosa to comfort her friend and assure her that all was happening as it should. Meanwhile, Hot was getting agitated still being tied to the pram; he knew something was happening and his doggie senses were on full alert. And now Little Ned was stirring – great, that was all she needed, Rosa thought. Surely they weren't going to have a repeat performance of when Theo was born in a big, soft dog bed in the Corner Shop! Lightning didn't strike twice, did it?

Oh God, she hoped not. Closing her eyes, Rosa clasped Titch's hand and prayed.

'I want Ritchie. I think the baby is coming,' Titch panted. 'I really do. I suddenly want to push down. The contractions came so quick. It isn't the same as with Theo. Please call Ritchie, I want him with me,' she cried again, her face bright red and tears pouring down her cheeks.

'It's OK, darling,' Rosa soothed. Then light dawned. Of course – Titch had a phone! 'Where's your phone?'

'I left it in the van earlier, remember? *Ooooooh!*' Rosa tried to support her as Little Ned, now wide-awake, screamed and Hot barked. Rosa knew she needed help from the operator but she couldn't hear anything over the din.

Rosa then gasped in fear as she saw a face looming at the window before realising it was Ritchie. So relieved, she lowered Titch gently and ran to the door to let him in.

Ritchie thanked her and went straight over to Titch, stripping off his coat and placing it over her. 'Oh, my baby girl.' He got down on his knees and gathered Titch into his arms. 'I wondered why you were so late. I came down to find you.'

'Thank God.' His frightened wife gripped his hand, causing it to go white. 'It's going to be all right, isn't it?'

'Yes, of course it is, my love.'

'Phone your mum, Theo is there.'

'You just worry about you and this baby now,' Ritchie said, planting a kiss on his wife's sweaty forehead.

Rosa went to talk to the operator, but she had lost her. Now that Ritchie was here, she could take Little Ned out of the pram and comfort him. Wrapping his blanket around him, and kissing his face that was wet from tears, she went to the main door to turn on the outside light so that the ambulance could see where to pull in. That was when she saw the figure of a man walking down the hill. Hugging the baby, she called out, 'Oh my God, Josh, is that really you?'

He started running towards her and immediately took her and Little Ned back into the warm after she had turned on the outside light.

'I thought you'd be at your mum's,' he said all in a rush. 'I tried to time it right, I got the taxi to drop me at Seaspray Cottage – and when Mary said you'd left I started walking back home and …and then I saw you and here you are, with our Little Ned.' He wrapped his arms around both of them. 'What's going on?'

'Titch is in labour. The baby's early. Come on, quick.'

Hot, who was still tied to the pram, jumped up at his master's leg and started barking his head off.

'You look after our two,' Rosa ordered. Josh immediately took the baby from her and put him over his broad shoulder, then released Hot from the pram handle and lifted him with his free hand onto a chair next to him, facing away from poor Titch to give her some privacy. Rosa snatched the other two blankets from the pram and took them over to Titch, to put under her head to make her more comfortable. Ritchie had managed to get a signal and was now on to the emergency services telling them that he was at the business end of the proceedings and that he could see that the baby's head was crowning.

Rosa took the young woman's hand again and held it tight.

'You've got this, my gorgeous, brave mate,' she encouraged her, then dared a joke: 'Sorry it's not as comfy as the dog bed in the shop. You really have got to stop making a habit of this.'

'*Ooooooh, huff huff huff.*' Despite the cold, Titch was now sweating badly and panting. 'Shut the fuck up, Rose.'

Both Rosa and Ritchie burst out laughing, relieved that Titch was still very much herself, despite the circumstances.

'Precipitate labour,' Josh shouted across the hall, with a now calm Little Ned hanging over his shoulder, making happy snuffling noises as he felt so secure with his daddy's voice and smell. 'It will be fine.'

'What are you on about?' Rosa asked.

'Precipitate labour – it means a fast labour,' Josh said knowledgeably, while Ritchie, barely listening, was whispering in his wife's ear, telling her how much he loved her and how proud he was of her, before crawling back to check on the patch of hair he could see at the birth opening. If the ambulance didn't come soon, he was beginning to feel terrified that the baby might not emerge. Might get stuck somehow. Ritchie Rogers had, beneath his usual kindly exterior, never been so frightened in his whole life. This was his baby, and his wife – and he didn't know what to do.

'It means when a baby is born within three hours of your contractions starting,' Josh was prattling on, repeating what he'd read in all the pregnancy books he'd studied. 'About two in one hundred women whose labours have started naturally will have one.'

Then Titch roared, drowning his voice, when a mighty contraction began and seemed as if it would never end unless she pushed – at which point the blessed blue lights of an ambulance could be seen flashing outside.

Realising help had arrived, Rosa gave a relieved laugh and took Little Ned from her husband. Sitting down beside a quivering Hot, she said, 'Quick, Dr Smith. Put your stethoscope down and open the bloody door, will you?'

CHAPTER FIFTY ONE

Rosa ran up the Corner Shop stairs as fast as her little legs would carry her and banged on the glass lounge door. Titch was lying flat out on the sofa with a throw over her and a cushion under her head, and Ritchie was gently rocking a little bundle wrapped in a soft white blanket.

'I can't believe it's a girl,' Titch grinned. 'All eight pounds of her – no wonder it bloody hurt.'

'It always hurts, doesn't it?' Rosa said.

'But no stitches, so that's good at least,' Titch said.

'I couldn't wait to meet her properly,' Rosa cooed.

'I did suspect a boy, to be honest.' Titch then added, 'She's long, just like her dad.'

Ritchie turned the baby around and cradled her in his arms so that Rosa could see her face. 'She's going to be a model, I reckon,' he said, gazing down lovingly at his baby daughter's tiny pink rosebud-like face.

'Aw, she's adorable – got your blonde hair by the look of it, Titch. I couldn't tell when she shot out. Well done Dad, too. I've never been so relieved to see anyone in my life when you turned up, Ritchie.'

'What is it with me giving birth to my children on floors?'

Titch wondered.

'And with me always there to be a very scrappy midwife,' Rosa reminded her, 'well, until our hero Ritchie took over.'

Ritchie leaned down and kissed Rosa on the forehead. 'If you hadn't had to go and put the key back, goodness knows what would have happened. I would have gone to find her but…it's not worth even thinking about.'

'Mary felt Titch's pain,' Rosa explained.

'Did she?'

'Yes, it happened just as I was collecting Little Ned after the rehearsal, so one of us would have found you, mate, whatever.'

'Josh was right about the precipitation labour thingy. How did he know about that?'

'He literally has read every baby book known to man.' Rosa grinned. 'He so wanted to come and see you now, but I thought it would be easier to visit alone. The whole Smith Family, which includes Hot, might be a bit much today.'

'You know me, everyone's welcome. Mum can't get up the stairs, so we are going to go to her this evening. She's itching to meet her too.'

'I bet she is. Has she still got Theo, then?'

'No, he's in his cot having a nap. He loves his baby sister, well, so far so good anyway.'

'Come on, I need to hold her.'

Rosa sat at Titch's feet on the sofa as Ritchie carefully put the baby in her arms.

'I can feel all my pregnancy hormones surging up to my face.' Rosa burst into tears. 'Just look at her. Does she have a name yet? I know you were struggling with girls' names.'

'Like I said, that's because I did truly believe she was a boy.'

Ritchie looked at Titch and smiled. They had both been waiting for this moment. 'You tell her,' Ritchie urged.

'So, Rosa Smith, I have great pleasure in introducing you to Elizabeth Rose Rogers. Lizzy for short.'

Rosa was speechless.

'I wanted to call her just plain Rose, but Ritchie rightly said it could be a bit confusing as we spend so much time with each other, but you're in the middle and it is most definitely in your honour.'

'I am very honoured,' Rosa managed.

'If she's even half the woman you are, Rose, well, she'll be one extra-special daughter.'

'Stop it. I need to get a grip, but thank you.' Rosa blew her nose.

'Good. Now that's sorted, when can I book you in for some babysitting?' Titch said bluntly.

Rosa's tears turned to laugher as she pretended to make a phone call, 'Oh hi Gladys, is that you? Yes, yes, a new-born now, that's right. You can take her? Excellent. Her name is Elizabeth Rose.'

CHAPTER FIFTY TWO

Rosa left Titch and Ritchie cooing over their baby at the Corner Shop and came down the hill towards the beach. She saw Lucas at the sea's edge, randomly picking up stones and throwing them into the water and could immediately tell that something was wrong. As Josh had written down all feed times and would be coping perfectly well with Little Ned, she wandered across the damp grey sand towards the waves. The beach was empty aside from a family and their dog venturing into the South Cliffs caves. The dull December day was making the sea look dark grey and uninviting, and even the gulls seemed less vocal than usual.

Lucas sensed her presence before she got to him.

He turned around. 'Hey,' he said, summoning up a weak smile.

'Hey.' She linked arms with him. 'I think while we've still got a bit of daylight and now that I have a resident babysitter, we could walk up the West Cliffs path together. What say you?'

Lucas just nodded. 'Are you warm enough?'

'Yes, I've got a string vest on under here,' Rosa joked.

'Mm, sexy,' Lucas murmured, causing them both to let out a little laugh. They walked up the hill, taking in the expansive vista of the horizon and a large oil tanker making its way to goodness knows where in the distance.

'It's Davina,' Lucas began. 'I dumped her. Well, I didn't have a choice; she not only stole a great deal of money off me, but she also planted a prawn in the hotel inspector's dinner while knowing full well she was allergic to them. Could have killed the poor woman – it has been known.'

'Shit!' Rosa's mouth fell open. Hercule Poirot had dealt with lesser crimes.

'Luckily, it just caused her to be very sick and not for her throat to swell and compromise her breathing. Fortunately we had proof that Davina was responsible, or me and Dan would be in prison. Thankfully, the hotel inspector didn't take it further or WPC Hunt could be up for attempted murder.'

Rosa shuddered. 'That's terrible.'

'And that's not all. Unbeknown to me, Joe Fox was our resident Santa, and she was shagging him as well.'

'Vile!' Rosa was genuinely shocked and also a little shaken. 'I'm so glad that Little Ned is too young to understand Father Christmas, or I'm not sure what I would have done. I can't believe you didn't realise it was that creep. I saw him at the bus stop the other day and his accent seemed thicker than before he left.'

'He disguised it. The whole Christmas Grotto thing was a scam. Davina was nicking cash and sharing it with him. What is quite funny though is that she said she needed four hundred quid for a reindeer. Turns out the reindeer was only his bloody Great Dane with antlers on.'

'Oh Luke, I'm so sorry.'

'And I'm sorry for even questioning you about the woman's allergy.' Luke grinned. 'Danny lamped him a good 'un. We won't be seeing Joe Fox in the Bay again, that's for sure. I mean, would you mess with Danny?'

'No, I wouldn't, but I know someone who might.'

'What are you getting at?'

'Amira.'

'Ah. That kind of messing.' Luke brightened. 'D'you know what? That's great news.'

'Yes, she told Nate she really fancies him, and that she loves the way he is with Alfie in the house. She can see he might be a good dad to Zaki too, I imagine.'

'He needs a boost, so that's really good to hear.' Lucas blew out a cloud of cold breath. 'I feel better now just talking about it all, especially to you. It could have been a lot worse. I took my eye off the ball, definitely, and they could have got away with a month of stealing, not just a few days. The only thing is, I'm short of a Father Christmas now. So, any suggestions would be most welcome.'

They reached Alec's thinking bench. Lucas sat down but Rosa immediately pulled him back up. 'It's too cold to sit, come on, let's walk to the top. That view makes anyone feel better.' They carried on up the path. 'Oh, and Luke, I found out from Jacob that the Seaside Star ratings are to be announced on Christmas Eve.'

'Oh, Happy Christmas for me then. *Not.*'

'Come to the Carol-oke concert, it will be a laugh if nothing else. See if Carly wants to come too maybe?'

'You're quite the little matchmaker, aren't you?' Lucas said.

'Jacob also said the Star results are to be announced by *South Cliffs Today* live on the radio.'

'Oh. So much for nobody knowing about it.'

'All the more reason for you to come then. If it's going to be public knowledge, anyway.' Rosa stopped for a second to take in the view. 'So, what was Davina's reasoning for wanting to cause such wilful damage to you and your business? I can understand the greed bit, but…'

'Um. She, er, she felt such a dislike towards me in the end, she wanted me to fail.'

'What the…?'

Lucas sighed. 'OK. She couldn't bear the fact that I am still so into you. She was arsy when you gave me the present for the anniversary and also that I rushed around to you when Amira broke in. She went all dramatic and said she felt like there were four people in our relationship. You weren't exclusive in her hatred, so don't get above yourself: Carly took a hit too.' Lucas smirked.

'Blimey, but that's what friends do, look out for each other, ain't it?' Rosa's eyes sparkled as the path opened up to a magnificent watery view. She put her arms out wide to embrace the sky.

'I do still love you, Rosa,' Lucas said, a pained expression on his face.

'I know you do, and like I randomly came out with the other day, I still love you too. But I am *in* love with Josh and I think you are fine with that now really, aren't you?'

'Accepting of it is the word, I think. I want you to be happy and you are, and I know this way you will always be in my life and that's what matters. I need you, Rosa.'

'You may think you do at the moment, but you won't always. Not like this, anyway. You will get stronger in yourself and won't *need* anybody. You will find your own strength within and somebody to complement you and your life. That doesn't mean I am going anywhere though.' Rosa put her arm on his. 'Talking of that, have you seen Carly yet?'

'Tomorrow.'

'Exciting.'

'Yes, it is. I'm single now too, so I have no excuse not to ask her on that date.'

'It's the law, Lucas Hannafore. And I insist. She seems just so lovely.' Rosa then sighed, saying dreamily, 'I will never ever tire of this view.'

'Me neither,' Lucas said, looking directly at Rosa who had already taken off and was swinging her arms in the air and running around like a child on the expanse of grass at the top of the cliff.

'Big Ned!' she shouted, laughing as she cried out his name. 'He used to tell my great-grandmother, you know old Queenie, that he loved her to where the sky touches the sea. Josh says that to me now.'

'I want to feel like that again about someone…other than you.' Lucas bit his lip.

'You will. It may even be Carly – who knows? But you definitely will. You are too lovely not to, and she said that too, so it must be true.' Rosa ran over and took his arm again. 'Come on, we don't want to get caught up here in the dark.'

As they started to walk back down the hill, Rosa debated whether to say what was on her mind, and in the interests of honesty felt she had to go ahead. 'Luke. I've got something to tell you and would rather you hear it from me than anyone else.'

'You're pregnant.'

'Oh, did Titch tell you?'

'No, bird. I've studied those tits of yours for three years now and they've gone from peaches to pumpkins in the space of two weeks.'

'Oh my God, stop! My bladder has gone the other way and shrunk to the size of a pea. Last one down buys the cream teas.' Rosa started running at full pelt down the hill.

CHAPTER FIFTY THREE

Rosa rushed inside Gull's Rest and rubbed her hands together in front of the log-burner.

'Bloody freezing out there,' she said, her teeth chattering.

'You've been ages.' Josh was stretched out on the sofa, with Hot stretched next to his legs and Little Ned sound asleep on his chest. 'How was the baby?'

'SO beautiful. They've called her Elizabeth Rose, the Rose bit after me, which is such an honour. She will be Lizzy for short. She looks like a Lizzy too.'

'Aw, that's lovely. I can't wait to meet her.'

'It's made me excited for our new little one now.'

'Come here and lie with us.' Rosa took off her coat and squeezed in next to her husband, stroking Little Ned's soft dark hair gently as she did so.

'I saw you on the beach with Lucas. How is he?'

'He's feeling better now. It seems Davina fleeced him, and it was her secret lover, that horrible Joe Fox, who was dressed up in the Grotty Grotto moonlighting as Father Christmas. They were sleeping together and collaborating in bringing Lucas down. She also put a prawn in the hotel inspector's dinner at the Ship Hotel and nearly did for her.'

'What!' Josh's face tightened. 'I'm glad I didn't know that about that bastard being there.'

'Danny hit him hard enough for all of us by the sound of it.'

Josh shifted restlessly. 'He's had that coming for years. I don't condone violence of any kind but, well, if anyone deserves it, Joe Fox did. That Davina – what a piece of work. Who needs criminals with police offers like her around! She was so wrong for Lucas, anyway.'

'I agree. He's meeting the woman who does his marketing for the Ship tomorrow, and I have high hopes for the pair of them. She's one of us, Josh. She's kind and I think she will be good for Luke.'

'Happy to hear that. Poor Lucas, he's had a bad run of it. It's sickening about the Seaside Stars too, but that will soon be forgotten and if this woman keeps on top of the marketing, he will always do well with that beach location.'

'Especially if she keeps on top of him too. Ever the businessman, aren't you?' Rosa nestled into her husband's sturdy frame, curving her arm around the baby and Hot so she had all her three boys in one embrace.

Josh gave her a kiss. 'Talking of that,' he said, 'do you think the Carol-oke concert will give the charities a boost?'

'For sure. In fact, it's so good you are back early as I need to get cracking on sourcing some decent raffle prizes and liaising with the radio and local paper to make sure we get maximum coverage.'

'I have got a bit of work to do to finish off this project, as that was the deal for me being allowed to come home early, but I can work around you with that and I want to make up for missing time with this little fella too; so you are both my priority, OK? Not forgetting our four-legged boy, of course.'

'We are a good team, me and you.' Rosa kissed his neck.

'We are, and we will have the football team I want if you keep having babies at this rate.'

Rosa was thoughtful. 'Who'd have predicted, when I moved into your flat in London all those years ago, that we would now be living in a beautiful beach house with the sausage dog I stole, or rather rescued, our first baby and another on the way?'

'You are OK about it – the new baby I mean – aren't you?' Josh asked, a little anxiously. 'I know I'm the one pushing for a big family.'

'I am actually. A month ago, I was happy with just Little Ned, but now Christmas is coming, and I've seen families at the fireworks and at the grotto, and now we are parents anyway, well, I like the idea. I grew up as such a loner. I don't want that for our lad. Are you desperate for another boy?' Rosa asked, and squirmed to get herself comfortable.

'No. I only joke about a football team. A mini-you would be perfect, or for Little Ned to have a brother. As long as they are healthy and happy, it's all good.'

'Something else I need to ask you.' Rosa yawned.

'That sounds ominous.'

'I would like to do Christmas here with Kit, Mum, Nate, Jacob and Raff and Luke, the Greens, Titch and her lot and oh, Amira and Zaki too, if you don't mind.'

Josh started counting on his fingers. 'So that's thirteen adults including us, five kids and six dogs, Rosa – if I've got the maths right.'

'I know.'

'Our table isn't big enough – and who's going to do the cooking?'

'Raff is the best chef, Nate and Danny are pretty handy too. We can get everyone to bring stuff and all muck in.'

'You've thought about this good and hard then,' Josh laughed, his chest going up and down, causing Little Ned to murmur his disapproval at being disturbed.

'We will make room. Queenie once said to me that if the home is a body, then the table is a heart. I love that. And what's the point of having this lovely big house and not filling it with joy and laughter?'

Josh hugged his wife tightly to him. 'And you, my gorgeous wifey, fill me with joy and laughter every day. And I promise I shall never leave you again.'

CHAPTER FIFTY FOUR

'Oh yeah, I have a message from Danny,' Lucas addressed Amira, who was busily preparing coffees for him and Carly, who had just popped into the loo at Rosa's Café. 'He says not to eat before he gets in, because I've just given him the night off and he would like to cook dinner for you.' The woman flushed pink. 'Is that OK?' Amira's head nodded furiously. 'Good, I'll tell him.'

With a huge smile on her face, Amira began to hum to the tune of 'Jingle Bells' as she finished off what she was doing.

'Well, hi there.' Carly flirted with her eyes as Lucas put her cup of coffee down in front of her. He hadn't noticed that Amira had finished it off with a heart on top. She winked secretly at him as she walked past to clear a table behind them.

'Aw, that's so sweet!' exclaimed Carly on seeing the heart.

Lucas shrugged, then noticed that Amira had done the same for him too.

'How are you?' they both said at exactly the same time and laughed.

Lucas spoke first. 'Well, I don't have a girlfriend any longer, there is the chance we may lose and not gain a Seaside Star and we have a new Father Christmas on his way as the other one was stealing the takings.'

'All going just great then.' Carly smiled. 'I phoned yesterday as your mobile was off and Tina did give me a little bit of a rundown. So, who's the new beardy man in town then?'

'I've no idea. Rosa told me to leave it to her, so I'm sure this one won't be a lying cheating scumbag. Danny punched the other one. I mean, we were all glad about that as Santa had it coming – but can you imagine if anyone had seen him do it! Another great article for the *South Cliffs Gazette*.' Lucas put on a BBC voice. '*So, not content with poisoning the hotel inspector, according to new reports coming in from the Ship Hotel in Cockleberry Bay, Father Christmas is also now lying dead in his grotto there, felled by a single hard punch.*'

Carly laughed. 'Joking aside though, how do you feel – about splitting up, I mean?'

Lucas took in the pretty, sweet young woman in front of him and he felt his heart do a little jump. 'I was never in love with her. We've been on a downhill slope for a while.'

'Good. I mean, good that you're OK. Oh heck, you know what I mean.' Carly sounded flustered, blinking her eyes and rubbing her face nervously, causing Lucas to like her just that little bit more.

'And you're not missing your ex, no?' he asked her.

'God no.' She took a deep breath. 'I'm single and ready to mingle.' Her dancing eyes looked right into Luke's. Then, looking away: 'OK, we are here to talk about the website and spring bookings, aren't we?' she said efficiently, jumping into work mode and pulling a folder from her bag. As she placed it down in front of her, Lucas put both of his hands on top of hers.

'Actually, no. I'm here to talk about something else.' He smiled at her awkwardly. 'You know how we discussed our imminent wedding?' Feeling this wasn't the moment to burst into laughter, Carly bit her lip and cocked her head to the side as the handsome man in front of her continued: 'Well, if it's not too forward I would like to propose…' he paused for dramatic effect '…that I take you out for dinner tomorrow night – if you are free, of course.'

Carly squeezed his hands tight. 'Hmm. I need to think about this.' She made him wait, and then her whole face lit up in a huge grin. Raising her cup, she chinked it against his. 'And I would very much like to accept your proposal, kind sir.'

CHAPTER FIFTY FIVE

Felix Carlisle flounced into the church hall wearing a cream fur full-length coat and his usual brown felt Fedora. Rosa was busy with Josh, setting the stage ready for tonight's Christmas in Cockleberry Bay Carol-oke Concert extravaganza.

'If I have to talk to, or even set eyes on, one more noisy, smelly, spoiled, ungrateful little brat this side of Christmas I will explode. *Explode*, I tell you!' Felix threw his hat, which landed directly onto a coat hook.

Rosa couldn't help but laugh. 'Ho, ho, ho! Good shot, Santa.'

'Not even remotely funny, dear.'

'And look at you with your fur on.' Rosa carried on placing tinsel around the main lectern. 'You will so look the part later. You do realise everyone else in our group is wearing Christmas jumpers though?'

'Faux, darling, it's faux fur and I obviously ignored the memo.' Felix stroked his coat. 'I always dig this out on Christmas Eve, since one can get away with it without too much of a scene. And with this belly, jumpers make me look like a Christmas pudding anyway.'

'Joking aside, Felix, I am so grateful you stepped up and agreed to help Lucas out. And to give me credit, I did negotiate a decent wage for you.'

'I know, I know – and as I had cancelled all my London gigs, it really was marvellous. Day work too, so no having to go out in the cold evenings to events, so I shouldn't complain really, darling. But note to self: I am never – and I repeat *never* – doing it again.'

'Hello Josh, darling, a vision as usual.' Felix sashayed past them both and went into the kitchen to find glasses for the bottle of fizz he had brought in with him. 'So what time is it all kicking off later?' he shouted through the hatch.

'Four o'clock.'

'Heck.' Josh checked his watch. 'We haven't got all that long.' He stood on a chair and began fixing the Carol-oke banner across the top of the staging. 'The Seaside Stars are going to be announced later too, aren't they?'

'Yes,' Rosa replied. 'The *Gazette* did a feature on it this week, as well. Poor Lucas – the anticipation of it all – and then to be shot down in flames like he's surely bound to be after what happened. He thought nobody would know about the awards but evidently somebody from the Seaside Star company thought it would be great publicity for them *and* the two venues – the Lobster Pot and the Ship Hotel – so it's being announced live on the radio, sometime after the Carol-oke winner is declared and before the raffle, I believe.'

'Tell me if I'm being stupid here, wifey, but why a judging panel, if there are going to be phone votes anyway?' Josh started noisily erecting the folding tables.

'It's just to add another layer of fun after each act really. Carly has designed some paddles with 1 to 10 on them, like they have on *Strictly*. The judges can just waggle them about for added drama.'

Nate poked his head around the door. 'OK to start unpacking

my stuff?'

Felix rushed out to the front. 'I'm free.' He waved his arm in the air at Nate.

The young man replied, smiling, 'Erring on the side of cheap, I'd say. Come on, give me a hand then.'

'Bubbles, anyone?' Felix then offered, stealing a glance at the young café owner and receiving a cheeky wink in return.

'It's reindeer men, Hallelujah, it's reindeer men!' The women from the St Michael's and All Angels choir, who had named themselves 'Angels' Delight', belted out their tune with gusto. With no thought of age or dress size, they were all wearing extremely short Santa's Little Helper outfits, red in colour, with a white fur trim. Their number finishing caused such a crescendo of applause and stamping of feet on the wooden floor of the church hall that Little Ned and baby Lizzy both started screaming, and the verger, after waving his 10 paddle around far too vigorously, had to take off his glasses to wipe the steam from them.

Jacob turned to Raff, lips pursed. 'There's more flesh on show up there than on Madonna's Rebel Heart Tour, New York, twenty fifteen. I mean, really!'

'The ladies are obviously in it for the win,' Josh said to Ritchie, as they did their best to pacify the babies and stop Theo from running up on the stage. Stuart Cliss had already had to leave the festivities and take his two boisterous boys outside to kick a ball around in the lit car park, while his wife Vicki pushed a double buggy to and fro; the twins inside it were, amazingly, sleeping soundly through the concert.

'Jesus, you wouldn't get many of them to the pound,' Danny noticed as, while bowing, the lead vocalist's mature breasts nearly heaved out over her bodice.

'You can't say things like that in this day and age,' Tina Green scolded him, looking around for Alfie, who had made his way under the food table and was shoving in a slice of chocolate log while no one was looking.

'I just did, but no offence meant, Ma. There's nothing wrong with appreciating the female form.'

'And you can remove your eyes off those stalks right this minute, Frank Moore.' Gladys Moore swiped her husband's arm.

'They stole my idea, Rose,' Titch said grumpily. 'I think we are mince-pie meat here. They sounded bloody brilliant too.'

The producer of *South Cliffs Today* at that point beckoned Mr Gunter, the Cockleberry Bay verger, up to the microphone. His voice when he spoke was still slightly shaky after watching the previous act. Geraldine Baker, the Polhampton vicar, was busy patting her group on their bare backs, encouraging them.

Mr Gunter cleared his throat. 'So that's it, everyone. You've heard and – for those of you lucky enough to be in the room – seen all of our acts, so now it's time to get voting.'

'Thank you, Mr Gunter.' The young radio DJ took over. 'So as the verger says, it's time for you to get your votes in online. It costs just one pound to vote and all of the proceeds go to the wonderful charities that encompass Ned's Gift – and of course our lovely ladies from Polhampton here have been singing their lungs out for a new church roof.'

'Quite literally,' Jacob whispered to Raff, squeezing his hand in a rare public display of affection towards his husband.

The DJ continued, 'And for those members of the audience who are here in person, you can either vote online, or just pop a cross on the paper slips dotted around the room, and put your donations in one of the collection boxes that are on show for the different charities. Dig deep and be generous.

'Right, it's song-time now while we gather the results in, and it's our old friend Robbie Williams, with his very amusing Christmas track, "Bad Sharon". Take it away, Robbie!'

Rosa went over to help Nate, who was busy dishing out mini pasties and warmed mince pies from the oven. Jacob and Raff were now serving drinks from behind their make-shift bar.

'That was hilarious, sis,' Nate told her. 'My sides ache from laughing. I do have to say I think Angels' Delight have got it though, purely for entertainment value alone.'

Rosa agreed. 'I know, they were bloody brilliant – put us to shame with our slightly dull Christmas jumpers and Indian Bells routine with not a knee-length knicker-leg – or any knee-length boobs, come to that – on show. Look, I don't mind who wins. It's all good for the charity.' She snaffled a mini-pasty and took a big bite.

Christopher came over and greeted his son and daughter. 'I am enormously proud of you for organising all of this, Rosa – and thanks for getting the plug in for me.' He put a mince pie on a paper plate and picked up a coffee.

'Thank you.' Rosa looked right up at the white-haired man in front of her and repeated, 'Thank you…*Dad*.'

Rosa smiled as Kit looked away and coughed to hide his emotion. A tingling feeling ran through her body. It felt good to be praised. It felt good to be part of a community, but most of all it felt good to be surrounded by the love of a family, something she had never thought would ever be possible. She went over to the DJ to get him to play another couple of songs so that people could carry on eating and drinking, filling the donation boxes and voting. Lucas and Jacob were now looking pensive as they knew that they would shortly know their Seaside Star fate. Titch came and stood by Rosa and grasped her hand.

The DJ sprang into vocal action again. 'So, that was "Starman" by the legendary Ziggy Stardust himself, which leads me nicely into talking to Mr Morgan, who is the Marketing Director of Seaside Stars Limited. For those of you who are not aware of this, Cockleberry Bay's very own Ship Hotel and the Lobster Pot had both applied to up their current Star ratings.'

The trainee reporter from the *South Cliffs Gazette* came running back in from having a cigarette outside, notepad at the ready as the DJ went on. 'They currently hold a worthy four Seaside Stars between them already, so let's see what happened after their visits from a mystery hotel inspector, shall we?'

Silence fell over the hall, and everybody held their breath as the DJ said smoothly, 'Mr Morgan, welcome to South Cliffs Radio and a very Happy Christmas to you...'

CHAPTER FIFTY SIX

Anna Wallace checked her watch, then put her finger up to shush her husband, who had just returned with a box of last-minute drink supplies from the off-licence. She had already tuned her phone into the Devon radio station online.

'So, firstly, to the Lobster Pot in Cockleberry Bay, with its current Seaside Star rating of two... Well, our secret hotel inspector said that it couldn't be faulted for cleanliness, friendliness, and standard of food, so we have no hesitation in offering it an extra star – which now makes it an accredited Three-Star Seaside-rated property. Big congratulations and an even bigger round of applause in the room to the proprietors, Jacob and Raffaele Fernandez-Johnson.'

Anna smiled as a big cheer went up in the background.

'Glass of Sauvignon?' her husband offered.

'One second,' she said brusquely, holding up her hand for silence. She carried on listening intently, hoping she might be able to hear some background voices or a speech at least. She knew what was coming. Putting the phone on speaker, she turned the volume up. The Ship Hotel had been exceptional; she couldn't have faulted it: the room was stylish, clean and with a great view, the bedding was as soft as fresh snow, and the food had been delicious. And, if she were honest, although she couldn't prove it, it was more likely the amount of Sauvignon Blanc she had consumed than any food that had passed her lips and caused her to be so ill. But how could she ever have admitted to that? It would have been mortifying.

After meeting him that once at the Corner Shop, followed by their session at the Lobster Pot, when Danny had appeared again at the Ship, well, it was like Christmas and her birthday rolled into one. He was not only incredibly sexy, but a thoroughly decent and likeable bloke – and who was she to ruin a place's reputation, let alone cause such a great lad to lose his job? The Lobster Pot had been an easy decision, the new Star well-deserved. However, with the Ship, and with it having become common knowledge that she had been ill there, it was her reputation which was on the line here. Just because Danny Green had given her the most mind-blowing sex she had ever had in her entire life, it didn't mean she could dish out Stars just to save his job – or did it?

Anna looked pained. She had thought long and hard about her final decision. She put her hand over her mouth in anticipation of the reaction as Mr Morgan carried on.

'And now to the Ship Hotel, Cockleberry Bay, also with its current Seaside Star Rating of two...'

CHAPTER FIFTY SEVEN

Josh chinked his fork against his champagne flute. 'Before we all sit down to stuff our faces, I would like to propose a Christmas Day toast.'

He had to shout over the noise of an excitable Theo and Alfie, who were running up and down holding new toy planes high above their heads. Rosa put her arm around her husband's waist. Little Ned was already sat in his new highchair bashing his plastic spoon as if in support of his father. Mary was next to him, clucking and fussing.

Gull's Rest could not have looked more Christmassy. Jacob had put a tree with lights on outside that could be viewed from the beach. Another huge tree, surrounded by a sea of presents, stood tall in the corner next to the log-burner, and the paper chains and garlands that Rosa had made with Titch the other day were draped around the huge open-plan room, along with various other chintzy decorations that she had got from the Corner Shop. She had even sprayed fake snow onto the bay window in the shape of holly leaves. The Christmas table, spread along the length of their large kitchen-dining area, was made up of their own bench seat, plus two of the long folding tables and some plastic chairs they had borrowed from the church hall.

'It's short and sweet, you'll be pleased to know,' Josh said loudly when the noise eventually subsided. 'I just want to say thanks for coming, you are all very welcome here at Gull's Rest today – and every day for that matter – and we'd like you to tuck in and enjoy the spread that we have all provided. Now, let's eat.'

'Who's missing?' Mary pointed to the four empty chairs.

'Lucas and Danny. They just called,' Rosa explained. 'They are just finishing up, as they had lunch guests today, but said for us to start and Nate has asked if he can bring a mystery plus-one, who he is evidently collecting from Polhampton as I speak. He shouldn't be long.'

'At last,' Christopher commented, holding a bottle of milk to Little Ned's mouth while the baby continued to bash away on the plastic tray of his highchair with his spoon. 'We need someone to make an honest man out of my lad.'

At the mention of Danny's name, Amira had smiled. Dinner the other night had led to another dinner and then to bed. He was adorable with Zaki and she had already seen what a good father he was with Alfie. Neither of them wanted to rush things but they were enjoying the moment, and right now, the moment felt good. She got up to check quickly that her little one was still asleep in his pram.

Jacob stood up. 'I'm putting the dogs outside while we eat, as I can't stand all this bloody barking.' As he waved treats in front of the six little wet noses, Hot, the Duchess, Ugly, Pongo, Saveloy and Mr Chips dutifully followed him in a crescendo of excitable barks towards the back door. Raff was busy carving the massive turkey he had brought with him. The potatoes he had also prepared, with love and goose fat, were just crisping up in the double oven. Titch, who had been taking a sneaky rest on the window-seat was now sparko, with milk patches forming on both boobs, while Ritchie, looking at her lovingly, cuddled Lizzy in his arms.

'Anything I can do to help, loves?' Tina Green shouted, helping herself from the huge platter of cold meats, bread and pickles in front of her.

'No, just get going on the starters, all of you.'

The front door then opened, bringing in with it a huge rush of cold air and a man wearing a recognisable faux-fur cream coat. Nate was following behind with two bottles of red wine and a huge bag full of presents, which he immediately plonked down in front of the Christmas tree.

'Oh, hello Felix,' Christopher said. 'Welcome to the madhouse.'

'Let's get this party started, I say,' the loud man boomed.

Josh stood up and handed him a glass. 'Champagne all right for you?'

Rosa checked on Little Ned, grateful to see that Amira had taken him out of his highchair and was rubbing his back to bring up his wind away from the table. She then grabbed Nate's hand and ushered him into the study.

'Your plus one as in an actual plus one?'

'Er…yep. I've been waiting for the right man to come along, and as Stephen Fry was already taken…well, it just kind of happened. You are happy for me, right?'

'I don't get why didn't you say anything to me? I had no inkling. You slept with Mad Donna from the bookies, didn't you?'

'I owed money to the bookies, that's why.' Rosa had hardly taken this in before her brother asked anxiously, 'You are OK with it, aren't you?'

'Nate.' She hugged him to her. 'Of course I bloody am. If you're happy, I'm happy. Shame it isn't Stephen Fry though. I love him. But Felix is great too.' To her annoyance, Nate then ruffled his hands through his sister's hair.

Joining Felix at the table, it was Nate's turn to tap on his glass.

'Here we go.' Rosa nudged Josh. 'Get ready for this.'

'I've got something to say before we all get started,' Nate told them all. Christopher smiled at Mary as his son continued, 'There's been a lot of secrets in this family of mine. Some for good reason but some not so good.' Mary tensed. 'So I thought, what better time to announce that I'm in a relationship with this wonderful man than today? I feel as if all my Christmases have come at once. Felix is kind, funny, clever, loud and – well, I'm just incredibly happy that I've met him.'

Jacob, now in from the cold and sitting back in his chair, nearly choked on an olive. 'I'm devasted,' he said, in true drama queen fashion. At this, the room fell silent. 'I really thought that *I* would forever be the one notable gay in the Bay.' He blew a kiss to the pair and grinned. 'But well done, and many congratulations.'

'To Nate and Felix.' Christopher stood up and raised his glass in the air. 'My son and his partner.'

Nate took a massive deep breath and downed his champagne in one. Christopher stayed standing up and felt for something in his pocket. He then walked around to where Mary was sitting and got down on one knee.

'If you can't beat them, join them, I reckon,' he announced. There was a collective gasp from the group. 'Polly Cobb, you stole my heart years ago and you've done it again. Not only did we create the most beautiful daughter together, but since the day I reconnected with you, we've been creating the most magical music together. We are also now blessed with the most adorable grandson and not forgetting you, Nate, my boy. Mary, you complete our little family. I love you. I love you a lot and I would be honoured if I could call you my wife.'

At that same moment, Lucas and Danny, arms laden with gifts, walked in to cheering and whooping. 'Whoa, what's going on?' they asked in unison.

'Nate is seeing Felix and Chris and Mary 'ere are getting 'itched,' Tina announced bluntly.

Danny patted Alfie's head then went immediately to Amira and kissed her on the cheek. Alfie then jumped up from his chair, knocking over his orange juice as he did so, and grabbed his dad's legs. 'Daddy!'

'It's all about celebrations today, isn't it?' Rosa came back through to the table carrying a huge tray of roasties and put them down on a coaster in the middle. 'Because it's not just a Christmas dinner that's in the oven.' She looked over at Josh to check he was OK with it, and when he nodded she put her hand to her tummy. 'There's another little Smith cooking in here too.'

She caught Lucas's eye. He smiled broadly, put his hand to his lips and blew her a massive kiss.

Mary looked dazzled. 'I'm not sure I can cope with any more surprises. But oh, darling daughter, I am so happy for you, Josh and Little Ned.'

'When are you due, sis? When am I going to acquire another nephew or niece?' Nate asked lovingly.

'Should be the same day as Little Ned's birth,' Josh spoke up, a massive, proud grin on his face as he took his son from Amira and strapped him back into his highchair.

'I told you,' Amira said in her soft accented voice.

'You did.' Rosa smiled. She then said to Lucas, 'It will be you next. Are you seeing Carly today?'

'Not today, no. She's coming over tomorrow night though.'

'And talking of celebrations,' Jacob chipped in, 'although it pains me to say it, I think a little toast is due for both of our Seaside Star rating performances, don't you?' He took a drink and winked at Danny, then lowered his voice conspiratorially. 'Although I can only suppose that one of you must have slept with the inspector to get you all at the Ship not one but two of the bloody things. Four stars! Unbelievable! Well done!'

Only Lucas noticed Danny choking on his turkey as Raffy lifted his glass and said romantically in his Italian accent, 'To stars, babies, weddings and love. To old friends and new beginnings. *Buon Natale* and Happy Christmas, everyone.'

A resounding, 'Happy Christmas!' filled the room.

EPILOGUE

Despite hiding cameras in the hotel bedrooms, Lucas had always felt too much of a voyeur to look at any of the video footage, but today, full of Christmas turkey, a large helping of Christmas pud and far, far too much red wine, an exception could be made. Half-covering his eyes in dreaded anticipation, he searched for the footage from the time of the hotel inspector's stay, and pressed play.

'A terrible mistake, you say,' Alabaster Anna was saying, as Lucas began watching the action, his eyes wide in fascination… and when a few minutes later she reached, 'Oh, Daniel. You bad, bad boy. Can't you make it four?' Lucas laughed out loud, holding his 4-Star Seaside certificate triumphantly in the air. First, he deleted all traces of evidence from the camera. Then, on reaching for his phone, he began typing a message: Danny mate, about your Christmas bonus…

THE END

ABOUT THE AUTHOR

Nicola May is a rom-com superstar. She is the author of twelve romantic comedies, all of which have appeared in the Kindle bestseller charts. Two of them won awards at the Festival of Romance and another was named ebook of the week in *The Sun*. Christmas in Cockleberry Bay is the fourth book in Nicola's bestselling Cockleberry Bay series. She lives near Ascot Racecourse with her black-and-white rescue cat, Stan.

Find out more at www.nicolamay.com
Twitter: @nicolamay1
Instagram: author_nicola
Nicola has her own Facebook page

BY THE SAME AUTHOR

The Cockleberry Bay Series:

*

The Corner Shop in Cockleberry Bay
Meet Me in Cockleberry Bay
The Gift of Cockleberry Bay
Christmas in Cockleberry Bay

*

Working It Out
Star Fish
The School Gates
Christmas Evie
Better Together
Let Love Win
The Women of Wimbledon Common (formerly the *SW19 Club*)
It Started With a Click (formerly *Love Me Tinder*)

CPSIA information can be obtained
at www.ICGtesting.com
Printed in the USA
BVHW041010301120
594472BV00014B/281